I0583542

The Collected Short Fiction of John R Little

Volume 2: Little Things

PUBLICATIONS

Lycan Valley Press Publications
1625 E 72nd St STE 700 PMB 132
Tacoma, Washington 98404 United States of America

Printed in the United States of America

LVP Publications Illustrated Edition

ISBN-978-1-64562-955-9

For Fatima, always and forever.
You are my inspiration and the reason I'm always happy.

TABLE OF CONTENTS

INTRODUCTION BY JOHN R LITTLE   xi

VOLUNTEERS NEEDED   13

TOMMY'S CHRISTMAS   27

GROWING UP   33

DOING DADDY   41

3:26 A.M.   49

THOSE LITTLE CAMERAS!   57

IN THE BOYS' CLUBHOUSE   67

EVER AFTER   77

WELCOME TO INFERNO   91

CLIMBING MOUNT TURNPIKE   113

THE JAMESON HOUSE   129

THE THIEF OF TIME   145

ACCORDION SEASON   165

THE OASIS   175

CRUEL EYES   189

THE SLOW HAUNTING   207

FOLLOWING MARLA   231

SAMMY   255

GEORGE'S HEAD   265

FLIES   273

My Little Jillian   283

The Wishing Stones   293

Placeholders   317

The True Story of Christmas   375

About the Author   397

Welcome back to the second volume of The Collected Stories of John R. Little. I'm thrilled you've decided to take a look at this new edition of *Little Things*.

Chronologically, most of the stories included here were actually some of my first published, but that doesn't much matter. Hopefully, you're interested in all four volumes.

As with the first volume, I'm including new introductions to each story, and each one also has a beautiful piece of art by the incomparable Luke Spooner. This edition also contains a story not previously collected.

Even though some of these stories are a little creaky with age, I still love them all. I've enjoyed revisiting them and remembering what was happening in my life when I dropped each one to print.

Next year, look for the last two books in this series. They'll both have a bunch of fun surprises for you! Here are the titles of all four books:

The Collected Short Fiction of John R Little:

Volume 1: Little by Little
Volume 2: Little Things
Volume 3: A Little Bit More
Volume 4: Lost Little Tales

John R Little
December 2019

Volunteers Needed

This was the first story I ever had published. Prior to this one, I'd written primarily science fiction, and it all horrid stuff. I can't believe I ever imagined an editor wanting to buy the dreck I came up with.

After a hundred or more stories didn't work out, I thought I'd try my hand at horror, and this story popped out of my fingers. Right from the beginning, I was really happy with it, but I had no idea where to sell horror. To fix that I looked to see where Stephen King had published the stories in his first collection, Night Shift.

He'd sold to many of the men's magazines, so I figured I'd try there, too. I sent the story to Cavalier, one of the mid-range publications, and they bought it almost immediately. I was shocked to open the letter from them with a check for $250.00 attached. It was the first money I'd made writing.

After that, I knew my calling was really horror (and later, dark fantasy). It just felt right, which is something every writer searches for.

Something I realized decades later was that Stanley Milgram performed a very similar experiment that I have in this story. He did it at Stanford University in 1961, and it seems that my story was somehow inspired by his work. I had no memory of ever hearing of Milgram, but I must have.

My version is much darker, but I do owe Milgram a tip of the hat.

I WAS LOOKING FOR A RIDE to the coast, but if they're handing out money for killing a couple of hours, who am I to turn it down? After all, a hundred bucks is a hundred bucks. I wasn't too sure of what I was getting myself into, but most of these psych. experiments are pretty lame.

The notice was stuck up in the student lounge, thumbtacked among vacancy listings, furniture sales, textbook coupons, concert announcements, and all the other crap that fills up any bulletin board on campus. All it said was:

VOLUNTEERS NEEDED
$100
APPLY: DR. NORMAN
PSYCHOLOGY BLDG. ROOM 842

I wandered over to the psych. building, a bright new ten-story granite box that looked more like an apartment block than a school, and walked in. There was no elevator that I could see, so I walked up the seven flights of stairs and went into Room 842. It was a waiting area of some kind, with magazines scattered haphazardly over a clear plastic table. A couple of tattered chairs sat alongside.

"May I help you?"

I jumped slightly as a receptionist slid into her desk after entering from a side door. She was quite good-looking. Somehow I always expect psychology people to be dumpy brunettes with horn-rimmed glasses and a pert, knee-length skirt arranged just so. A hot blonde was a nice surprise, even if she was ten years too old for me.

"Sure. I mean I'm here to be a volunteer. There was a notice over in the math building."

She blinked and rested her chin on her hand, leaning over her desk.

"Do you know what you're volunteering for?"

"Not really. I figure it's probably a stress analysis program or some such crap."

She smiled and took a drink of her coffee. The mug was stained dingy brown on the inside. "It's a three-part experiment dealing with conditioning."

"Three parts? How long's this going to take?"

"Not long. An hour. Maybe two."

"And I get a hundred bucks for this, right?"

"Free and clear." She reached into her desk and pulled out a manila file folder. "Payable after completion of all three sections of the experiment, of course."

"Okay. Is Doctor Norman around?"

"I'm Doctor Norman."

"Sorry. I thought you were a receptionist."

She shrugged. "Are you in?"

"Sure. Where do I start the experiment?"

"Right here. Fill out this form. That's the first part. I'll be back in a bit. Bring you a coffee?"

I nodded and grabbed the form as she left the room. It was a three-page questionnaire. As usual, it was filled with useless questions. These things were tricky sometimes; they threw in garbage questions to hide what they really want to know. I've gotten pretty good at reading behind the questions to find out their real interest.

This one started out the same as all of them what is your sex, age, height, weight, etc. I rattled them all off quickly. Male, nineteen, six-foot-one, a hundred seventy-five pounds. Any college student can rattle off the standard set of answers without thinking, they get asked so often.

Most of the rest was a series of multiple-choice questions. Those are trickier, because the answer you want to pick is never one of the possible choices. The first one was, "Do you feel that capital punishment benefits society? Yes or no." No place for well, maybe sometimes, depending on a whole lot of stuff.

I checked *yes* and moved on. I thought that was the answer they were looking for. Dr. Norman arrived back with my coffee in a Styrofoam cup and placed it beside me. Black. I wanted cream but didn't bother asking.

I flicked through the better part of the questionnaire. I'd guess there were somewhere around forty or fifty questions. Finally, the connection formed as to what they were really after. A lot of the questions had something to do with violence or death of one sort or another. "Do you believe in euthanasia?" "What percentage of rapes do you believe go unreported?" "Have you ever experienced pain so bad you wished you were dead? If so, explain."

I thought of the time my bike skidded out from under me while going too fast around a hairpin curve down the coast highway, sliding into the oncoming traffic and being smashed by a shiny new Toyota Camry. I checked *yes* and quickly wrote a summary of what happened, not wanting to dwell on the memories.

There was a lot of camouflage in the questionnaire, too. "Who did you vote for in the last election?" "What is your favorite drink?" But it was the violence aspect that permeated the questions. The last two were the clinchers. "Would you be capable of killing another person if you thought the situation warranted it?" I quickly stroked *yes*. "Would you be capable of torturing another person if you thought the situation warranted it?" I doubt if the test would have proceeded any further had I answered no. *Yes.*

Dr. Norman gathered up my answers and carried them through a rear door. "Wait here, please."

I finished my coffee while she was gone. It was already cold, but what the hell, coffee's coffee. Even black.

She was gone about ten minutes before the door clicked open and she was beside me again.

"This way, please." She waved at the direction she had just come from.

The door led into a hallway which looked like it ran the

length of the building. The floors were tiled, and the click-clack of our shoes echoed hollowly from the far wall. She stopped at an unmarked door on the left side of the hall and punched some numbers on a keypad.

"Here we are," she said. "All set for part two?"

The door opened into a small room. There were windows on two of the walls, both covered with black curtains. Some buttons were sitting on a control panel in front of each window. The rest of the room was empty except for two gray metal stools near the center.

"All set, I guess."

The room couldn't have been more than about eight feet square at most, and I was a touch claustrophobic as she closed and locked the door.

"Great." She moved the stools in front of the left window and gestured me to sit down. Pushing one of the buttons caused the curtains to withdraw with a small hiss. I don't know what I expected, but I jumped a bit when I looked into the room and saw a large brown rat staring back. Large? Christ, it was as big as a football, with a long snaky tail dragging lazily behind it. Patches of fur were missing and scar marks covered the bare spots.

The rat was chewing on something wet and sticky. I didn't ask what it was. I didn't want to know.

"It's a budgie bird."

I flinched at the sound of Dr. Norman's voice. Somehow she smiled, staring at the remains intently.

"You'd never guess it," I said. My voice was a bit shaky, but I was calming down. It's not every day you see something as horrid and disgusting as that creature ripping hungrily into a bird.

"Look at the strength in his jaws. He doesn't just bite and chew his meat, you know. He rips the flesh from the body and swallows it in chunks."

I nodded, wondering what this had to do with the experiment. The rat soon finished with the bird, leaving the unrecognizable carcass behind, sniffing around the corners of the room for fresh food or a quick exit. He scratched at the walls a couple of times and snapped his tail across the floor.

"Okay. You see this knob the red one here? The second part of the experiment is simply for you to turn it. To turn it in a complete circle. As you do that, the floor of the room the rat's in will become electrified. This gauge will show the amount of current being passed through the floor."

I looked at Dr. Norman and then back to the rat. "You're joking."

"Why, no. You said you could torture a human being, but you won't torture a rat?"

"That was only if the situation warranted it."

"Yes, well this one does. I told you the research I'm doing has to do with conditioning of people. How much can a person be convinced to do? It's only a rat, after all. And remember, you don't get the money unless you complete all three phases."

"I just turn the knob?"

"That's all. Clockwise."

I reached for the knob and started to turn it. After it had gone about one-quarter of the way around, the rat stuck its nose in the air and squeaked. Its tail flopped up and down, a whip angrily beating the floor. I continued to turn the knob as the rat squeaked louder and lifted its front paws in the air. It started to run around the room in circles. As I increased the current, its ugly face was having spasms. The needle on the gauge was near the center of the range, and I felt myself sweating. My heart was beating faster, and the rat's hair was standing up on end. It was grotesque, an obscene porcupine convulsing with pain.

The rat squealed louder, and I turned the switch as fast as I could to the end position. The rat leaped into the air, screamed loudly, and fell to the floor with a sickening thump. Its eyes stared accusingly at me, and its legs continued to twitch spasmodically.

I jumped back from the console and rubbed the sweat from my eyes. My heart was pounding loudly, and I huddled into the corner to try to calm myself and get away from that awful image of the rat's eyes, half popped out of its head staring at me, staring at me in utter terror.

"Very good," Norman said. She clapped her hands loudly once. "I rather enjoyed that. Most people can't actually go this far. Only about twenty per cent or so."

I just stared at her, trying to catch my breath.

"Just relax," she said. "There's no hurry."

I thought I could smell the scorched body of the rat through the walls. Maybe it was only my imagination.

"The government is very interested in the results of these tests, you know. They want to know how people react under pressure to do things they normally consider brutal or repugnant."

I reluctantly climbed to my feet and brushed my palms down the sides of my face. I looked through to the charred carcass. "You like this, don't you?"

She smiled. "Why, yes. Yes, I do." Her face was a stony challenge.

"What's the third part of the experiment?"

A bell rang out sharply, and I jumped.

"Whoops. Excuse me a minute. I have another volunteer out front."

She tripped out the door, and I heard it click behind her. *What the hell was going to come next?* I wondered. I stood and stared at the rat. Steam rose from its body, its eyes white like a well-cooked trout.

After a few minutes, Dr. Norman returned.

"There. He's working on the questionnaire now. We're going to have to move on. Haven't got all day, you know."

I nodded.

"Good. Now, this section is very deceptive. Please notice that we have a window on this other wall similar to the first. We're going to go through a similar experience, except this time there's a human being in the room instead of a rat."

"No. You can't be "

"The human," she interrupted, "is a volunteer similar to yourself. He's aware of what's about to happen. He's in no danger and will not be in any danger at any time. Yes, he will receive a *small* electric shock, but not the amount that our furry friend over there did."

She paused and seemed lost in thought. Her eyes were wide open, her pupils dilated as if she were on drugs. I knew she was high from just the excitement. She loved this.

"The subject, however, will *appear* to receive a fatal

amount of current. He'll only be acting, and that's what he's being paid for. The challenge is that he'll be paid double if he convinces you *not* to complete the experiment."

"So I should can it, to help him, right?"

"Oh, no. Because then you don't get your money. Just remember, he's in no danger. After all," she chuckled, "we can't go around frying all our students now, can we?"

She pushed the button, sliding the curtains open. The room was about the same size as the one we were in small, but sunk lower, so the guy in the other room came up only to my chest. The room was painted a godawful pink color with a white ceiling.

"He can't hear or see us. We also will not be able to hear him like we heard the rat. Nobody ever completes the experiment when they can hear through."

The subject was about my age, maybe a year older, with blond hair and a beard to match. He looked very athletic compared to me. My only exercise these days is walking to the coffee machine down in the lounge and back. He was pacing around the room nervously and glanced in our direction every once in a while. He never made any gesture that he could see us.

"There's the dial." She pointed. "Go ahead. Turn it."

I reached for the knob and turned to face her. "I don't—"

"You *said* you could do it. Now *do* it."

I scratched my temple and then grabbed the dial firmly and turned it a fraction. The guy stopped pacing and looked down. The hair on his arms was starting to stand up a bit. He swirled to face us and screamed at us. No sounds came through, but it wasn't very difficult to figure out what he was trying to get across.

"Are you sure this guy knows what's happening?"

"Don't be ridiculous. Keep going. You're doing fine."

Slowly, I turned the switch—turned it a quarter of a circle. The guy was jumping up and down to get away from the floor. He was still screaming, and then he started to pound on the glass separating us.

"Hey!" I stepped back. "That guy doesn't want to be there."

Dr. Norman frowned. "There is virtually no current in that room. Listen! I'm ordering you to complete this! He's an actor, only an actor, who wants to double his earnings. He's been through this before. Now, get to it!"

My heart was pounding a march again as I took hold of the knob. Sweat rolled from my upper lip. I turned my back to the console and clamped my eyes shut. Quickly, I reached behind me and turned the knob completely around. I thought I heard a sudden yelp, but that, too, could've been my imagination.

I fell to the floor and passed out.

The room seemed hazy for a few moments as I tried to stand. My rubber legs betrayed my queasiness. I'd been moved into some type of rest area.

I staggered to my feet, leaning against the brick wall beside my cot. I couldn't help but wonder about the other guy. Visions haunted me visions of him being burned to a crisp, his eyes bursting into flames, and his charred skin flaking off. Silly, but...

"You're back with us."

Dr. Norman strolled nonchalantly through the entrance and sat on the rumpled cot. "Feeling okay now?"

I nodded. "Was the other guy alright?"

"You won't have to worry about him. Here's your money."

I counted the five crisp twenties and stuffed them quickly into the pocket of my jeans before she could change her mind.

"Thanks," I mumbled.

"No problem." She was as cheery as ever. "Send your friends over if they need a bit extra."

Not bloody likely, I thought.

She opened a door. "Right through this way."

After I walked through, she grabbed the door violently and slammed it shut behind me. I tried the handle from instinctive fear and found it was locked. I turned around and saw I was in a familiar room. I shook my head to try and clear it. There was a large mirror on one side. The walls were painted a godawful pink, and the ceiling was white.

It took about an hour before I felt my hair beginning to rise and my feet starting to tingle. I looked through the mirror and thought I could see a pair of shadowy figures watching me.

I screamed and pounded on the mirror, knowing it would do me no good. 🦋

Confession time.

I got the idea for this story one day while I was at work and supposed to be writing a computer program for a now-defunct retail chain. The idea came to me fully formed around lunch time.

I spent the rest of the day pretending to work, hiding my screen from any supervisors who happened to walk by, writing this story, cackling with laughter as I wrote it. Although I knew I should be working, I couldn't. I needed to write the story.

It was one of the earliest stories that I knew without a doubt would sell. The only question was where to?

At the time, there were a number of horror/fantasy magazines on the newsstands, and I went for my favorite. I sent the story to The Twilight Zone, and sure enough, T.E.D. Klein (a wonderful writer himself) bought it, and the story appeared in their Christmas issue.

The story was subsequently published many times in both American and European anthologies. Possibly my favorite is the Italian anthology, Un Fantastic Natale, where my story lives alongside work by Charles Dickens and Nathaniel Hawthorne, a feat unlikely to ever be repeated.

The little boy, Tommy, in this story was inspired by my son, Christian, who was a young child when I wrote it.

I WAS BEING NOISIER THAN I should have been. Goddamn kid. I never even hear the little bastard come into the room until he cried, "Santa!" Then, he ran over and hugged my leg.

"Hi there, kid."

He rubbed his eyes and yawned. He was maybe three years old—four at the most. His hair was brown like a sparrow and stuck out at odd angles.

I swallowed and slowly put the silver candlesticks back on the mantel over the stone fireplace beside me. The burlap sack was almost full anyway. If I could just get rid of the damned kid, I would leave the rest of the loot and just split.

"Did you bring me toys, Santa?" He was wide awake now and staring up at me in awe with big blue eyes.

Christmas Eve is usually my busiest night of the year. The parents are all too drunk to wake up, and the kids are normally too worried about scaring off Santa Claus to get out of their beds if they hear me.

"What's your name, little boy?"

"Tommy."

"Well, Tommy, has Santa ever disappointed you?"

He shook his head. "Well you di'nt bring me a Hot Wheels Road Race set last year like you promised."

The place had seemed like a perfect setup. I had cased the joint pretty good—the parents were sleeping in a small bedroom in the basement, and only the two kids slept on the main floor. Maybe I hadn't been careful enough because it had seemed so easy.

The house was all decorated for Christmas inside, and the family had gone to bed with all of the lights still burning on the tree. There was a set of Royal Doulton figurines in a china cabinet in the dining room. I had been careful to wrap them up so's they wouldn't chip.

There was also a good heavy crystal set and a couple of hundred bucks stashed away in an oak bureau drawer.

A grey and white cat was meowing loudly around me when I first got in. That's probably what woke the kid up. I picked the cat up by its neck and tossed it out the back door onto the porch overlooking the yard. It looked at me and hopped down the steps.

I had drunk the glass of milk and ate the oatmeal cookies that the kids had left out for Santa Claus. A can of Green Giant niblets corn was sitting on the coffee table beside them; I guess it was a snack for the reindeer. The milk was warm.

"How come you got Danny next door a Hot Wheels set and not me?"

"Can't have everything you want, Tommy. You'd be spoiled."

"That's what my mommy says."

I bit my lip. Never did like to deal with little kids. "You'd better get to bed, you know. You ain't supposed to be up when Santa comes."

"You really Santa Claus?"

"Sure I am, kid. Why?"

He twisted his head and scratched his ear. "I dunno. How come you din't know my name?"

"I always get you mixed up with your brother, kid."

He thought this over and said, "You don't look like you did in Sears. Maybe I better get my mommy."

I grabbed his shoulder. "Hell, no, kid. Don't do that." He looked scared. "Big people don't believe in Santa. You know that, don't you?"

He nodded slowly. "Aunt Betty does."

"If you wake up your mommy, I'd have to leave and take all of your presents with me."

His eyes brightened and grew wide again. "*Presents!* What did you bring me?"

"Why, I brought you a Hot—"

I looked behind Tommy and saw an older boy walking down the hall toward us. "Oh, damn."

"Tommy?" he said. Then he saw me. "Hey, what's going on?" He looked to the staircase leading down to the basement.

I grabbed Tommy and covered his mouth with one hand. "One word and I'll break his neck." Tommy squirmed and tried to get loose, but I kept a tight hold on him.

The older boy was about ten, tall and skinny for his age with short blond hair. He wore a light green robe over brown flannel pyjamas.

"Put those candlesticks in the sack for me. Fast."

He walked over and did as I asked, frowning with dismay as he saw the rest of the silver and china I had lifted.

"What are you going to do with Tommy?"

"I'm getting a bit old for this business," I said. "Need an apprentice. He'd be okay if'n you don't try anything stupid."

The idea hadn't occurred to me until I said it, but maybe it was time. Whoever heard of a fat old man like me breaking into houses?

"You just stay put, kid. One move and your brother's dead."

I grabbed Tommy, picked up the sack, and quickly climbed up the chimney. Prancer and Vixen didn't like him at first, but they'll just have to get used to him. ✖

Growing Up

Over the years, I've had a reputation as that horror guy who writes stories about time. Time has been a fixture in my writing since the beginning, and this is the first story I ever published that dealt with the nature of time.

This story was also inspired by my son. The family was driving home to Vancouver from a vacation to Disneyland and my son was upset about some perceived slight. He pouted and said, "Just you wait until I get older and you get younger!"

Well, I almost drove the car off the highway when he said that. The story here appeared to me full-blown as soon as he chastised me.

The story went to the other major horror/fantasy magazine I dearly wanted to be published in: Weird Tales.

George Scithers bought this one and published it in an issue alongside stories by Stephen King, Robert Bloch, and Ramsey Campbell. When I got my contributor's copy and saw those stories, I think my jaw dropped and crashed on the floor. I was dumbfounded and couldn't believe how fortunate I was.

I still feel that way.

After this story was published, I didn't write any more stories at all for about a dozen years.

Why? I'd written a horrible novel (science fiction, having not learned my lesson earlier apparently) that nobody would touch, my children needed my time, I was climbing the corporate ladder at work, and I was depressed about life in general. I quit writing cold turkey, missing it every day.

HARRY SELKIRK WAS THIRTY-THREE years old before he realized something was missing. Not that he was missing much, mind you—he was a successful chartered accountant, and nobody could miss the twinkle in Old Man Kolfax's eye when he watched Harry. He would be the next partner of the firm.

Harry owned a silver BMW and lived in a huge ranch-style house in North Vancouver overlooking the Pacific. Although the house was mostly owned by his bank, Harry did own outright a modest cottage in the interior, where he faithfully spent three weeks each summer, fishing and enjoying the quiet.

But on his thirty-third birthday, he had a revelation so clear it jolted him awake at 6:00 a.m., an hour earlier than normal.

Harry wanted to have a son.

Not a daughter and not even a wife, although she would likely come with the package, but a son. Harry could remember his mother's overpowering voice booming when he'd left home.

"Gotta get yourself married, boy. Get yourself some

kids. They'll keep you young at heart for the rest of your days."

Well, Harry thought. *I don't know about that.* But he did know he wanted a son.

Harry had rarely dated women. When he was fifteen, he had charted out his own future carefully, culminating with his own accounting firm by the time he was forty. So far, everything was dead on track, and it irked him that he hadn't thought to put a son into the plans.

As he was shaving, Harry ran through the possibilities. He could afford to hire a woman for a year to bear his son, but that seemed a bit too crass.

He could adopt, but that wouldn't be right, either. He needed a boy that carried his genes.

There didn't seem to be many other alternatives; he would have to get married.

He cut himself with his razor as he realized this. *Damn,* he thought. *Who would want to marry me?*

The question remained unanswered until he went into work that morning and said hello to Cathy, the office receptionist.

"Hi," she answered.

Harry was about to walk past her into his office when he looked back at her more closely. Pretty, more or less. Nice personality.

"Would you be interested in dinner tonight?" he asked.

Harry and Cathy were married three months later. Harry woke up the morning after with a smile on his face. He knew that Cathy was now carrying his son.

Nine months later, on Harry's thirty-fourth

birthday, Harry Selkirk, Jr. was born.

Harry, Sr., doted on the baby to the exclusion of all else. He immediately took his three weeks holiday to play with baby Harry, spending every minute with him. He wouldn't allow Cathy to breast-feed the baby, since that would take him away from his father for fifteen minutes at a time.

It was hell for Harry to finish his holidays. He phoned in sick with a fictitious flu to add an extra week with the child, but after that he ran out of excuses and had to go back to the office.

"Babies must agree with you," said Old Man Kolfax when Harry showed up at the accounting firm. "You look great."

"They say kids keep you young," said Harry.

For six weeks, Harry dreaded night time, since that meant morning would come soon, and he would have to leave Junior for eight straight hours to go to work.

Cathy grew more and more frustrated and soon gave up and left Harry. She had been totally ignored since the baby was born and just wanted to get away. Harry didn't try to stop her, but rather encouraged her to leave. He went in to work the next day with Junior in his arms and smiled as he handed a neatly-typed resignation letter to Kolfax.

"You can't leave," said Kolfax in disbelief. "We were about to promote you."

Harry knew he had no choice. People would soon begin to notice too much.

"Sorry," he said. "I've got more important things on my mind."

"But what about your papers and—"

"Help yourself to whatever you like. So long."

Harry stopped at the first realtor that he saw and asked her to sell his house as soon as possible. They scrambled to find a buyer a week later, and Harry made a thirty thousand dollar profit on the sale. He moved all his belongings out to his cottage and settled in to enjoy the peace and quiet.

Harry loved spending all of his time with his son. When Harry, Jr., was eleven months old, he started to walk, and he was talking steadily soon thereafter.

Harry held a joint birthday party for them both. He was brimming with joy when his son turned one and he turned back to thirty-three. Junior seemed to like the party, even though there was only the two of them present. Harry brought out party hats and bought a boy Cabbage Patch Kid for a present.

The years passed quickly, and with each that passed, Junior grew to be more and more like a little boy instead of a baby. By the time he was five, Harry had turned back to twenty-nine and had lost all the excess weight he had put on. He felt trim and spent most of his time running through the wilderness with Junior or teaching him how to swim in the lake. Winters were a bit tiresome, since he was afraid to keep the boy out in the harsh wind and cold snow for long periods at a time, but that only made them both appreciate the hot, dry summers all the more.

Harry Junior loved his dad in equal part. He never knew that living alone wasn't normal, although he was always particularly excited when they would go for their monthly grocery trips into town.

Every second year, Harry would change the grocer

that he used, since he didn't want any questions being asked.

By the time that Harry was twenty-four and Junior was ten, the townspeople started to think of them as brothers, rather than father and son. Even Harry sometimes thought of it that way.

Harry and Harry, Jr., both celebrated their seventeenth birthday on the same day. To mark the occasion, they double dated two sixteen-year-old girls from town. Harry's date was a blonde girl who worked at the grocery store, and Harry, Jr.'s was a darkly-tanned girl who worked part-time at the tennis club. They went to an evening showing of *The Night of the Living Dead* and then talked the girls into skinny-dipping off the end of a deserted pier.

The two boys shared a secret smile as they dropped their dates off later that night. They knew they couldn't date the girls for long without raising suspicions, but it was fun while it lasted. Both thought it was the best birthday they had ever spent, although Harry, Sr., sometimes had trouble remembering some of his older birthdays.

At fifteen, Harry started shaving only on alternate days, and soon gave it up altogether as his facial hair pulled back into his chin.

As Junior grew older, he started to pick up the responsibilities that his father could no longer handle. He was the one who now organized the shopping trips, holding his father's hand as they crossed busy roads.

By the time that Harry, Sr., was four, he was small enough for his son to cuddle with. He had only vague recollections of his past, which were no more real than the flighty imaginings that any little boy has. Harry, Jr., loved the boy with all his heart and spent every minute with him, racing through the forest, wading in the lake, or whispering lullabies at night.

Harry, Sr., turned into a cranky baby, but by the time he was eleven months old, Junior hardly noticed. He carried his dad everywhere they went, although they didn't go quite as far as they had in the past, when Harry had been bigger. Junior put on quite a bit of weight from the lack of activity, and small worry wrinkles crept into his brow.

And soon, Harry Selkirk, Sr., disappeared.

Harry, Jr., was heartbroken, even though he had known that the day was coming. It was his thirty-fourth birthday, and all he could thing about was his dead little father.

Junior spent a depressed month, drinking steadily. Finally, he managed to accept his father's death and built a small monument at the back of the cottage, near the woods.

He was lonely and looked up the little brunette he had started to date on his seventeenth birthday. They had kept in touch over the years, although nothing serious had ever developed. She still worked at the tennis club.

Harry asked her out more often, since he had nothing much else to do with his time, and a couple of months later, they were married.

Harry, Jr., smiled the morning after their wedding night. He knew that his wife was now carrying his son.

❧

Fast forward to 2003. Kealan Patrick Burke was editing an anthology called Tales From the Gorezone, a reference to an online message board I frequented occasionally.

I felt this overpowering need to write a story for Kealan. In fact, over the course of three days, I wrote three stories. It was one of the most productive times of my life, as the decade of not writing seemed to explode into fragments spilling all over the floor.

Kealan bought "Doing Daddy," but because this was a charity anthology to help abused children. He suggested removing the first word from the title, to avoid anybody getting the wrong idea about the story, so it was published originally as "Daddy."

The main character was loosely based on my father-in-law, who was suffering from dementia at the time.

I HAVE TO KILL DADDY AGAIN.

It's 5:30 in the morning and he just phoned me. He says he can walk through walls. "It's amazing, Jeannie," he says with a slight stutter to his voice, as if he's surprising himself as much as me. "Right through the walls."

"Daddy, you know you can't walk through walls."

"Yes, I know." He pauses and adds, "They were coming to meet me. They called me last night."

I pinched my lips, not knowing how to reply. "Who called you?"

"It wasn't you, was it, dear? Did you phone me?"

"No, no it wasn't me," I said.

"I knew that. They called me and wanted me to take some papers to them."

"What papers are you talking about?" As soon the words left my mouth, I knew it was a mistake. No point in encouraging him. "Daddy, where are you? Are you in your room?

"I'm at... at this place. They should be here."

"Your room?"

No answer. My fingers hurt where I was clenching the phone.

"They called me last night, that's right. They called me and said to bring the papers to them. I've got them packed in my suitcase."

"Are you in your—" I cut myself off. I knew he was in his room, because his name was displayed on my phone before I answered it. That was good.

"But I couldn't find them. I went out to the road—" *The fucking four-lane highway outside his rest home*, I knew.

"—and I walked back through the walls. I know how that sounds, but I didn't want to walk around to the front door so I just walked through the walls."

5:30 in the fucking morning. I closed my eyes and wished for a rest from him. From watching over him every god damned day and every god dammed night. He was ninety years old and I wished he were dead.

There's nobody else to do it, I reminded myself. *No brothers, no sisters, just me.* To add even more guilt to the mix, I remembered all the times he had looked after me when I was so young and so sick, no mother, no other relatives, just him. It's payback time.

Now it's time to kill him again. I wiped a small tear from my eye.

Daddy lives in a high-end residential complex for seniors. He has a small room about fifteen feet by ten, meals supplied in a large dining room, where a hundred other half-dead old farts meet for tasteless food and mindless conversation. I think they spike the coffee with something to make them all docile, since I've never so much as heard a single one of them raise their voice at anything.

The knives are plastic.

He doesn't have a stove or anything like that in his room. Nobody wants the place burned down. He is allowed a small fridge, but the only thing he keeps in there is a small canary he found near the road one day. It used to be yellow.

I pay twenty-five hundred dollars per month to keep Daddy and his moldy canary at Cedar Gardens. It's not tax deductible.

The attendants hate him. "You look tired," they say all the time. "Shouldn't you go back to your room now?"

Shouldn't you go back to your room now? I wonder how many times I've heard that over the years. I'm sure it's the mantra of the place. "Shouldn't you go back to your room now? Please put that knife down. Really, please, put it down and go back to your room now." Sometimes they surround him, four or five of them, hands held out in front so he stays calm. As if he could do them any harm with a stupid little knife like that.

My life has been devoted to my Daddy. Jeannie, the perfect child, always there for dear old Daddy. I was only nineteen when he moved into Cedar Gardens. I'm... so much older now. Thirty? God, who knows anymore. I feel like I'm seventy. How old would that make him? I laughed at the thought. It would make him dead.

Again.

After I hung up the phone, I decided this time he needed to stay dead forever. I opened my small closet, its door complaining with several small squeals. "Haven't had to go in here for years," I said to myself. "Decades."

The thin cardboard box was hidden at the back of the closet, on top of a rickety old hat rack. It was the size of a box I might have received from Amazon.com, but this box didn't hold the latest bestseller. I lifted it carefully over to my dining room table and unfolded the flaps. Dust clouded around me.

The revolver felt as new as the day I originally bought it. I always knew that one day it would come in handy. With the gun was a small velvet pouch. More carefully, I opened the pouch and reached in, gently lifting out the six silver bullets.

Six silver bullets melted down two decades earlier, waiting for the right time to kill him one last time.

My mouth was dry as I slipped the bullets into their chambers. They clicked and snapped into place, and with each new snap, I could feel my power growing.

Ready.

I walked out into the hall and down to the dining area.

"Shouldn't you go back to your room now?"

Nuisance noises.

"Jeannie?" I turned and saw an orderly looking at me. "Are you okay? Shouldn't you – "

He stopped when he saw the gun in my hand. "I have to kill my Daddy again."

"Jeannie, just take it easy." He looked around and a few of the other orderlies carefully walked towards me.

"Just give me the gun now."

"He called me and said he was walking through walls. I have to kill him again."

"Your father couldn't have called you, Jeannie. You know that."

"They wanted papers from him."

The orderly nodded but his words didn't make any sense. "Now, Jeannie, you know your father was killed more than fifty years ago. Just before you came to live with us." In a softer tone, "You already killed him."

I frowned.

"Please give me the gun," he said. Trying to smile.

"He called me," I said. "He's here again."

Then, I saw him. He was wearing a white jacket, but that wasn't going to fool me. I turned and fired, the first silver bullet hitting him right between the eyes. I killed three more of him before they took my special little gun away.

Maybe now he'll leave me alone. 🦋

This is the second of my blast of stories written over a three-day period. It was a bit of a gross-out story, and I loved it. I laughed out loud while I wrote it, while simultaneously having no freaking idea who would ever want to publish something like this.

I tripped across the Horror Fiction Review, and they were occasionally publishing short fiction. I figured I had nothing to lose, and I was really pleased when they bought the story.

In many of my stories and novels, I use the time of 4:42 for things to happen, for reasons explained in my introduction to "Dreams in Black and White" in the first volume of my short fiction.

This is the only occasion I've used a time as the title of the story, and it's always bugged me that I didn't use 4:42. I was tempted to change it for this edition, but that's kind of cheating.

AT THREE TWENTY SIX IN THE morning, Ada's eyes popped open. It was time to check on Bill.

She stretched her body out as far as she could, to try to wake up the sleeping muscles. She didn't wake as easily as she did thirty years ago, when she first started checking on Bill every night.

Ada was two years shy of her seventieth birthday, and sometimes she felt every day of every month of every one of those years. Her left leg cramped a bit as she climbed out of bed.

"Move, Scamp," she said with a dry mouth. She swept the fat, sleeping cat away as she rearranged her bed sheets. She hated to come back to a messy bed.

Ada slept in the basement of their home, the coolest part of the house. Bill slept on the main floor, where the summer heat was far too stifling for her to sleep. He on the other hand always complained that the basement was too cold.

Great team we make, she thought from time to time. Overall, though, the years had been kind and they had been happily married all these years.

They had only had one bad year together. 1972. That year had started out wonderfully with the birth of their only child, their daughter, Stella. Stella was a surprise, since the doctors had told them that children would be extremely unlikely, due to Bill's low sperm count.

He sure didn't like hearing that he was to blame for not having children, not being able to look forward to growing them, teaching them, loving them.

Stella came along well after they had given up on any hope. Ada was thirty-eight and Bill past forty. The doctor called Stella a miracle baby.

When she was six months old, she died in her crib.

The doctors couldn't explain her death any more than they could explain her birth. "It's God's will," was all they could offer as an explanation.

Ada was disconsolate after Stella's funeral. She blamed herself for leaving the baby in her crib unattended. Logic made no impact on her; she felt she should have been there, every second of the day, watching over her little miracle, protecting her.

Ada had let Stella down.

But, she would never let Bill down.

Every night, between one and two o'clock, she would awaken, quietly go upstairs, and peek in Bill's bedroom to be sure he was sleeping peacefully.

Every night, between three and four o'clock, she repeated the process.

For thirty years, she had made the trip up and down the stairs, twice every night. She had only ever missed two nights, when she was hospitalized with a bleeding ulcer that almost put her in the grave alongside her daughter.

Ada was mathematically inclined, thank God, since Bill was useless that way. She kept their bills paid, their checkbook balanced, and their investments growing steadily. The most important number in her focused life, though, was twenty-one thousand, eight hundred ninety-three. That was the number of times she had made her mid night climb to check on Bill.

"Twenty-one thousand, eight hundred ninety-four now," she said under her breath, as she pulled on her faded yellow terrycloth housecoat. "And counting." She always chuckled over the same small joke.

Bill never knew that Ada checked on him. He would have been astonished to find out that she did it even occasionally, let alone, twenty-one thousand, eight hundred ninety-four times.

Bill snored loud enough that he frightened Scamp, which is why the cat always slept in the basement with Ada, even though Ada hated her. Scamp had lived with them since twelve thousand, three hundred and eight, and that meant Ada had swept her aside nine thousand, five hundred and eighty-five times.

"Damned animal," she muttered.

Ada snored too, just not as loudly as Bill. Of course, she always denied snoring, but sometimes her deep sounds rumbled up from the basement, and Bill could hear her if she fell asleep before him.

Her legs hurt as she climbed the fifteen steps from the basement to the main floor. She hugged the left side of the stairs, so that they wouldn't creak. Over the years, she had woken Bill only three times. That gave her a success rate of 99.986%. *Not bad in the scheme of things,* she thought.

As she reached the top of the stairs, she knew that something was wrong. She couldn't hear any snoring. *Damn* she thought to herself. *Must have woken him.* She quickly calculated that this would lower her success rate to 99.982%. She frowned.

At the top of the stairs, she looked down the hallway to her husband's room. He slept in the middle of three bedrooms. The other two were empty shells. They had bought the house when still hoping to fill the empty rooms with children. When Stella went to sleep and never awoke, they kept her furniture for a while, but eventually it was too hard, and they sold it all. It was easier to have empty rooms.

Ada stood silently, hoping to hear Bill's snoring re-start. After five minutes, she still heard nothing. *This is silly just standing here*, she thought. *Better take a look.*

She moved down the hall, her right hand sliding on the wall for balance.

Then, she heard a small squeak. She stopped and hunched forward a bit. "What the heck?"

She could hear other small noises, scritches and scratches and rustling, and maybe a hiss.

Someone's there.

Ada felt goose bumps on her arms. She was breathing in quick gulps. She convinced her feet to move, backwards, and she ducked into the kitchen at the far side of the house. She kept looking behind her as she slowly opened the cutlery drawer and pulled out a long carving knife. It was her only weapon.

She swallowed and steeled herself. It had to be a

burglar. No way she was letting a petty thief get away with anything in her home.

She forced herself back forward down the hall. Bill's bedroom door was open, as always, and as she got closer, the strange sounds got louder.

At the door, she held the knife tightly and reached around the frame to switch the light on.

The brightness temporarily blinded her, but she quickly recovered and stared into Bill's room.

The floor was covered with fur. Moving fur. It took a moment for her conscious mind to realize what she was looking at. *Rats.*

Hundreds of them.

Many of the rats were a foot long, and dozens of them stopped and looked up at her. Their pink eyes seemed to shine with aggression and she could see some of them baring their teeth at her. They were all pitch black, snaking dark tails swishing behind them. A few rats were fighting among themselves.

She forced herself to look at the bed.

Bill was covered with a frenzy of rats. She could see them gnawing on his flesh, all of his flesh. His bedclothes were gone. His fingers, toes, and genitals were only forgotten stubs, and his eyes were pools of goop. Bloody bites and punctures covered what was left of his body. Rats gnawed on bones that they had surfaced.

A smaller rat had crawled into Bill's mouth, forcing it wide open, and as she watched, the disgusting rodent disappeared down his throat, only its shrinking tail a reminder of what had gone before.

Ada lowered the knife and backed out of the room.

She closed the door to the bedroom, vaguely remembering that there had been thumping noises sporadically coming from the attic in the past few months. She remembered now that she had asked Bill to check on the sounds, but he always claimed to be too tired.

She put the knife back in the cutlery drawer and yawned. It was 3:44, and she quickly made her way back down to her own bed. The damned cat was in her way, so she shoved her aside again. "Will you never learn!" she scolded.

She started to fall asleep, drifting off to the wonderful thought that twenty-one thousand, eight hundred ninety-four was it. She smiled as she thought of finally getting a solid night's sleep.

Now we're at the third of the three stories I used to get my writing career back in high gear.

The title of this story came before any idea of what it would be about. At the Pacific National Exhibition in Vancouver each year, there was a booth selling small donuts that were made while you watched. The booth was called "Those Little Donuts!"

Well, somehow, I substituted cameras for donuts and had my title. I've always been a bit of a reality show junkie, so that part of the story came naturally, too.

This was the first of a group of stories I sold to Dark Discoveries magazine. I loved the magazine and was thrilled to be in their fourth issue.

GOOD EVENING, LADIES AND gentlemen of our studio audience and all of you out there in TV land. Welcome to tonight's episode of *Those Little Cameras!* The show that invades (ha-ha)—more like destroys— the privacy of one of our citizens.

My name is Chad Jameson, and I'll be your host tonight.

[Pause for live audience applause.]

Tonight's contestant is Jimmy Melenstein of 163 Amherst Street in Brooklyn, New York, who was nominated by his ex-wife, Marsha.

Marsha has supplied the necessary deposition, stating that she believes that Jimmy has broken the law at some point in the past. That's enough for us to have installed two hundred of *Those Little Cameras!* in his house while he was at work yesterday. We've gathered the most interesting parts of his night, and we're all about to watch Jimmy's routine together.

[Smile to camera. Look humble.]

Our regular viewers know how the game works, but for those of you who might be tuning in for the first time, let's run through the rules of our game.

Our hidden cameras are made by using nanotechnology. They are built atom by atom and are so small that they can't be seen by the human eye.

[Superimpose video of lab worker using aerosol spray.]

Our team has developed a spray of nano-cameras that cling to any surface. After applying the spray, millions of the cameras stick to the surface of a cupboard, a window, a computer, whatever. Our programmers then select two hundred different cameras to transmit, and we're in the snoop business!

[Applause and cheers. Focus back on Chad.]

Tonight, we have a very special show for you. This may be a winner! Marsha Melenstein, I know you're out there watching us. If the tip about your ex ends up as the best backstabbing of the season, you're going to be a million dollars richer. That's one *million* dollars.

[More applause.]

Now, let's look to see what Jimmy was up to when he got home last night.

[Cut to Clip 22A.]

It's 6:00 p.m. Jimmy's been home for an hour and he's already had dinner. Now, he's surfing the Internet. What's he looking at, you ask? Watch as our camera focuses onto his monitor. What do you see?

[Audience yells, "PORN!"]

Porn! That's right! He's a member of the *Live Sex Acts* site. Let's back the video up and watch him log on.

There. You can see that his user id is "Bigcock" and his password is also "Bigcock." Boy, this guy isn't very imaginative, is he?

[Jeers from the audience.]

Feel free to sign onto *Live Sex Acts* using Jimmy's id. We've checked and he has almost five thousand dollars available credit limit on his Visa card.

[Back to Clip 22A.]

And look! If we pull back into a wider angle, we can see that he's not wearing any pants and he's masturbating while watching the site.

Incidentally, he's pretending to be a girl. Is he pathetic, or what?

[Pause as camera zooms in.]

Not very well endowed for his name, is he?

[Long laughter.]

Enough of this. It's not like he's got anything that we haven't seen before. Oh, there he goes making a mess.

[Switch to Clip 137B.]

About forty-five minutes later, he's relaxing and he runs a line of cocaine. Take a big snort, fella!

Now, here's the first time that Marsha gets to score. Every illegal act that Jimmy undertakes will be rated and a point value assigned. Let's look at a few common scores.

[Switch to standard list of penalties.]

ACT	POINTS
Illegal Drug Use	100
Tax Evasion	300
Fraud	500
Sexual Abuse	1,000
Rape	2,000
Torture	4,000

Of course, in the past, we've hit many more crimes than are listed here, and we have point values for almost everything.

However, in the event that our contestant performs an illegal act that isn't listed, we have our distinguished panel of judges who will provide a point value. Let's hear it for the judges!

[Applause.]

I see it's time to sell some product. When we return, we'll get to the good stuff. What kind of trouble is our contestant going to get himself into? And how many points is Marsha going to count? She will have to hit twenty-eight hundred to beat our current high score for the season.

[Wink.]

I think she's got a good shot.

[Go to commercial.]

Okay, we're back. I'm Chad Jameson, your host for tonight's show and we're now going to get into the meat and potatoes.

Let's check in with Jimmy and see just what he's up to.

[Switch to Clip 62C.]

Well, look at this. Marsha, I hope you're paying attention...

Our friend Jimmy really ought to have paid attention when the latest round of amendments to the Patriot Act were passed last summer, allowing us to peek into his life whenever we have reason to believe he's involved in criminal activity.

[Audience cheers for the Patriot Act. Video starts, deliberately out of focus. It's not completely clear what the contestant is doing.]

Can we get a better resolution, guys?

[Video focuses.]

Ah, there we are. Audience! What's he doing?

[Mumbling in the audience. Planted member yells out "Torturing a dog!" Gasps among the others as they now see what is happening.]

That's right—a border collie to be more precise. Did we get the right guy this week or what? Hey? Hey?

[Slowly, audience starts to applaud.]

The dog's already out for the count, but just look at that precision. Jimmy *really* knows how to wield a scalpel, doesn't he?

[Pan through audience, various people nod.]

And I really like the way he's got that stainless steel table set up in his garage. Very sterile. The drains are well spaced for the blood to run out. [Chuckle.] Hell, we could spend the whole show just watching this.

But we're not going to do that.

Why?

Because Jimmy is only getting started. Before we leave this clip, though, judges, we need to know how many points to award Marsha for the dog torture.

[Cut to the three judges, conferring. One holding the official point sheet, one rubbing her chin, the third trying not to laugh. After a moment, the first judge rings in the result, and it pops up on the official scoreboard beside Chad.]

Fifteen hundred points! Halfway between spousal

abuse and rape. I can buy that! Marsha, you must be just jumping with joy out there. Your ex-husband may be making you a millionaire today.

We're not done yet, folks! Not by a long shot. I promised you a very special show and now, our friend Jimmy is about to deliver.

But first, a word from our sponsor.

[Cut to last commercial.]

Welcome back, folks! I'm Chad Jameson. [Humble smile.]

We're checking in on Jimmy Melenstein of 163 Amherst Street in Brooklyn, New York. We're getting quite a look at Jimmy's life today.

We have one more clip to show you.

Remember that nice stainless steel table in Jimmy's garage? Hey? Hey?

[Audience yells, "YES!"]

Well, you didn't think we'd seen the end of that, did you?

Jimmy's a very neat fellow when it comes to his little hobby.

[Switch to clip of contestant cleaning the table, running at ten times normal speed. Spikes of laughter from audience. Interlace with a few short clips of Chad nodding and smiling.]

I'll tell you, ladies, he cleaned that table a helluva lot better than I could have.

[Muted laughter.]

So, here's his nice sparkling stainless steel table. And look at this, he's dragging over—what is it, audience?

[Someone yells, "It's a person!"]

Yes, it is a person. But not just any person. Let's watch as he undresses her.

Jimmy doesn't worry about any preliminaries; he's just in it for the gold. Look at how he uses his scalpel to slice off her clothes and toss them aside. There's efficiency.

[Switch to audience, all leaning forward in their seats, focused on the video feed.]

I want to ask the studio audience to look carefully at the woman. You can see her breasts rising as she breathes, proving she's still alive.

At least for a few more minutes. [Chuckle.]

We didn't have *Those Little Cameras!* rolling when he kidnapped this woman, so we can't show you that part of his illegal act.

Now, look at his work. The symmetry of his cuts. And there! Did you see that? Let's show that again in slow motion.

[Slo-mo video of contestant pulling all internal organs out and dropping them to the floor. Audience murmurs, some gasp, a few applaud.]

And now for the big finale. Look at that chainsaw. He can maneuver that thing like nobody's business! See how he gets her chopped up into such small pieces? They'd almost fit in the garbage disposal!

[Laughter.]

Almost done.

[Cut video. Focus on Chad.]

Now, was that a criminal act or was it not, audience?

[Hooting and furious applause for twenty seconds.]

Judges, we need a score.

[Focus on judges again. One is shaking his head, clearly disagreeing with the other two. Eventually they work it out and display the score on the screen.]

Well, looky here! *Six thousand points!* Adding that to the score that she already has, and Marsha is now way in the seasonal lead with a total of—

[Looks up at the score board. Pauses until total shows.]

Can you believe it? Seventy-six hundred points!

Marsha, you must be one very happy woman right now.

[Pause. Breaks into a broad smile.]

Actually, ladies and gentlemen, that may be an exaggeration. Because we've been holding out the biggest surprise of all for you!

[Pause.]

Jimmy's friend that he was having that fun with...?

[Looks to audience expectantly. Eventually, they clue in and start to chuckle and whisper to one another.]

Now you're getting it.

Marsha, your *heirs* will be very happy.

[Outpouring of laughter from the audience.]

And that's our show for tonight! I'm Chad Jameson and this has been another edition of *Those Little Cameras!*

Until next time!

[Roll credits.]. 🐝

In The Boys' Clubhouse

When I was a teenager I was a baseball junkie, and the Detroit Tigers were my team.

I watched every game I could on TV, knew the statistics of every player by heart, and when my father drove me to Detroit to watch a game in 1968, it was one of the most memorable days of my life.

That was the year that Denny McLain won 31 games. No pitcher has won 30 games since that season. During the pre-game warm-up, McLain stood at home plate and hit about 50 fungos. These were normally fly balls hit to help the fielders have a bit of practice. McLain didn't want the fielders. He hit all of his balls into the left field bleachers, every one a home run.

I still cherish that memory. One of the best pitchers of my lifetime hitting home runs for practice.

This story is one of those rare cases where the entire plot came to me all at one time, in a flash. Most often, I start writing a story without any idea where it's going or how it's going to get there. It seems to work for me. This one though, came fully formed, imprinted on my mind.

It's one of my favorites.

NELLY STARED OUT INTO CENTER field. Even in the dead of winter, with the lonely seats covered with six inches of hardened snow, Tiger Stadium still caught her breath and made her smile.

The wind whistled through the stands as Nelly walked towards home plate. The snow crunched under her feet, and she shivered as her cold metal bat numbed her hands.

"I made it, Gramps," she whispered. "We've finally got another Bryant in the stadium."

Nelly was nineteen years old, almost twenty. Outside, the cold temperature was twenty-five degrees below zero, and it felt even colder inside the stadium. The night before, twelve people had died of exposure in Detroit. It was the coldest Nelly could ever remember, but nothing was going to stop her. It was Christmas Eve, the anniversary of the day her grandfather died four years earlier, and she was carrying the Bryant name back into Tiger Stadium. She'd remember Gramps in her own way.

She had often thought of breaking into the

stadium, but until this year she hadn't thought of trying in the middle of winter. *Can't imagine why it didn't occur to me*, she thought. *It's the only right time of year to come.*

The Tigers themselves had abandoned the stadium years earlier; only ghosts played here now.

Nelly felt a chill run down her spine as she moved to where home plate hid under the packed snow. She carefully lowered her pail of balls and looked out to center field. "Gramps played here," she said. It was a bit after noon hour, and the shadows hadn't started to creep across the infield yet. Soft flakes of snow drifted down and sparkled as they caught and held onto the balls and bat.

She looked in awe up to the three levels of decks in the left field bleachers. They seemed so close to her.

"Ya gotta love baseball, Nelly, girl," Gramps had said. "Ya gotta love it. It's in you blood same's you coal black hair."

"They won't let me play real baseball, Gramps. I'm only a girl."

"Ain't *nothing* you can't do iffen you want it bad 'nough. Don't you be givin' me that damned nonsense."

Nelly silently remembered. Gramps had taught her how to play. How to judge the spin on a ball as it was being thrown at her, how to slide into bases without injuring herself, how to shield the sun with her glove so she didn't lose high fly balls, how to drag a bunt down the first base line.

But more. He taught her how to love the game, how to watch for the slight movements that would telegraph what a pitcher was planning, how to look for the positioning of the opposing players to know how they judged her. "Strategy's the name o' the game, girl. Don't let no asshole tell you no diff'rent. Iffen you know how the other team plays, you halfway round the diamond already."

Gramps had given Nelly her first baseball glove when she was eight. She practiced throwing an Indian rubber ball against a red brick schoolhouse wall for hours to break the glove in. She applied her grandfather's lessons on hitting and was the star of every team she played for.

The boys hated her. Nelly heard their fathers ridiculing them for letting a girl better them.

At thirteen, the boys decided enough was enough. If they couldn't be better ballplayers than Nelly, they'd just get rid of her. She became the constant target of beanballs, her face often swelling up after being hit by "wild" pitches. Her legs bled from being jumped on when she slid into bases, and her nose was broken three times in two years by stray elbows.

Worst of all, whenever she was hurt, she could hear the boys snicker.

When Nelly was fifteen, she gave up. She'd never get beyond little league without a fight, which meant that the majors were out of the question. It didn't matter how good she was; she was a girl.

She was reminded of a boys clubhouse with a hand painted "No Girls Allowed" sign hanging on the door. Nelly gave up trying to rip down the sign that kept her from being a professional ballplayer. Maybe it wasn't worth enough for her to try, when there were easier things in life to aim for.

She never told her grandfather.

When Gramps died, Nelly had been with him. He was stuck in a narrow metal hospital cot, with clear plastic tubes running up his nose, down his throat, and into his arms. Cancer had spread through his body, and most of the time he was delirious, not recognizing anybody and rambling on about the old teams and games. He smiled whenever he talked about the pinch hit homer that he hit in the '68 World Series.

But there was one last time in the hospital that he recognized Nelly. Suddenly his eyes lost the cloudy fog that lived there most of the time, and he nodded his head, smiling. "Hi there, my little tiger. How's your sluggin' percent today?"

"Fine, Gramps. We'll be leading the league any day now."

Even as they spoke, snow drifted down outside the hospital windows. Christmas Eve. As Nelly watched him in his cot with his hair all fallen out and his face drawn and limp, she knew that she never would tell him about leaving baseball.

"You'll be playin' at Tiger Stadium one day," he said, trying to keep his smile. "I can tell, you'll be hitting fungos into the crowd afore the game and they'll be cheerin' just like you was Dennis McLain back in '68. Wish you could've seen that bastard hit the fungos afore the games. Crowd loved it, just ate it up. Most o' the other players you know, the hitters were out warmin' up their arms, but old Dennis, he was their star pitcher, won thirty-one games that year, he'd stand behind the first base line and hit a bucket o' balls into the left field bleachers just like nothin' else."

Nelly smiled. "Sure, Gramps. I'll be at Tiger Stadium one day. You'll be proud of me."

"I'm already proud o' you." He tried to lift his hand off the starchy white sheets to her but couldn't. "We're a strong family, the Bryants. His voice became steady and clear as he spoke his last words. "Me and my friends, we'll be watching you."

She shivered again in the cold and held her bat between her knees while she unzipped her winter coat and tossed it down. The coldness bit into her instantly, making her take several deep breaths. Goosebumps popped up on her bare arms. She looked to the dugout and yelled, "I made it past the sign, Gramps! I'm in the boys' clubhouse!"

She could imagine the roar of sixty thousand fans as Gramps hit his World Series home run, making him an overnight hero in Detroit. The autumn heat would be hanging in the air, and the excitement would be so concrete, you would almost be able to feel it move through the crowd.

She picked up her ball bucket and moved back behind the first base line, back about ten feet towards the dugout. She was wearing her homemade Tiger uniform, Number 28, the number Gramps had worn, with a large BRYANT stitched neatly across the back of her shoulders.

She hefted the bat, picked up the first ball, and rubbed the snow off before tossing it into the air. Her fingers were already starting to numb.

Nelly swung and felt a satisfying thunk as a painful sting traveled down the length of the bat to her hands. The ball landed about twenty feet short of the left field bleachers, sinking into the snow without a trace.

"That's okay, Gramps," she called. "Just warming up."

The coldness was making Nelly's whole body tremble, and she had a sudden urge to just sit down in the snow and forget this nonsense before she froze to death, joining Gramps in his grave.

No!

She missed the ball with her next swing, but the following shot landed just into the bleachers, and she let out a loud cheer. The fans called to her as she circled the bases. Everyone was watching her, cheering. *"Nelly, Nelly, Nelly!"*

She couldn't feel her toes anymore, nor her ears. Her lungs didn't want to work.

You doin' just fine, girl.

The next three balls all landed in the bleachers, and the coldness didn't bother her. Baseball was all that mattered. And the memory of her grandfather.

She picked up another ball from the grass beneath her. That one landed in the second tier of bleachers, smashing into the bright metal chairs near a group of fans. Two teenage boys chased after the ball as it bounced among the seats.

Nelly no longer cared about the frigid temperature; it could damage her no longer.

"That's as good a ball as I ever hit, you know. You keep'm flyin' like that, you be tossin' my memory right outta this place and be takin' its place with you own."

Nelly laughed. "Nobody could ever replace you, Gramps."

"Quit you blabberin'. The folks ain't here to watch you flap you gums. Give 'em a show."

Nelly turned back to the crowd and hit more fungos. With each one that she hit, the fans grew more and more excited, watching each one to see if she would better her previous distance. Occasionally, one of the balls didn't quite make it to the stands, and one of the outfielders practicing nearby would pick it up and toss it back to the infield. Even on those misses, the crowd would give her polite applause.

"Standin' room only today," said Gramps, looking at the crowd. "We gone be startin' the game pretty soon, girl. Mebbe you'd best be wrappin' things up."

Nelly sighed and stared up again into the sun. She was sweating so much that her uniform was soaked. She was getting a bit tired from the exercise and would need a break before the game started, so she knew that Gramps was right. She knocked a few more balls into the stands and then saluted the crowd with a tip of her cap.

"Good hittin', girl. Welcome to the team."

Nelly smiled as she joined the other ghosts, walking into the dugout to get themselves focused for the game.

Ever After

Without a doubt, this is the most controversial story I've ever written. If you read it, you'll understand why.

It's a story that started with no clear idea where it was going. All I knew at the start was that an older man was sitting chatting with his daughter. I had no clue where it was going from there, and I was damned surprised at who the man turned out to be. I think I was more surprised than my readers!

I wrote this and had it workshopped at the Borderlands Boot Camp by F. Paul Wilson, David Morrell, Thomas F. Monteleone, and Richard Chizmar.

Chizmar is the editor of Cemetery Dance magazine and about a huge number of extremely fine anthologies. He bought the story for his anthology series, Shivers IV.

For short stories (as opposed to novellas), this has to be my all-time favorite of my own work. To the best of my knowledge, there's no other story similar to it.

(Watch, after typing that, I'll pick up an old magazine tomorrow and find a similar story...)

TIRED. DEAD TIRED.

Philip sat in his old blue suede armchair, the one with the worn patches where his elbows rested. He rocked slowly, breathing long sighs, just trying to rest.

"Dad?"

He forced his eyes open and smiled at his daughter sitting on the couch beside him. His smile was forced, but his love for her wasn't.

"What's up, Janie?"

She pulled her legs out from under her and reached for the remote, fumbling with it as she hit the mute button.

Philip didn't mind. He'd seen *Casablanca* countless times before and could almost recite the dialog by heart. He took a drink from his glass of wine and sat forward, forcing himself to pay attention. It wasn't easy sometimes. The days at the loading dock seemed to grow longer and longer, especially in the frigid, cold winter. Sometimes Chicago really sucked.

A thought crossed his mind: time to move someplace warmer. Florida. California. Maybe even

Arizona again. Haven't been there in ages.

"Dad, we need to talk."

"Sure. We can talk."

He rubbed his eyes and looked at her again. She was staring at him. Well, two could play that game. He looked at her, really looked at her for the first time in years. Twenty-five years old last month. He knew she was plain looking: mid-length mousy brown hair, chipmunk cheeks, thin lips. She rarely had dates, but in his eyes, she was the most beautiful girl in Chicago. *Wish the guys her age would see that,* he thought.

She took a sip of her Diet Coke. "You see, the thing is..." She paused and then seemed to force herself to continue. "You and Mom. You know, like we never talk about her. About you."

Philip forced himself to keep a smile on his face. "Your mother was a wonderful woman. You know that."

"Of course I do. That's not what I mean. I just wish we could talk about her. I wish we had some pictures of her."

Philip thought of Marie, formed a complete image in his mind. Over all the years, Marie would never fade. Janie resembled Marie in some ways, but where Janie was soft and weak, her mother was strong and firm. Marie's eyes had been crystal blue, hypnotizing, her hair long, flowing, a beautiful chestnut river.

"I'm sorry, honey, but we don't have any pictures of her. You know that."

Philip took another drink of his wine.

"And why is that?"

Philip told the same lie he always told. "It's too hard

for me to look at her. She meant so much..."

His voice choked slightly.

She reached across to touch his hand.

"You must have kept some. You *must* have. How could you not?"

He shook his head. "Janie, she died more than a dozen years ago. I "

"And I thought the attic would be where you'd keep them."

Fuck, he thought. *Janie, what the hell are you up to?*

"So, it took a while. It's a mess up there."

"Janie, you don't want to do that."

"You know that your wedding pictures are there, right? In that steamer trunk by the back? It took a while to find them, almost two weeks. Every day while you were at the dock."

Philip knocked back the rest of his wine.

"Gotta get a refill," he whispered.

He shuffled into the kitchen, grabbed the bottle of chardonnay from the fridge, and poured a big gulp into his glass.

Looking to the ceiling, he implored, *Please, God, don't make this happen. Not now.*

But his prayer was ignored.

"Dad, are you coming back?"

Philip took a deep breath and went back to the living room. He sat in his comfortable old chair. *Maybe the last time,* he thought.

"What did you find?"

"Well, you know, like I told you. You had your wedding pictures. You and Mom."

Her eyes wanted answers.

"I didn't want the pictures taken." He shook his head slowly. "Your mother insisted. 'I'll only get married once,' she said. And I loved her. You know that."

Janie nodded.

"She wanted the pictures, and..." He shrugged. "I should have gotten rid of them after she died." He laughed. "After all those years of wanting to get rid of them, there was my chance. But, when it came right down to it, I couldn't do it."

"I don't understand how you look the same. Exactly the same."

There, he thought. *It was out in the open now.*

"Yeah." It was all he could think to say.

"It's been thirty years. You haven't gotten any older. How is that possible?"

"I don't know," he said. "I've always been like this."

"What do you mean, always?"

He thought back to when he was thirty-four. The dim recesses of his memory sparked as he struggled to find the event hidden in the broken file cabinets of his mind.

He cringed. *Nobody should ever have to go through that.*

"Dad?"

In the olden days it was easier.

Back when.

Back when he was young for the first time. So long ago, so many hundreds and hundreds of years ago.

Thousands.

Never aging. Never dying. Just stuck in an endless purgatory.

Philip appeared to be about thirty-five years old. When he was young, he'd aged the same as anybody else. Nothing unusual about him that way.

Then, that life-changing event. After that, he stopped aging. All because of that one terrible experience.

He remembered when it first hit him. He had been living in a small village for twenty-three years, just trying to be a simple farmer. Married to Nira, the daughter of the local tribal leader. One day, he woke to find Nira staring from above him in their bed. At first, he thought she wanted his love, but it wasn't that kind of stare.

"Nira, what is it?"

"James, you don't age."

He didn't know what she meant, and he shook his head in confusion.

"You have no lines in your face. Your hair doesn't gray or fall out. Your strength is that of a young man, like Nathan. And your skin. It is still rosy, still plum."

"Nathan is twenty years younger than me, Nira. What are you talking about?"

"Look at me." Her voice was forlorn. "My face is pitted with age. Most of my teeth are gone, and the ones that remain hurt all the time. My color is gray, not pink like yours. I am so tired and sore, ready to die. But not you. Why don't you age?"

"You're talking nonsense. Of course I age."

"Not since the day we first met."

He pulled her down beside him. She *was* talking nonsense.

Five years later, he buried Nira, and by then, the entire village could see he looked almost the same age as his oldest son, Nathan. They could be brothers. The villagers began to fear him. Even his three children avoided him.

He left on his horse, the only possession he took.

"I should be dead by now," he said to himself. "My sons can split what I leave behind."

James rode for two fortnights, finally settling in southern France. He took the name Abdullah and said he was from a vague area to the far east.

Abdullah pitched hay in an inn, a job he felt he was well suited for. He sometimes laughed without really knowing why. He kept to himself and slowly learned the language. It took almost a decade for the people of the small town to accept him.

Another decade, though, and that acceptance turned to whispers in the dark, as his new town, too, noticed that his body refused to age.

Abdullah left in the middle of the night, becoming Richard when he settled in Rome.

Janie was still waiting for him to answer. Her eyes were wide. He almost wished she still wore glasses instead of contacts, so he could have a shield to stop the sharpness of her glare.

"I don't know why I don't age."

Philip didn't want to lie to Janie, but she hadn't given him much choice. He could never tell her the truth, couldn't tell her about the pain that left him almost lifeless and how he overcame so much.

"So, tell me about it. How old are you?"

Again, he shook his head. "I don't know any more." In his thoughts, he added, *I was born before calendars were commonplace.*

Now it was her turn to be speechless.

Philip couldn't help himself any longer. The memories of that day flooded through him. He hadn't thought of it in at least a century. Probably longer.

He woke after being beaten, stuck in a dingy cell filled with shit and rats. There were no windows, and little light came in from the front of the building.

Three other men were in the stinking dungeon. One was dead, and rats nibbled on his feet. He imagined maggots feasting on the rest of him, but he didn't go close enough to check.

The other two prisoners were common thieves of some kind. He knew little about them but prayed for their wellbeing in any case.

His own wellbeing was not in doubt. He knew he would die today.

He was nodding off when the guards pulled open the heavy wooden door and one of them stabbed him in his foot with a spear. "Get up, you fool!"

He did as he was told. The guards efficiently chained the three prisoners together.

Everybody knew the rest of the story. How he was

forced to carry his own cross to the crucifixion, how the nails ripped into his flesh.

And the awful, awful pain, he thought. The nails went through his wrists, not his palms, and he still imagined pain in those same wrists, every night.

"My God, why hast thou forsaken me...?" Everybody thought he was dead when they pulled him down and buried him in a cave later that day.

But a spark of life remained. A spark that grew brighter and stronger. Three days later, God completely returned his strength to him.

As he left Jerusalem, he vowed never to allow anybody to torture him again. He swore to live in obscurity and die the same way. The price of being God's son was too high, and he was unwilling to pay it.

Jesus walked south, into the forsaken desert of the Sinai. He used a sharp rock to cut off much of his long hair and beard. He looked and acted like a lost beggar, and by the time he reached the small village where he met Nira, he had cast off his old persona. He became James, taking the name of his younger, quieter brother.

He lived happily for many years, until Nira aged naturally and he aged not at all.

James, then Abdullah, then Samuel, then...

After a while, he couldn't remember everybody he'd been.

It was as Samuel that he finally understood why he wasn't aging. He had cast off his ministry, his public pronouncements, his followers. He knew that the Holy Father was telling him that this was unacceptable; his body was on hold until he continued spreading His word.

He realized this while sitting on the banks of the Tiber River one hot summer night. It was the only thing that made sense.

"You'll wait forever, Father."

Samuel thought he heard the wind whisper back at him. "We'll see..."

Philip took another drink of wine, clenching his fists, feeling the imaginary pain in his wrists once again.

Samuel, then Christopher, then Michael...

"Come on, Dad," Janie said. "Tell me what the real story is."

"I don't know what to tell you. I feel the same as any other person, the same as you or your mother. It's all just an illusion. Some weird disorder or something that makes me look the same as I did thirty years ago."

He licked his lips, feeling the same old lie coming out between them. *Father, why do you make me suffer so?*

"It's a medical thing. I went to Doctor Hardaway a long time ago. He was puzzled at first, too, but he did some research and came up with a long Latin name for some rare disease." He shrugged. "I don't remember what it was. "Didn't much matter once he figured it out."

She seemed to want to believe him, but she hesitated. "It'll last as long as you live?"

"Don't know. Doc didn't have a prognosis. Didn't know if it would affect my lifespan either." He shook his head. "I really can't say it matters much without your mother."

Janie went to him and held him, moved by the phony tears in his eyes.

He hugged her closely and cried. As he held her, he knew what he had to do, and the tears turned real.

That night, Philip woke at a little after four a.m. He shuffled down the hall to Janie's room and eased open the door, listening for her heavy breathing before pushing the door all the way open.

He watched as she slept, so peaceful. He loved her as much as he had loved Marie.

But Janie would never stop watching him now. She was probably already thinking of searching the Internet, and if she did, she would find no medical disorder matching what he told her. She might even call Doctor Hardaway, who would protest at first, but who would eventually tell Janie that there had been no such conversation. His secret would come out. He would be forced into the spotlight again, and that he could not allow.

Philip reached for the pillow and crushed the life out of his beloved daughter.

Dan Marciano was taking longer than usual to acclimatize to his new name, his new life. Los Angeles was too big for him. He was back to thinking that Arizona would have been a better choice.

Two months had passed since he left Chicago with Janie's lifeless body in the trunk of his car. Nobody would miss her for long. She had no boyfriend, no real friends of any kind.

He imagined that after a few days, the neighbors might notice Philip and his daughter had pulled up stakes. They'd talk among themselves for awhile, and there might be a short investigation, but nothing would come of it. Dan was an expert at disappearing without a trace.

He buried Janie in southern Montana.

But her memory still haunted him. As had Marie before her. And Claire before *her*. And Jasmine. And Diana. And on and on. Ever after.

JOHN R LITTLE

One of my favorite books is Inferno, written by Larry Niven and Jerry Pournelle. It was published in 1976 and was loosely based on Dante's famous epic poem of the same name.

I've never re-read the book but still have very fond memories of it.

Came time to write a story and I wanted to write a bit of a spin-off of Niven and Pournelle's novel. I have no clue why. It just felt like the thing to do!

I still need to go back and re-read the novel one day.

THEY BUILT INFERNO IN THE middle of nowhere. Twenty miles southeast of El Paso, Texas, just off I-10. In August, the temperature easily passes a hundred degrees. Thank God there wasn't much humidity.

I could feel my face burning after only a few minutes. The latest and greatest theme park was set in the middle of a *real-life* inferno. Must have made the planners chuckle. Whoever *they* might be. I was still betting Disney was behind this, even if they wouldn't admit it.

I stood in the middle of the massive parking lot that was filled with cheap Japanese imports. American as apple pie.

Laura climbed out of the passenger side and immediately started in on me, shaking her head as she complained. "I told you we shoulda waited until a weekday. Look at that lineup. And it's *so* hot."

"I wanted to be here on opening day."

"You didn't have to bring me."

"Oh, sure, like the *Times* is going to publish my story without pictures."

She just shrugged. *Hell is a good place for you,* I wanted to say. But I kept my mouth shut. Laura might be a pain in the ass, but she was the best photographer I had ever worked with.

I wished that Bobby had come with me instead. He wasn't interested, though. Wanted to just stay in the little townhouse we share in Jersey. "Ray," he'd said with a hug when I left our place to head to the airport. "You go get the goods and tell me all about it." He punched my shoulder for luck.

I gave him a kiss on the cheek and waved as I left. That had been two days ago; I missed him already.

"Well, c'mon," Laura said. "Let's go if we're gonna do this thing."

"Yeah," I mumbled. "Just a second. Gotta catch some first impressions."

I grabbed my mini-recorder and stared at the massive theme park in front of me. I knew I'd never recreate the same feelings if I left it to the end of the day.

"The first thing you see is a massive chain link fence. We're about five hundred feet away, surrounded by a rainbow of dusty old cars; even they seem like they're wilting in this terrible heat."

From the corner of my eye I saw Laura shaking her head impatiently. *Good you can wait,* I thought.

"The fence looks to be about fifteen feet high, stretching out as far as we can see in either direction. This is a big fucker. Looks like a concentration camp crossed with Disneyland. High lookouts every—oh, let's call it every two hundred feet—can't see who's in them. Maybe nobody. Maybe actors. Maybe animatronics. Maybe demons. Beyond the fence in the distance, I can see towers, spires, colorful rides or something."

Finally the heat was getting to me, too, and I pulled my Yankees cap down farther over my forehead and wished I had brought a bottle of water with me. I walked toward the entrance, and Laura trailed along behind me. As much as I disliked her, with her holier-than-thou attitude and her squeaky voice, she could yank that camera of hers into place in a second and had the fastest and most true aim of anyone at the *New York Times*. I had to grudgingly admit that I wouldn't be where I was without her.

But that didn't mean I had to like her.

After sidling between the empty cars, we eventually reached the front entrance, and I added some notes to my tape. "The sign says 'Welcome to Inferno,' and there's a caricature of a devil rising up above the turnstiles. A happy go lucky kind of guy, red steam swirling off him as he laughs and waves the tourists inside."

Laura shot several photos of the entrance. I wasn't sure we'd be using any from this angle, but what the heck; it got her in the spirit of things.

I watched as she finished up. Her cool eyes seemed to be focused even more than the lens of her camera. Damn, when she took herself seriously, I could see why most guys were drawn to her: long dark hair flowing back under her hat, a slim figure, pouting lips. She was photogenic in a weird way. Not my type, though.

The main entrance had a crowd of people milling

around, trying to squeeze themselves through the turnstiles and into the park.

We walked over to one side, toward the "Groups and Press" private entrance. Much smaller, less gaudy, and no lines, which made us happy.

"Mr. Jenkins! Ms. Chambers! Welcome to Inferno."

A pudgy forty-something guy grabbed my hand and shook it vigorously. He looked like a bobblehead as he nodded back and forth between me and Laura.

"Hi, glad to meet you," I said.

"My name is Virgil," he said, still nodding.

Of course it is, I thought. *Dante's guide.*

"All our guides are named Virgil," he added. "An in-joke for some. For the rest, just a name that's easy to remember."

"Quite a setup you have here." I pulled my hand away, waving at the grounds. "Must have cost a lot of money." I had my tape recorder going; you never know when you'll pick up a worthwhile quote.

"Not my department, I'm afraid." He shrugged. "Please, let me escort you inside."

Virgil was about five foot seven and fat. His handshake was damp. Even without knowing who the other guides might be, I wished for a different Virgil.

Laura frowned. We followed him through the gates.

And into hell itself.

"Oh, my God," said Laura. She brought her hands to her mouth in surprise.

I whispered into the mic, "Optical illusion of some kind. The park seems to stretch forever."

The fences were no longer visible from inside the park. We were in the middle of a for lack of a better word   landscape, that was as foreign to us as Manhattan would be to an Eskimo.

The ground was soft to walk on, like putty. Light blue, mimicking the sky outside the park. In contrast, the sky here was blood red, streaks of dark purple running through it like racing cirrus clouds. I recorded the colors and added, "But it isn't dark, like you'd expect. And there's no indication of a ceiling. The sky looks a million miles high, just the wrong color."

"Gets 'em every time," laughed Virgil. His mouth was stretched wide by his grin, showing too many bright and sharp teeth.

Laura uncharacteristically grabbed my hand. "I have a feeling we're not in Kansas anymore, Toto..."

I didn't answer her. I was too busy staring at Virgil. It was more than the sharpened teeth, which I hadn't noticed outside the gates. His face was now drawn thin and his ears larger than they should have been. I looked down and saw the scaly red fingers that hung like charred twigs from his wrist.

Quick change artist.

Actually, more likely a different guy. Switched while we weren't paying attention.

Laura looked over to me. "The effects are amazing." Virgil just looked back and forth between us again.

"Tell me how this is done," I finally said.

Virgil barked another laugh, and I could see his pointed tongue. "Our marketing campaign says this really is part of Hell. An arm reaching out from the core if you want to think of it that way. Who am I to say different?"

I tried another tactic. "Off the record. Call it deep

background. I don't want to spoil it for anyone, but is there some kind of lens above us, changing the color? It doesn't look like a roof up there."

Virgil just laughed. Then his voice turned to a whisper. "Do you feel safe, Ray?" I didn't know what to do, couldn't seem to move my feet or even mutter a reply. I found myself staring into his eyes, his irises swirling like miniature kaleidoscopes, swallowing me. I've never seen such convincing contact lenses and couldn't take my eyes away.

"Ray!" Laura had moved to me and shook me out of my trance. "Ray, what's wrong with you?"

I swallowed and took a step away from Virgil, staring down at his feet. "Not a very friendly welcome, is it?"

"Ah, just having a bit of fun with you. I promise to be good." He laughed, with a hidden implication: how much was his promise worth?

I grabbed the mic and started rattling off some quick descriptions of the buildings I could see. There were so many of them that it was pointless to try to be thorough. We'd be seeing the key ones as part of the tour, but I wanted to have a few words about the general overview. Some large boxy buildings, some cylinders, a lot of small stands where people could buy souvenirs. Teeshirts, figurines, plastic drinking glasses. The usual crap, all emblazoned with "Come Back to Inferno" in bright red letters.

"Advertising," said Virgil. "Gets more customers here. Same as your story will."

"Don't count your chickens yet. The story might not be very positive."

Virgil nodded. "Probably won't be. Doesn't matter. Anything you write will get people to come, just to see how you could possibly have gotten everything wrong."

"No such thing as bad advertising," added Laura.

"You got it. And there's a sucker born every minute. Maybe you'll run into old P.T. himself later on and see if he still believes that."

Laura had taken a few shots, including one of Virgil. He posed for her. "Don't bother me none," he said. "I like this better than the way I look on the outside. A fat P.R. hack."

"Do you live in El Paso?" I asked.

"Not even close."

We kept walking.

"In order to get through the whole park in the few hours we have available, we're going to take the express tour. Sorry, but if you want the deluxe experience, you'll have to come back as a paying customer."

I couldn't help but smile. "What's the admission fee?"

Virgil gazed at the guests and didn't immediately answer. I followed his stare to my right, and it hit me that there must be thousands of people who had preceded me into the park. Men, women, and children. I scanned around and waved at Laura to take a picture. "Mostly children," I said.

"Yes, we do attract kids. That's part of the allure of being a theme park, of course."

He waved to us, directing us toward a large building that had a bright green sign on it. "Visitors' Orientation."

As we got closer, Virgil said, "The admission is very competitive with other theme parks, of course."

"If this is supposed to be an arm of Hell, how do you explain why Hell would want money?"

"Why indeed? That's not our currency. Souls are."

Laura jumped in. "But you can't have somebody's soul until they die."

I couldn't help but be irritated by her comment.

"Aah, yes, the old expectations coming out once again. Of course, we're very patient. All we want right now is a promise." I thought I heard him add, "...or a deed," but I couldn't swear to that.

We went into a side entrance, once again to avoid the crowds. "Private, faster showing," said Virgil. "Here you see a map of Inferno."

A red cross marked "You Are Here" was at one edge of the map. There was no scale, but it seemed that the canvas covered a huge area. The grounds were built like concentric circles numbered from one to nine.

A recorded voice started to speak, to explain the map, but Virgil waved his hand and the voice stopped immediately. "No time for all that. Dante had nine circles of Hell, as I'm sure you know. We thought it'd be fun to use the same concept. Of course, a lot of years have passed, and some of the rules have changed, so we've modernized things somewhat."

That didn't sound right. "Isn't a sin a sin? Why would that change over time?"

"Well, we move with the times. After all, Ray..." he smiled at me with those rotating hypnotic eyes again. "...when Dante was writing, sodomy was a terrible sin, sentencing those who did it to the Seventh Level of

Hell." He laughed. "Are you sure you don't like progress?"

I looked at Laura, but she didn't seem to be paying attention. I never hid being gay but didn't flaunt it either. She just kept staring at the circles on the map.

The Seventh Level. I wondered what that meant; maybe I should have read Dante more carefully before coming here. I'd only skimmed the book. Way too hard to read.

Virgil answered my unspoken question. "You'll find out."

For the next thirty minutes, Virgil told us a condensed version of how Inferno was laid out. I held my mic out to catch his speech rather than having to dictate it all back later. The place was a lot more complicated than I expected; suddenly all I could think about was the engineering problems.

Virgil cut that thought off as soon as it crossed my mind. "There are no engineering problems. Remember, what you're seeing is simply an extension of hell, not newly manufactured buildings."

Right.

He stared at me, almost as if daring me to contradict him, which I had no intention of doing.

"Okay then," he said with a nod. "Be on your way."

Laura said, "Hold on. Aren't you coming with us?"

He smiled, those pointed teeth gleaming even more brightly. "No. You must travel Inferno by yourselves, the same as you go through your lonely little lives."

In front of us, a door appeared. It had been hidden

behind a swirl of mist. The door swung open and all we could see was another fog behind it.

"Go!"

Laura and I took tentative steps forward. I kept reminding myself that this was just a theme park, intended to frighten us, no different than the haunted houses at any amusement park.

"Remember what I've told you." Virgil lowered his voice back to a normal level and chuckled. "Or read your notes if your memory isn't good enough. Level One awaits you."

We stepped through the door, and I felt Laura's hand grab onto mine; I didn't mind at all.

The door slammed shut behind us and the fog subsided, as emerald lighting rose from... somewhere. We could see again.

"Ray, what was Level One? I can't remember what he said."

"In Dante's *Inferno*, it was Limbo, a place for people who hadn't really done anything wrong, just hadn't done anything right, either." I remembered Virgil saying there was no longer room in Hell for people who didn't belong there, so Limbo was somewhere else. He hadn't said where. "Nowadays, Level One is for the small stuff. Cheating at a casino, lying, that kind of thing."

The fog had lowered enough that we could see people in the distance. They were wandering aimlessly, lost in the desert. And a desert it was, a lot worse than the land surrounding El Paso. The heat hadn't hit us immediately but was rising second by second. I stared in horror as steam rose from my arms, sucking every bit of moisture out, leaving my skin feeling like ancient parchment. Laura dropped my hand and rubbed her arms. "Too hot!" she cried.

"Let's move it."

Although we couldn't see exactly where we were going, Virgil had told us to walk in a straight line in each level. We walked quickly, feeling dehydrated and thirsty as we moved. There was no moisture in my mouth   nothing to swallow. It was hard to talk. Blisters popped up on my lips.

The inhabitants of Level One moved slowly, like zombies, trapped in this eternal oven.

And still it seemed to get hotter.

After a few minutes, another door appeared in front of us and we stumbled through it. I thought I would scald my hand on the door, but that didn't happen. I didn't question why. We fell inside, into the first way station. A cool breeze kissed our faces, and a small stream meandered by.

Laura jumped into the water without waiting, and I was right behind her. I knew from our orientation that the way stations were safe.

I swallowed some of the sweet water and let my body sink below the surface. All I could see of Laura was her head angled so that her mouth and nose were above the water.

Time to think. Time to feel. The way stations were where we were supposed to digest our experiences.

All I felt was irritation at Laura.

It was weird. As I had walked through the heat, it was like the sky and the ground acted like an amplifier, bringing out the small sins that Level One contained.

Nonsense. But I did think about whatever stupid things she must have done.

I felt the petty jealousies and heard the lies she had told in the past. She would be full of them. Exaggerations told at the office Christmas party in return for better assignments. She stole fifty dollars from petty cash once. And the biggest one: she lied to my face, told me that she was proud to work with me. Now I knew she hated me, hated the fact that I would never be attracted to her. She took this assignment to make me fail.

The bitch.

I kept a straight face as I climbed out of the water and watched her emerge a moment later.

"That was hard," she said. "Maybe we should go back."

"You really should have listened," I snapped. "The doors are oneway."

Her eyes widened. "Okay," she said. "We'll get through this together."

"Let's go. The sooner we finish, the happier we'll both be."

She picked up her camera and followed me to the next door.

Level Two was for lust. Cheaters and womanizers. The landscape was covered with an ocean filled with whirlpools, and inside each one was somebody who had spent their days lusting after another. They continually drowned, or almost drowned, choking for all eternity as water washed down their throats and only occasional gulps of air let them breathe.

"Terrific animatronics on this level," I said to my recorder.

We walked over a bridge about ten feet above the water. This level of Hell didn't harm us directly.

Laura stared at the women and men below her. They were naked, some fat, some thin, all waterlogged and covered with a green slime.

"Disgusting," she said. Her hand tried to find mine, but I rejected her.

You stupid bitch, I thought. I thought about all the times that she had screwed men, had their cocks rutting up inside her while she clawed at their backs. The vision made me sick. All she cared about was her own pleasure.

I wished I could banish the feelings that washed over me, banish the dirty secrets that spilled out of her gutter of a mind.

"Fucking pig."

"What? Ray?"

I didn't know I had spoken out loud. "Virgil," I said quickly. "I was thinking of Virgil."

She nodded and slowly took a few pictures with her telephoto lens. Probably just wanted to see the damned men's cocks.

After a moment, I grabbed her arm and pulled her toward the next way station.

The next few levels were uneventful.

Level three was for Self-indulgence (formerly Gluttony). Here was where overeaters ended up as well as alcoholics and drug-users. It was a slushy, half-frozen landscape, and as we walked through it without shoes, our feet began to freeze. It was like marching through a Slurpee. The inhabitants were tinged with blue, and it seemed like they could barely move. We rushed through as fast as we could.

Laura's history of drug abuse came to me along with the vision of many nights she had spent drinking alone or sitting in a sleazy bar, picking up random men. She loved to be high on heroin. She just revolted me.

Level Four was for Fraud, no longer Dante's sin of Avarice. Identity theft and email scams were the sins of many recent arrivees. There was a large plain that seemed to stretch forever, and everywhere we looked, there were battles, sinners continually fighting to see who would possess large boulders. I assumed the fights lasted forever with no winners and no losers. There must have been a loop, but I couldn't detect it for as long as we watched.

Laura's frauds bubbled around inside me, and I knew she had picked up credit card numbers when she once worked in a restaurant, kept the numbers and used them herself later. And she had often used her business credit card from the *Times* for purely personal purposes. Once, she even bought a new high definition television on credit, thanks to the *Times*.

Level Five was for Greed, replacing Dante's Ill Temper. I almost laughed at the thought of ill temper being a sin halfway through Hell. Who wouldn't end up here?

Around us were crowds of people, the greedy who hurt other people in their desire to want more, to own more, to have more than anybody else.

Like Laura.

Greed oozed from her, and I knew she planned on taking complete credit for the success of my article about Inferno. She wanted the money and the prestige. She wanted my chance at a journalism award. She wanted my job. She wanted my life, for Crissakes.

Well, she wasn't going to get it that easily.

I kept my distance from her as we watched the people wandering beside us in the mucky filth of the River Styx. They were being pulled down into the marsh, gurgling among the reeds as they spit out the mud they swallowed.

This is where she belongs, I decided. Of all the levels of hell we had seen, this is where Laura belongs. Among all the other scum and filth-eaters.

"Ray, are you okay?"

I looked back to her. "Sure. Why?"

She shrugged and gave me her fucking phony smile. "You just look a little upset. And you're not taking any notes."

"Yeah, well, don't forget I've got a good memory."

This time she started walking to the next way station, and it was me doing the following.

Virgil was waiting for us inside, smiling. "Welcome to what we call the Interface. It's the way station separating Upper Hell from Lower Hell."

His face seemed to be crawling with maggots. I don't know why I hadn't noticed that earlier. Even so, I felt more comfortable around him than Laura. She was the true evil, hiding behind a pretty mask.

"Can we just skip to the end?" she asked Virgil.

He just laughed again. "No, there's no short cuts for you." He offered us a drink of water and a chance to rest. Then he added, "It's noon now. You should get moving if you want to get out of here in a reasonable time."

"Hold on," I said. "How is it possible that you think people will ever return here after seeing how horrible it is?"

Virgil nodded, as if he were thinking of the question for the first time. His irises started that spinning thing again and his answer was almost a whisper. "Nobody's really bothered in the long run. They remember the adventure, maybe some thrills, the cute Disney-like figures who seem to enjoy their time in Hell. It's like river rafting or hiking. A bit of risk adds to the reward." He shrugged, not caring.

I thought of the article I was going to write and the photos that Laura was taking. "Us, too?"

He laughed again. "Guess you'll find out when you see what you end up writing."

"This just isn't a nice place. My tape recorder has been on. And she's taken pictures. We'll get it right."

"Ah, they're just trinkets."

And then he vanished. I reached out to find the hidden mirrors but couldn't find them.

We walked though Level Six quickly. Dante had reserved this level for Heresy, which seemed pretty laughable today. In this new Hell, Level Six was for

Anger. The inhabitants were in terrible pain, being entombed in fiery graves, screaming endlessly. We could see them burning in their coffins because the ground and their caskets were glass. We couldn't get out of there fast enough.

Level Seven was violence.

Level Eight was Organized Crime. Big-time drug traffickers and Mafia members showed up here. In Dante's version, it was for people who had committed fraud. Small potatoes now.

Level Nine was Mass Murder, Terrorism, and Crimes Against Humanity, something Dante never had to worry about. His Level Nine was only for Treachery.

We didn't get as far as Level Eight or Level Nine.

As soon as we walked out to Level Seven, Laura looked at me with those big blue eyes of hers, and just for a moment I remembered the other Laura, the one with the public face of professionalism, the one that most people liked and most men wanted. She had me for a moment until I regained my thoughts.

Stupid cunt. God I hated her.

"What?" I asked.

"We should just walk through as fast as we can. Get to the end and get out of here." She pursed her lips and touched my arm. "We've got enough material for the story now."

"Maybe." I walked to the next door and pulled it open.

This was the Seventh Level of Hell, where Virgil said that the old sin of sodomy was punished. This also once included suicides. I wondered if that was still a sin.

The stench hit me as soon as we walked through the door; it was the most horrid smell I'd ever experienced. After a moment, I knew what it was. Blood. A river of blood lay in front of us. It was deep red, flowing slowly, like a current of filth. Large sections looked like burned rafts: coagulated sludge. The illusion was totally convincing.

There was no escape from the smell of rot, the stench of dead animals magnified a thousand times. I almost vomited, but somehow I managed not to.

In the river were the lost souls that had performed violent acts in their times. A teenager flowed by on the current, and I could imagine how he had held up a liquor store, killing the owner by stabbing him twenty times with a paring knife.

Another floater went by. He looked like a wife-beater.

Most of the sinners were men, but I could see a few women in the distance. On the far bank was a group of centaurs holding something that looked like assault rifles. They were guarding the sinners and occasionally would randomly shoot at one of them. The centaurs laughed when they hit one and then would sit quietly until they got bored again.

Thousands of bodies floated slowly by, each one covered with sticky blood and scabs. I could now see that the river-blood was boiling.

"Ray, I can't do this one." Laura held her hand to her mouth. "I can't breathe. I'm gonna puke."

"There's the bridge," I said. "We have no choice." I

pulled her roughly to our left, toward the narrow wooden bridge spanning the blood.

As I touched her, I gasped with horror as I felt a vision in my mind.

Laura last summer. Walking in Times Square. Late. Midnight or later. A side street. She sees a man wanting something. She smiles. Goes down the side street toward him. He whispers something to her, but it's not what she wants. Or maybe it is. "Fucking homo!" she says. She pulls out a gun and shoots him in the knee. He falls to the ground. As he screams in pain, she kneels down and grabs his head, smashing it over and over again on the curb until his brains fell out.

I pull my hand away from her and blurted, "You're a gay basher!"

"What?"

"Don't look so innocent. I felt it. How could you do that? What did he do to you?" I moved toward her, feeling my anger rising.

"Ray, I don't know what "

She didn't finish; my hands were crushing her throat. I wanted to break her neck. I looked into her eyes as they slowly glazed over. Her arms fell limp, but I kept squeezing, making sure that the evil bitch never again practiced her hate crimes.

It felt like hours that I held her, not willing to let her drop, but eventually I did. My arms were numb from the pressure. She landed on the bank of the river, and I kicked her dead body into the flowing blood.

Behind me, I heard familiar laughter. Virgil.

He patted me on my back. "Good job, Ray! Better than I could have done myself."

"Bitch."

"Well, yes, you could say that." He squeezed my shoulder. "Of course, you could also say that everything you thought you knew about her was just a bit of suggestion on my part."

At first I didn't know what he meant. I was so convinced of how awful Laura was. "You mean she didn't?"

"Kill someone? No, of course not. No drugs, no theft, none of that other stuff, either."

I couldn't believe what I was hearing. "But, you let me kill her." I glanced down to see Laura's body floating away in the blood and filth.

"We all make choices, Ray."

Virgil started to walk me to a door I hadn't seen before. "Don't worry, she won't end up here. She's going upstairs."

I was numb. *I killed her?*

"Enjoy writing your story. You won't remember much of this, of course. You'll be surprised to see that Laura got lost on the way home and somebody mugged her, killing her." He nodded. "She was a good girl."

"I can't write about this place," I said.

"Sure you can. But, take one last look at the river of blood before we go. Our Level for Violence." He turned me around to see the swollen bodies spitting out blood as they flowed down the river. "After all, you'll be back."

Climbing Mount Turnpike

I haven't written many ghost stories. For some reason, it's just not my thing. This story is a bit of an exception.

It started out as a pure adventure story. I had a dream where I was climbing up a cliff, just like the boys in the story, and I couldn't get back down. The only place to go was to jump to a ledge across a chasm. In the dream, I didn't make it, and I woke, absolutely terrified from falling.

I'm quite scared of heights, so that didn't help.

Fortunately, I know what to do with my nightmares, so I got out of bed immediately and started typing. It was the middle of the night, but that wasn't going to stop me. I wrote the first section that night with no idea where the story was going to go next. I thought I might end up abandoning it if something interesting didn't come to me.

When I woke in the morning, the rest of the story had worked its way out in my subconscious, so it was all there, ready to blast out of my fingers when I was able to get back to the computer.

This story was originally published as a limited-edition chapbook, supposedly to give away with the limited edition of The Memory Tree, my first novel.

As far as I know, though, only 10 copies were actually printed and I ended up with all of them. If you have one, you have an extraordinarily rare item. You're also probably a sister of mine, one of my children, or a close friend.

I WAS TWELVE YEARS OLD WHEN my father died. Killed, actually. His car was blasted to bits by a two ton screaming down the turnpike. The guy at the wheel was half asleep after driving eighteen hours without a break. He had a deadline. I was told he shrugged when the cops arrested him. He asked for a coffee after his hands were cuffed behind his back.

That was June 15, 1992. The start of my most miserable summer.

My mother tried to make things better. Every morning, she'd gently wake me, breakfast already on the table. She cooked more that summer than I could ever remember. Bacon, eggs, pancakes, sausages, toast, ham, muffins, and everything else you could think of. She had some kind of a rotation so that every day had something different, but I didn't much care.

I smiled and pretended to be happy. I knew she wanted to be there for me, to help me, but the muffins tasted like coffin sawdust, and I could see my father's blood running when I cut into the over-easy eggs.

The summer before that—1991. Now, *that* was a summer. Dad took a whole month off work. Well, I found out later that the shoe factory he worked at had shut down production due to slow sales, but he said he was taking time off to be with me.

"C'mon, Sport," he'd call to me. "Rise and shine. The day's a wasting." He never called me Jimmy, always Sport.

I'd always jump out of bed when he called me, toss some clothes on, and run down from the back bedroom to the kitchen to see what he had planned for the day.

Fishing, hunting, playing ball, whatever it was didn't matter. Every day was a magical surprise. No kid in Kansas was happier than me that summer.

Dad always punched me lightly twice on my shoulder when it was time to get going. One of those funny little habits that people have.

I sure missed that shoulder punch the following year.

"Hey, Jimmy! C'mon. You can't stop now. We're almost there!" Scott was a few steps ahead of me and I craned my head to look up at him. His shoes were just above my head.

"It's too steep," I said. "I can't make it."

"Pussy."

That got me climbing again. Scott looked down and smiled. "Dad wants you to do this."

"How do you know what he wants? He's dead."

"Yeah, well, I'm the older one. I knew him better than you."

I shook my head and mumbled, "Did not."

The hill started off gently at the bottom, but it quickly veered upward. Trees and bushes at the bottom made it easy to climb at first, but now, there wasn't much to hold onto other than small holes we'd poked in the walls of the cliff.

Dirt fell down on me as Scott climbed another couple of steps.

I couldn't look down. From the bottom, looking up, it hadn't been that scary, but halfway up, I glanced down and it was a *long* way down. I felt dizzy and started to panic, grabbing at the last bits of shrubbery beneath my hands. I felt sure I was going to fall.

Scott saw the panic in my eyes. "Just close your eyes, like I told ya."

I did, and after a moment, my heart stopped pounding quite as much. I kept climbing and didn't look down again.

It was okay to look up, though. When I did, it seemed like I was getting close, maybe only another twenty feet to go.

At the top was the turnpike where Dad had been killed. I could see the bottom of the guard rail that was supposed to stop anyone from falling off. It was a joke, since it was right on the edge.

Scott thought that climbing up the cliff would be a pilgrimage to our father. I suppose he thought that the effort would somehow provide closure to the summer of hell we had been through.

He was fifteen that year, and somehow much more mature than those extra three years should have allowed. On June 30, only two weeks after the accident, he came home and told me and Mom he had gotten a job and wasn't going back to school. Mom tried to talk him out of quitting school, but no dice. He was taller than her, stronger, and somehow, seemed older.

"It's my turn to take care of us," he said.

What he didn't say was that he took Dad's job at the shoe factory. No education required, and the work needed to be done by somebody, so the foreman signed Scott up without flinching. So, I'm told, anyhow.

The summer of 1992.

Beautiful sunshine that I never noticed. Friends dropping by to shoot hoops or go wander the woods. I always shook them off. All I could manage was to smile at Mom and pretend I wanted to stay home and be with her. All I really wanted to do was to spend one more day with Dad, to feel him double punch my shoulder one last time.

The worst part was never having the chance to say good-bye.

The casket was closed at the funeral. The undertaker couldn't salvage enough of his face to allow an open casket. All I saw at the service was a long shiny brown box. It wasn't real, somehow, but I knew I had to make it real. I just didn't know how.

We were nearing the top of Mount Turnpike. Another clump of dirt fell down on me. I shook it from my head, and as I did that, I accidentally looked to the side and could see how high we were.

"Holy crap."

I froze again, not able to get the sight out of my mind. Before we started, I knew we'd be climbing about a hundred feet. That didn't sound so bad, but when you looked down, it was terrifying. It was the same as clinging to the outside window ledge in an office building, ten floors up.

There was nothing more to hold on to. We were climbing completely vertically now, had been for the past ten feet or so, and the only thing holding us were outcrops of rocks or clay. I didn't believe they would hold me.

Scott yelled down to me, "I'm there!"

I looked up and saw that he was close to the lowest rung of the four yellow bars that hung down below the edge of the cliff. I suppose they were there to stop erosion. Scott was trying to reach the first bar but couldn't quite make it. At least his feet were in a stable place, so he seemed like he was out of danger.

Not me.

I reached up and grabbed onto a rock. It easily pulled out of the cliff and fell. I quickly put my hand back where it had been before and froze.

I couldn't hear any noise when the rock landed.

Still about five feet for me to climb.

Scott worked every day that summer, even July 4. I didn't know much about household finances back then, but Mom sure seemed to appreciate when he brought his paycheck home every second Friday.

He never became a father figure to me or anything, but he was always there in the background, trying to help out. Even though he wasn't around much during the day, he couldn't have helped notice I was depressed and hurting, but he never said anything about it.

Until Labor Day.

"C'mon, Jimmy," he said when we woke that morning. "We're going somewhere."

"Where?" I kept the blanket covering my head, just wanting to keep sleeping.

"You'll see."

Until that day, I'd never heard of anyone climbing Mount Turnpike. We all called it that, even though it didn't really have a name. It was just a cliff beside the highway.

Although some older guys had talked about climbing part way up, I never heard anybody claim to go all the way to the top. But, that's where my father was, so Scott's idea somehow made a weird kind of sense to me.

My hands were slippery. The sun was blazing hot, a typical Kansas heat, and I had to blink sweat from my eyes, too.

I wasn't sure if I could make it any farther. I was scared, but more than that, I was tired. We'd been climbing for a couple of hours, and I wasn't sure I had any strength left to finish. Even five feet now seemed like a million miles.

Scott looked down at me and shouted, "C'mon, Sport. You can do it."

I stared at him, saw his gawking face smiling down at me. He had never called me *Sport* before. That was Dad's name for me. I wasn't sure how I felt about Scott using it.

"Maybe I should go back," I said after a moment. "I don't think I can make it."

I forced myself to look up at him again, wondering if he could even hear my weak voice.

"You got no choice." He paused and then added, "You'd never be able to climb back down. Up is hard enough, but down would be impossible."

Part of me knew he was right. To climb down, I'd have to *look* down in order to find places to put my feet, and I knew I couldn't do that.

I almost started to cry. Might have if Scott wasn't looking down at me.

"C'mon, Sport, you can do it."

I blinked back the tears and pushed myself up. The next rock I grabbed held firm, and I was able to move up another couple of feet without trouble.

Scott waited for me. I'm not sure how long it took, but soon we were close to the same height. I felt a feeling of relief wash over me; maybe I could do this after all.

"What now?" I asked. Even though this was new to both of us and I could see the same things he could, he was the leader.

We had separated a little bit on the way up. He was about six feet from me, but both at the same level. It just felt so good to be able to see him face to face.

We both had our feet on outcropped rocks, so we were very stable, and our hands held onto bits of clay near our shoulders.

The problem was that I couldn't see any more outcroppings above us. In fact the last few feet of the cliff looked very smooth and seemed to curve out above us. There was nothing to help get us up.

The lowest bar of the guard rail was tantalizingly

close, maybe three feet above my head. May as well have been three miles.

"What do we do?" I yelled this time, feeling a sinking feeling.

"Hang on. I been thinking while you caught up with me. I'm pretty sure I can reach it."

I held onto the clay with all my strength, suddenly wondering if I could crush it accidentally, making me fall to my death, crashing silently at the bottom along with the rock that I had dropped.

"We shouldn't have come," I said. "I'm scared."

"It's okay. We can do this."

The light breeze gusted at that moment, just when Scott was going to make his move. He held back and waited for the wind to die down.

Then, he stretched himself up, holding on with his left hand, reaching for the lower yellow rung with his right.

He grabbed onto it and yelled, "Yes!"

I smiled and watched as he reached with his other hand and slowly scrabbled his way up, grabbing onto the next rung and the next.

Scott took his time, but he eventually made it all the way to the top and over the guard rail, back on solid ground.

And I was left alone.

Scott was about six inches taller than me. He could barely reach the rung, and as I cautiously reached up above me, I knew there was no way I would make it.

I froze. All I could think of was how easy the climb looked from the bottom and how impossible I now knew it was.

I couldn't go up and I couldn't go down.

The muscles in my legs were starting to complain.

"Scott?" I called up.

He didn't answer immediately, and just for a moment, I had a fleeting thought that he had abandoned me here.

"Can you reach it?" he finally answered. I couldn't see him back behind the rails.

I stretched my arm out. I clutched firmly with my other hand, but I was a good four or five inches shy from the bottom rung. I couldn't get any closer.

"No," I whispered. "I can't do it."

"What?"

I took a deep breath and yelled, "I said I can't reach it. I can't do anything."

"I've been looking for something to help, but there's nothing up here. Just the highway. No trees or anything, just dirt and grass. I thought I could get a branch, but..."

I nodded.

"Sport, you gotta hang on. I'll go for help, okay?"

"No! You can't leave me!"

"I don't see another choice. I can't get you up."

Scott must have been frustrated, but he didn't seem to realize the terror I was feeling. It felt like he was leaving me the same way Dad did.

"Okay, Sport?"

I didn't want to answer, but I knew there was no choice. If he didn't get help, I was going to fall. "Yeah."

"I'll run all the way down. Just hold on!"

And then he was gone. After a few seconds, I yelled up to him, just in case, but of course he didn't answer.

I traced the path of the highway in my mind. I was pretty sure it curved to the east and the exit that led down into town was far away. I remember after seeing where Dad died, it took at least ten minutes driving to get to the exit, and maybe another ten to get into town.

How long would it take Scott to run that far? I had no idea.

But I didn't think I could hold on that long. My fingers were starting to cramp. I took turns clenching each fist, but that only helped for a few moments.

It was deathly quiet after Scott left. No voices, no birds, no animals, no cars above, even the wind died down to nothing.

A twenty minute car ride to town. Averaging maybe sixty miles an hour. That would mean twenty miles.

Scott had been on the football team and could run a long way without stopping. Even so, maybe he could run six miles per hour? I shook my head, trying to do the math, anything to keep my mind off of the height.

Twenty miles at six miles per hour. More than three hours.

Then if he got help, another twenty minutes driving back.

No way I could do it.

I had to find another way.

My father always told me there were no limits to what I could do.

"You just gotta put your mind to it, and you *do* it." He must have told me that a hundred times. I always wanted to ask why that didn't work for him. Even as a boy, I knew that working on the floor of a shoe factory was nobody's version of an ideal job.

Just do it.

I looked up to the yellow rung taunting me and reached one more time, hoping that I had grown in the past ten minutes or some other miracle would bring the rung closer.

Nope.

There was only one solution. I shut my eyes, terrified at the thought. "Gotta be some other way," I said. I just needed to hear the sound of my voice— anything to break the silence surrounding me.

I stared at the rung, trying to calculate how far it was from me. Reaching again, I looked at the distance with a calculating eye. Four inches or so from my outstretched fingertips.

I had to jump for it.

"Scott!" It was futile, but I called to him anyway.

My fingers were slick with sweat. Even if I could somehow jump to the rung, I might not be able to hold on. I rubbed my hands on my tee shirt, preparing for a plan I knew I couldn't follow through with.

I started to crouch down a bit, figuring if I could get a good leap, it really wasn't all that far.

Four inches.

When I crouched, I had to find new handholds, and again, a rock went spiraling down below me. This time I thought I heard a small thud after about five seconds.

Five seconds would be a very long time to fall.

"Stop that," I said to myself. "It isn't helping."

I pressed my lips tightly together and looked up.

The rung was still there, farther now that I was crouching.

"No other choice."

I closed my eyes, trying to gather my will.

And jumped.

I was in the air less than a second, but it seemed like an hour. I felt myself flying and just focused on the bottom rung.

Finally, the hour ended and I grabbed the pipe as hard as I could, half expecting my momentum to pull the whole damned guard rail from its moorings. Everything held, though, and I found myself swinging in the void.

Both hands were grasping the bottom rung, but my body was so far now from the cliff that there was nowhere to put my feet. I was dangling, and I could immediately feel my arms weaken as they tried to hold me up.

The next rung was about a foot higher. I tried to reach it but didn't have the strength any more. I could barely reach up two inches. I'd swing wildly, one hand the only thing saving me from the fall I knew would come.

"*Scott?*" I was close to screaming.

No answer.

The road was so close, but so far.

I steadied myself, took a deep breath, and looked down between my legs. If I let go, I'd fall about twenty feet before hitting the side of the cliff. From there, I'd skid off the surface and bounce down the remaining eighty feet.

No chance of surviving.

I could see the town in the distance and wondered if my mom might be looking over to Mount Turnpike while hanging the laundry in the back yard.

Just do it, my father would say.

I looked back up and stretched again. No luck.

My fingers were weakening. I was running out of time.

I didn't want to see what was going to happen, so I closed my eyes. I would only be hanging on for a few more seconds.

I felt myself get angry at the utter stupidity of trying to climb Mount Turnpike. Stupid brother. What was he thinking? And why did I follow?

The anger grew, and I tried one more time to grab the rung above me.

This time, though, I felt a push from below. My legs lifted up as if Scott were hoisting me over a chain link fence. I was too stunned to do anything but grab the next rung up.

"Got it!"

I had one hand on each of the two bottom rungs, and I used the adrenalin rush I was on to keep going. Again, I felt something push my legs up. I grabbed the next rung, and then I could get my feet onto the bottom rung.

I was safe. The rest of the climb would be nothing.

I looked down.

There was nothing below me. Nothing at all that could have pushed me up. Just the smooth surface of the cliff and empty space.

I climbed up the remaining rungs to the top of the cliff. As I pulled myself over the rail, I felt two light punches on my shoulder. I swiveled around, saw nothing.

But that double punch was real.

I rested on the grass beside the highway and looked over the cliff, waiting for Scott to come back. I spent the time reliving memories of Dad, knowing that he was sharing the same memories with me.

The Jameson House

The haunted house in this story was real. It was about a block away from my childhood home, and all us neighborhood kids used to sneak up on it and get as close as we could before we got too scared and ran the fuck away.

I've always liked this story, because the main character has my name. I tried to capture the fear I'd felt of that house all those years ago, and giving the character my name seemed to help amplify that fear.

The house was knocked down when I was a teenager, and a hamburger joint was put in its place.

I never ate there. I bet the food was haunted.

Wʜᴇɴ I ᴡᴀs ᴀ ʙᴏʏ, I ʟɪᴠᴇᴅ ɴᴇᴀʀ a haunted house.

Of course, my parents never bought into that, but they didn't see what happened one summer afternoon. Come to think of it, I never heard a single adult ever refer to the old Jameson House as haunted. Rundown piece-of-shit rat hole was a pretty common description, but "haunted"? Never spoken. Never believed, most likely.

I asked my Mom once, and she just frowned. "Of course there's no such thing as a haunted house, John. You've been watching too many of those *Outer Limits* or that *Twilight* TV show, whatever it's called."

"*The Twilight Zone.*"

"Maybe you should read more. Those shows are rotting your brain."

I'm not sure why I thought back to that old rat hole today. Maybe it's because I just turned fifty. Maybe because the sounds of construction next door are irritating me and causing my mind to drift back to the similar noises of the Jameson House being boarded up. Maybe just because there should have been another birthday this week.

Markie should have turned forty-five the same day I turned fifty, but he never had a chance. He died when he was seven.

What's that phrase from the old Barbra Streisand song? Misty watercolored memories...

It's true my memories may be fading a bit. Sometimes I can't remember what I ate for breakfast the day before, but I like to tell myself that's just not very important to me.

But the Jameson House. *That's* another story. My memories are crystal clear on that matter.

I grew up in a suburb of Vancouver called Coquitlam. All the kids loved the name because it was an old Indian word meaning something along the lines of "stinking fish slime." What kid could resist having fun with a name like that?

Back then, Coquitlam was only half-built, twenty miles from downtown, dirt roads, septic tanks instead of sewer lines, wilderness more common than civilization.

Pete Boyle was my best friend when we weren't yelling at each other and fighting. Both of us housed short fuses and would raise our fists at any perceived slight. The summer I turned twelve, I think I sported blackened eyes or split lips more often than not.

Pete called me one August morning. "Hey, Spud. We're gonna explore the Jameson place today."

"Yeah? Who?"

"Me, you, Markie."

I cringed a bit on the phone. Markie was just a kid, and we hated having him around us. Pete wouldn't have asked him to come along on his own, so he must have been ordered to look after him for the day by his folks.

My pause must have told Pete how I felt, although I'm sure he didn't actually need any assistance in figuring that out. "Shit, it wasn't *my* idea you know. Cripes, I gotta take him."

"Yeah, sure," I said. "To the Jameson place, though? You sure?"

"Scare the crap out of him, most likely."

I didn't mention it'd probably scare the crap out of Pete and me, too.

"Yeah, okay. I'll be over soon."

It was a hot day, but not as hot as some places. Mid-August would see the thermometer hit eighty-five or so. All in all, we never had anything to complain about that way.

Pete had called midmorning, and I wasn't even dressed yet. I threw on the same light brown teeshirt I wore the day before and a pair of dirty brown cords.

Pete and I were the oldest kids in the neighborhood, but there were plenty younger, and we always managed to throw together a game of pickup baseball three, four, sometimes five times each week. Rain or shine, didn't matter to us.

In the winter, we mostly hung out indoors, which wasn't nearly as much fun. It never got cold enough for hockey, and it was too rainy for football, so TV and board games seemed to win out. We were both sick of Monopoly, Life, and Mouse Trap by the time the spring brought us baseball again.

A couple blocks away, there was a large grassy field with a frost fence about two hundred feet away. It was perfect. None of us could hit the ball far enough to lose over the fence, although Pete and I both tried our damndest, mostly just to be able to say we beat the other one to it.

A forest crowded behind the frost fence. Well, it looked like a forest back then a thickly wooded area probably only fifty feet deep, but when you're twelve, that's a forest. I think they were mostly Pine trees, but I'll grant you that's one part of my memory that does seem a bit hazy.

I do know they were evergreens, since we couldn't see through them even in the dead of winter.

Behind the forest sat the old Jameson House.

We had tripped across it the summer before, when Pete and I were both eleven.

"Dare ya," he said.

"What?"

"Go to the haunted house in the forest."

I shrugged. "No such thing."

We went together, winding our way through fallen boughs and crusted limbs. The Pines did a great job of blocking the sunlight, and that first trip through was pretty spooky, even though it was after lunchtime—a perfect afternoon.

We could have walked around the side, to get to the house from Cumberland Avenue—there was a long gravel driveway winding right up to the old bastard place, but we didn't know that then.

Besides, Pete had double-dog dared me to go through the woods.

No Coquitlam kid ever turned down a double-dog dare. At least not from a guy who'd never let you live it down.

"Who says it's haunted?" I asked.

Pete just shrugged. He was a bit taller than me and three months older. Somehow those three months seemed so much bigger than they really were. I always felt like he was the older kid. Maybe that's why we fought so much; I always felt I needed to prove I was in his league and not in Markie's.

"Heard a lady at the corner store. Talking to that guy who always carries the white cane even though he ain't blind."

"That's it?"

He glared at me. "I've heard it before. Just can't remember where. Doesn't matter. We'll find out ourselves anyhow if you ain't a chicken."

"I'm no chicken. I'm going, aren't I?"

A moment later, the forest ended as suddenly as it started, and we were standing in an overgrown area that had obviously been abandoned years ago. Brown weeds had killed most of the grass except right up near the house.

"Holy crap," said Pete. "Look at that thing."

I couldn't hardly do anything else. The house was bigger than anything I had ever seen. Four floors rose above the ground, and it looked like a basement hid below.

The windows were all either broken or boarded up with big sheets of plywood. A couple of the sheets had crashed to the ground and sat rotting.

I didn't know what to say. I couldn't help take a sideways glance at Pete, hoping he was as slack-jawed as I was. He just stared in silence, too.

The house was once painted white with dark green trim. Now, the green seemed to drip off the house like slime, the paint peeling in long strips. The white was covered in dirt and odd splotches of other crap.

The front door had a large red X painted across it. Some of the paint dripped to make a third leg coming down from the center of the X.

I never knew who drew the X or why, but it totally messed with our minds that day. There was the biggest omen we could imagine yelling at us to *get the fuck out of there.*

Instead, we took a step forward, each of us. Neither of us was going to be the one to crap out and run back through the forest to safety.

"You wanna keep going?"

Pete turned to me. "Scared, Spud?"

I didn't answer, just took another step.

There was a weird smell in the air. Like burning rubber or maybe rotting food. I took a big whiff and saw Pete do it too. He scrunched up his nose.

"Fuck it," he said. "Nothing worth seeing here."

I let him take the easy way out and ran along behind him back through the forest.

We didn't return for a year and two weeks, till that warm day in midAugust, when Pete told me he wanted to return to the Jameson House and take Markie along.

Hell, we never even *talked* about it, let alone walked back.

"Yeah, okay, I'll be over soon."

I didn't care if my brown teeshirt was dirty. It was like my summer uniform. Once in a while my Mom would take all my clothes and wash them. Maybe every second week or so. Kids now sometimes change their clothes twice a day, always wanting to be clean. Times sure change.

Fifty seems a lot younger than it used to. And forty-five seems a lot younger than dead; some things don't change all that much.

I met them at Pete's house, sitting on the front step. Their house was a bit rundown and sagged from age, but no more than mine or any of the other wooden houses that had sprung up in Coquitlam thirty years earlier. Everything and everybody eventually showed their age.

"'Bout time you fucking showed up, Spud," Pete said. The "fucking" was mostly to shock Markie, but he was probably immune to it, since his older brother used that tactic way too often to still have any effect.

Spud was my nickname. Some people called me the less imaginative Little John, like the character out of Robin Hood, but that was pretty lame, and Pete refused to follow what everybody else did. He called me Spud because I loved french fries. I didn't care. I thought it sounded like Stud, and that was cool.

Pete stood and I could tell he was really mad about having to babysit Markie. He started marching off towards the baseball field, leaving us behind.

"Hey," I called. "Wait for us."

He swiveled and yelled, "Hurry the fuck up then."

I could feel my own temper rising and knew before the end of the day, one of us would have another bloody shirt. Most likely both of us.

Markie hobbled along behind me as I followed Pete.

We looked like a weird little parade marching off to the haunted house.

We reached the forest without speaking, and that was probably just as well, as I could feel the tension between us floating away as we walked. Quiet was good.

"Is it really haunted, Spud?" Markie looked up at me with his big blue eyes. He had short blond hair and almost never smiled. He was a serious kid, but man, those big blue eyes just hypnotized everybody.

"Nah. It's just an old house. Abandoned."

He didn't look convinced, but maybe that's because I didn't sound all that convincing, even to myself.

"We're going inside this time."

I looked at Pete and wondered if he was serious or if this was a dare we both knew we could work around and back down from.

Nope. He was serious. He still looked pissed, and he glared, waiting for me to give him an excuse to take a swing.

Still standing at the edge of the ball field, with the sun beating down on us, and the house a distant and likely distorted memory, it didn't seem all that brave to agree. "Sure thing. No sweat."

Ten feet into the dark forest, my confidence withered away. I thought to myself, *What the hell are we doing?* but my feet kept moving behind Pete.

I couldn't back down first, even as I could feel my heart pounding and sweat trickling down my back.

Pete started to slow down, as if he were walking in molasses, and I slowed in step with him. *Maybe he'll give in,* I thought. *Just maybe we won't have to go through with it.*

But then, out of the blue, Markie started to sprint ahead of us, his smaller body easily winding through the trees. He actually laughed as he got in front. "Wooses!" he called.

"Fucking pig!" called Pete. We both stepped faster and before we knew it we were out of the forest.

The Jameson House loomed just as big as it had the year before.

I couldn't remember which pieces of plywood had already fallen to decide if more were lying on the ground, but there was definitely more wear to the green painted trim.

The smell was worse than I remembered, and the scarlet X on the door looked like fresh blood warning us away.

Pete and I stopped just outside the trees and caught our breaths, staring at the monster house.

"Hey, you wooses! Over here!"

Markie was already at the front door and pushed it open. Part of me wondered why it wasn't locked, but not for long. Nobody in my neighborhood locked doors in those days. There was no reason to. There were no monsters going door to door kidnapping babies or raping little old ladies.

Why wouldn't the Jameson House be unlocked the same as any other?

"Fuckin' moron," muttered Pete.

I was pissed at the kid, too. I still hoped for some way to avoid going inside, but that thought evaporated with Markie's first step.

We ran over to the door. I could swear the red X

was fresh. It looked wet. My chest felt tight, and I *really* didn't want to go inside.

Pete pulled the door open, and we could hear a long creaking sound that seemed to be taunting us. It echoed back from the trees.

Hadn't done that when Markie went in.

As we walked through the doorway, the temperature dropped. It was dark but not pitch black. Just gloomy enough to wish we had a flashlight.

"Stay close, Spud."

No worries there. I wasn't going off on my own.

The floorboards all creaked, and I could feel them bend beneath my feet. Rotted.

A small hallway led us to a large sitting room. It looked like it was two stories tall. There were a dozen or so framed portraits hanging on the walls. My eyes were adjusting to the darkness, and I could see the portraits were all of old men, mostly with bushy beards or sideburns.

There was no furniture in the room.

"Why'd they leave the pictures?" I asked.

"Fuck if I know."

I couldn't see Markie anywhere. Probably a good thing for him. I wanted to grab him and shake the life out of the rotten brat.

The smell was worse inside. I was sure it was rotten meat, and I had a vision of dead bodies being eaten by maggots and worms. Maybe in the basement. Maybe upstairs.

Maybe there was somebody else in the house.

Maybe he was watching us right now.

In fact, I could feel his eyes boring into me. I turned

around in a circle, quickly looking in every direction. My bladder was close to bursting.

"Spud?"

I looked at Pete. "Yeah?"

"You see Markie?"

"Nope."

I got my courage up and yelled, "Markie! Where are you?"

Pete almost crumbled to the floor when I yelled, fear overcoming him. He bounced back straighter than ever as soon as he gained control of his body. Nobody would ever cause him to cower for long, and in the middle of this nightmare, I was too scared myself to appreciate it.

Then we heard a laugh.

From upstairs.

"Markie!" Pete ran to the staircase in the far corner, and I played his shadow, following him as closely as I could. I'd seen loads of scary movies; I knew we had to stay together if we were going to get back home safely.

I called to Markie, too, and as we climbed out onto the railing at the top of the stairs, I saw his small outline down at the end of the hall.

"Fucker," I said. I was secretly relieved he was okay, but now I was really mad. Pete too.

We walked down to him. He just smiled up at us. "Chickens," he said.

Sometimes, shit just happens. Life hands you a twist in the gut that changes you forever. It doesn't always take much. A car running a red light. A doctor frowning at a test result and taking off his glasses to speak to you. Tripping across a lover in a place they

shouldn't be. Single snapshots that change...
everything.

That one snarky comment was the shit that
happened to me. "Chickens." From a fucking seven-
year-old punk. Sneering up at me.

I lost my temper and swung at him the same as I
had swung at his older brother a hundred times.

He was so much lighter than Pete, though, and I
smacked him like a twig. He fell over the banister and
fell down to the sitting room far below.

He started to scream just a split second before his
life was snuffed out.

The echo of his body hitting the floor seemed to last
a million years.

Pete and I were both frozen. I knew my pants were
soaked from me peeing myself.

"Markie!" We both yelled his name at the same
time. No answer.

It didn't take long after we ran down the stairs to
confirm he was dead. His head must have hit first and
snapped his neck. All the angles were wrong. His neck,
arms, and legs. All wrong.

We ran out of the house as fast as we could and
didn't stop until we hit the other side of the forest.

By then, our faces were both covered in tears and
we were breathing in big gulps, both from the race
through the woods and the horrible realization about
what had happened.

We collapsed against a big tree that had moss
growing on it. For a few moments, neither of us said
anything.

Then, it just came to me. "We were playing catch on

the field." I pointed out to the ball field. "Got tired and just lay down. Just like now, only lying on our backs, eyes closed, talking about whether Mickey Mantle was better than Joe DiMaggio."

"What the hell are you talking about?"

"We talked for a while, maybe even fell asleep. When we woke up, Markie was gone."

"Gone."

"Listen, Pete. We can't tell what really happened. I'd end up..."

I wasn't quite sure where I'd end up, but I was also damned determined not to ever find out. I grabbed his shirt and held my fist back, ready to beat the crap out of him if he didn't go along. All at once, I was leading things, not him.

He nodded quickly, and I pushed him to the ground.

They found Markie's body the next day.

The house was checked and they also found some dead dogs in the basement. At least that's what I heard, but somebody else heard they were wolves.

The front door was taken down and replaced with a solid door that was kept bolted shut. I don't know who kept the key. All the windows were boarded up firmly as well.

I never got back inside the Jameson House. Sometimes when I was a bit older, I'd go back, alone, and I'd place my ear to the door. Sometimes I'd swear I could hear whispers on the other side, calling me chicken.

If the house wasn't haunted before that day, it definitely was after.

Life-changing moments, they're called.

That speeding car and the nearsighted frowning doctor. The kid falling to his death from the banister. Everybody has something. Sometimes, though, the changes aren't what you'd expect.

When we ran out of the forest and slumped against the tree, I knew Pete was feeling sorrow and fear. My tears were equally real, but by the time we sat, I knew they were tears of exhilaration and joy.

I had just found out how much fun it was to kill children.

My life changed forever that day, and now that I'm fifty, I can look back at that one crystallizing moment as the single pivotal event of my life.

I'm a happy member of society, still live in Coquitlam. Never been married, but that was a deliberate decision.

My hobby really demands that I spend a lot of time alone. Me and my little friends. ❧

The Thief of Time

My friend Steve Savile, a fabulous writer, was editing an anthology called Monster Noir, in which all the monsters in the world were penned up in a town in middle America.

Each contributing author would write a story about one of the monsters, but we all had a common background and we knew about the monsters that the other writers were using, so we could include them in our story if we wanted to.

It was a very cool idea, but for one reason or another, the anthology never materialized.

I still liked my story a lot, though, so I've included it in this collection.

I KNEW WHAT JANIE WANTED: the one thing I couldn't give her.

She kept looking at me from across the table at dinner. *Sammy's Drive-In* wasn't an actual drive-in but rather was dressed up as one. It was a wide, long restaurant filled with empty shells of sports cars. The patrons climbed in, sat on the faux leather seats and played a selection of the latest beach songs from the chrome radios set into the side. The ceiling was as high as a gymnasium, to further give the impression of being outdoors.

Our waitress rollerskated to the car and pretended to talk to us through a small speaker. Somewhere to my left was a large screen playing a silent movie, but nobody ever watched it as far as I know.

We all went for the ambiance. Sitting in a fancy convertible in November, I could almost believe we were on a beach, my arm around Janie, wondering if I would have enough nerve to kiss her.

"Tom?"

I chuckled at my little daydream and focused back on Janie. "Sorry, I was just thinking."

"That's okay. I was wondering about later."

Later. There it was again.

She added, "Maybe we could go for a walk back to my place. It's not that far, and you've never seen it."

I smiled.

Janie smiled back, and I felt my stomach lurch. My eyes locked onto hers, and I knew I was in trouble. After all these years, I had fallen in love.

It was her eyes, I think. I've never seen such bright green eyes, emerald tinged with flecks of gold. Over the past month, I'd often found myself lost in them, wondering how any woman outside of a Harlequin Romance could have such hypnotizing eyes.

Janie did.

I licked my lips and grabbed one of the few loose french fries on my plate.

Her hair. Her second stunning feature. She had shoulder-length naturally blonde hair that she usually wore in pigtails hanging down and framing her face. In sunshine, her hair looked like spun gold.

The face of the Goddess of Love, I'm sure. Perfectly smooth skin, teeth whiter than white, lips beautifully sculpted, high cheek bones. She told me she was thirty-six, but nobody would ever guess she wasn't still in her twenties.

The only way she showed her age was her comfort with others and an outlandish sense of humor. She also had a stringent work ethic and high standards of community service well, as high as possible in Nyxon.

I had it bad.

"Would you like that? To come back to my home?"

"Sure. That'd be wonderful. I've wanted to see your place since we first met."

Just not your bedroom, I added silently.

Janie grinned, took her glass of Merlot and held it up to me. "To us," she said quietly. "To our future."

I clinked glasses and chugged the half glass of wine I had remaining.

More than anything, I wanted to fuck Janie, wanted to feel her body next to mine, wanted to please her, and at the same time to have her please me.

Her eyelids lowered a bit while she took a sip of her glass and then licked her lips. I stared at the tip of her tongue and imagined.

I was getting hard just sitting there, thinking of being with her. Knowing at the same time that I would have to find some way to turn her down.

My wine glass sat there, lonely, asking to be refilled, but I knew if I did that, I'd never have the will power I'd need later.

"Tom? You're drifting again."

I pulled back and started to chuckle. "Getting old," I said.

"Oh, right. You're barely forty. It's not like you're my grandfather or anything." Her eyes twinkled. "Cause that would be really weird."

"Weird?"

"Well, sleeping with my grandfather. That would be really weird."

We both laughed, but my mind was racing. There it was right out in the open. *Sleeping with.*

My hand reached across the table of its own volition

and grabbed onto hers. I must have looked like an idiot, grinning from ear to ear at the thought of hopping into the sack with her.

"Let's get the check and blow this pop shop," she said.

I pushed the red button on the convertible door handle, and the waitress slowly skated over and dropped the bill. "Everything okay?" she asked. She blew a bubble with her gum.

"Perfect," answered Janie.

I paid the check. We climbed out of the car onto the tarmac and headed to the front door. Several other waitresses skated around us as we went.

Outside, autumn was turning into an early winter. I felt a cold breeze kiss my cheek with a promise of frosty delights to come. Janie shivered. She wore a light blue overcoat. In the zapping fluorescent lights above the restaurant, her hair seemed to be streaked with purple and green.

I pointed at the lights. "Your hair looks normal in the glow here."

"Huh. Normal to you isn't normal for me." She pretended to pout. "Blonde is a perfectly acceptable hair color in Los Angeles."

I put my arm around her, and we walked to her place, about four blocks away, all the while me planning how to escape.

As we got close to her rented house, I felt something I hadn't felt in years, and a sense of dread came over me.

The Need.

It was back. I could feel it growing in the back of

my mind, awakened by the sexual arousings Janie had brought about in me.

It'd been five years since I last felt The Need. Five long years of careful restraint, holding back, not allowing myself to make love to a woman.

I slowed my walk as the urge coursed through my body. It was a rush of energy, a flood of endomorphins stronger than any street drug, and I felt my sense of control starting to fade.

"Tom, what is it? Are you okay?"

She stared at me, and all I could see was her outline, a body I could steal time from. I wanted to fuck her more than ever, to capture her youth, to steal the very life force from within her and leave her a shattered husk.

"Tom!"

I licked my lips and leaned over to kiss her. I had to have her.

She kissed me back, hard, and grabbed me in the cold. Neither of us cared if anyone else was watching. I felt her body through her coat and imagined a few minutes from then, when I'd be in her bed, fucking her, sucking her dry

"Jesus."

I pulled back, taking every bit of will power I had to do so. *What am I doing? I love her.*

"What? Are you sure you're feeling okay?"

"Janie, I've got to go."

"Go? But "

"No buts. I've got to go. I'll call you."

"Tom?"

I started to run away in the opposite direction from

her house, away from her youth and vitality, hating myself for leaving behind such a precious commodity, hating myself more for wanting to destroy her.

An hour later, I ended up miles away, in the part of town called Lower Nyxon. Sometimes, it was more casually called Pit Nyxon, which was a more descriptive name. I'd walked through there a couple times shortly after moving here, just to see a different part of town than I was used to. Pit Nyxon was where the scummiest monsters and freaks lived, the outcasts that had trouble fitting in, even in a place full of outcasts.

The area was only accessible by a winding road leading down to the river edge from above. The streets were covered with mud and slime, since the river overflowed its banks every spring, and nobody cared enough to ever clean it up. The air stank, but the inhabitants stank worse.

Only a few hundred people lived here. No Normals, of course, just the dredges of the monsters.

Ahead was *The Red Light District*. It was a combination bar and illegal whorehouse, a small skuzzy converted church. Religion never much caught on here, but at least the building was useful for something.

I paused to catch my breath, and pulled my coat tighter around me. The wind was colder, as it flew across the water from the empty fields beyond.

Below my coat, I still had an erection, and along with it, I was being overpowered by The Need.

Subconsciously, I'm sure that was why I was at the *District*. I pushed open the silly wingtip doors at the front and then the *real* doors that opened into the main bar.

Cigarette smoke blued the air, and the smell of beer clung to me like precious ghosts.

I hadn't been inside before, and I wasn't sure I was keen to be here now, but The Need was too strong. I needed a woman.

It was always that way.

I can't remember not having The Need. Even when I was in my early twenties, back God knows how many centuries ago. I remember being young, barely more than a kid, feeling that rush come on me. It was all-encompassing, so possessing and overpowering. I never had a choice.

Once every year or two was enough to satisfy me. The craving would be stifled, pounded back into sleep for awhile.

It was harder then. Women were hidden behind castle walls or fathers' purses. I got good at kidnapping and rape. It wasn't that I wanted to be that way; it was a necessity.

Stealing a woman's youth was always so sublime. Normals love their sex, but they have no concept of what true ecstasy is like, taking back a year of life, discarding decades of hers.

"Getcha sumtin?"

The woman behind the bar had a gray furry face and only one eye. Half a beard seemed to grow on her left side.

Catwoman. I'd vaguely heard of her. She was a

mutant who'd lived in Nyxon since being abandoned there as a baby.

"Beer," I said.

She snarled and wandered to the other end of the bar to pull me a draught. I sat on a bar stool and looked around the room.

There were about a dozen patrons, all men. Well, "male" would be a better term, since some of them weren't recognizable as men. There were no Normals, of course. Most were freaks. Horribly disfigured, oozing pus or slime, one guy must have weighed five hundred pounds, another sat on the floor with no legs, yet another had hundreds of prickles on his head as if he wore a porcupine wig.

All here to get drunk or get laid. Or both.

The women serving them weren't much to look at, either.

I didn't care. All I cared about was it not being Janie.

I drank half the beer before a tall, purplish woman sat beside me and put her hand on my thigh. She had no eyelids, and her face was a mask of veins crawling across a surface of warts. A steady trickle of blood dripped from one corner of her mouth. "Haven't seen you before," she said. As she smiled, I could see more wet blood on her teeth.

"First time," I said.

I guessed her to be about fifty, but monster ages were always tricky. Who would guess I was more than nine hundred years old?

"Drink?"

"Maybe one," she said. "I'm working."

Catwoman brought us two more pints of beer and I chugged most of mine. The Need was rushing me. No point taking time.

We negotiated a price, and I let the purple ghoul escort me to a private room in the back.

Thirty minutes later, I left a crinkling husk gasping in the bed and walked quietly out the front door of the bar, back into the cold, dark night.

The Need was satisfied again, and I felt the renewed vigor of having been youthed by a year. Every time I made love to a woman, I gained a year of my life back, and it always felt amazing. A year crawls, so I never noticed the tiny slowing of my step, the small aches that poked at me, the slight tightening of my vision, and the fraction of my hearing that trickled away.

Gaining a year back unwound time and instantaneously regained all those tiny lost bits, making me feel more whole.

I always wanted to do it all again, to gain *another* year. Then, a shroud of loss predictably followed the joy, knowing it would be a long time before I would get my next chance. The Need only came when it wanted. At most other times, I was impotent. At least a few months would pass, but this time it had been five years. Now Janie would be safe.

I changed in those five years. Surprising myself, I learned to accept aging, to realize that eternal youth wasn't everything it was cracked up to be. Being the thief of time had often sent me spiraling into depression, knowing I was only alive due to my thefts.

I often felt shame and regret over the pain I had caused.

Five years. Maybe The Need would never return; maybe I was past all that. Funnily enough, I was happy about that thought.

Now...

I was back in my little routine. Fucking for my lost youth.

I climbed back up the lonely road to the main part of town, and then down Main Street back to my apartment.

As I climbed into bed and drifted off to a dreamless sleep, I thought of Janie.

And a stir went through my loins.

The next morning, my mouth was dry when I woke, but otherwise, I felt fantastic. I jumped out of bed with a renewed vigor and smiled as I walked to the mirror in the bathroom.

Several small wrinkles were gone. I hadn't really noticed them before, but now that they were gone, their absence jumped out at me. A bit less gray in my hair, too.

"You're looking good there, Mr. Thomas Johnson," I said to my reflection.

Janie was right; nobody would think I was past forty. Smooth skin, nice smile, eyes that some people thought were as hypnotizing as Janie's own were.

I rinsed my face and brushed my teeth, cleaning a bit of blood leftover from kissing the bleeding ghoul at the bar. When I had a shower, my thoughts went again to Janie, and a rumble shook my body.

"No!" I gasped. The Need was back. It hadn't been satisfied by the ghoul.

By the time I dressed and left the apartment, I was trembling with desire and purpose once again. In almost a millennia, this had never happened before. Never had The Need hit me twice in a row, and I knew it was because of how I felt about Janie. She was the only woman I had ever truly loved, and The Need wouldn't be satisfied until I had taken her youth.

The coffee shop on Main Street was mostly empty surprising for a Saturday, which was usually the busiest day of the week. The Brothers were cramped together in a side booth, whispering new conspiracies, and from the corner of my eye I could see Gill-Man walking past the shop outside.

I thought I was alone otherwise until I saw a mug on the counter lift itself into the air and the coffee disappearing when it spilled over the lip. Some invisible guy.

I got my coffee, added some sugar, and sat in a booth where I could see the door. It was just a few minutes shy of ten o'clock, and I wondered if Janie was going to show up. We'd set the coffee date during dinner at *Sammy's Drive-In*, but that was before I ran away from her. She must have been mystified, wondering what had come over me.

"Moon River" played on the radio, its lilting tune drifting around the coffee shop. I tapped my toes and listened, killing time. It was uncomfortable to sit at the cramped table with an erection this large.

I should leave.

You can't, I answered myself.

Janie and I had met right in this coffee shop, at this very table. It was crowded that day, a month ago, and I was reading the *Nyxon News*, catching up on the issues in the upcoming local election, bored to tears.

Then, she was standing beside me. "Can I join you?"

I looked up and into those sparkling green eyes and found myself just staring at her.

She laughed and tossed her pig tails as she indicated the rest of the shop. "There's not really any other place to sit." There were only four tables in the coffee shop plus a few stools, and most people never bothered to stay, preferring to take their coffee with them.

I found my voice finally. "Sure. Of course." I pulled the paper off the table.

"I've only been here a couple months. Just in from California. I wanted to live someplace different, exciting, you know?"

"Well, I'm not sure how exciting Nyxon is, but it's different."

We talked for two hours that day, and by the time we were done, I knew I had finally found my soulmate. She assumed I was a Normal like her, and I never dissuaded her from that assumption.

"Tom?"

Janie'd come in when I was daydreaming. I glanced at the clock over her shoulder. 10:20.

I stood up and gave her a hug, careful not to let her

feel how hard I was. "I'm glad you came."

She shrugged. "Another coffee?"

My cup was still full but cold. "Thanks."

She picked up the coffees and squeezed into the booth across from me.

"What happened last night?"

I didn't expect her to be so blunt and wasn't sure how to answer. Part of me wanted to tell the truth. *Janie, I can't make love to you because I'd...*

I couldn't even finish the thought in my own mind, let alone out loud. I'd scare her away. Both parts of me didn't want to lose her.

"Tom? I felt so ashamed. Abandoned. I just don't know what I did wrong."

Her pig tails were braided today, and I wanted to reach out and caress them, to feel the tiny turns in her hair. I wanted to know and experience every little part of her.

"I just got scared," I finally said. "I've never been with somebody I love so much." I heard a hitch in my voice. I was actually telling part of the truth, just not the important part.

She reached over for my hand and smiled. "It's okay. We can take our time. I've been pushing you, and that's not fair."

The rush came over me at her touch, an almost painful onslaught of desire. I looked into her eyes and tried to smile, but I'm not sure how successful I was. "Right now," I whispered. "Let's go."

"It's okay, Tom. I can wait until it's the right time."

"Really. There's nothing that I've ever wanted more." Inside, I was shouting at Janie. *Get away from me!*

I stood and gave her a longer, closer hug, being sure to let her feel me.

"Oh! I guess you *are* interested." She laughed and put her coat on, pulling me behind her out the door.

Janie clung tightly to my hand, seemingly unwilling to give me any chance to change my mind. We hurried to her house, barely saying two sentences to each other along the way.

As we walked, my body shook with anticipation and greed. My feet carried me forward and my face smiled and my hand grasped hers and my cock throbbed with need.

And I silently cried.

Since I'd lived for almost a thousand years, and I now looked about forty, I had made love to about nine hundred and fifty women. A year gained from each at the cost of decades of their lives. Never had I much cared about them. Never had any of them imprinted themselves on me.

How would I ever face Janie after I stole her youth? I imagined her being sixty or seventy years old, her life ruined, hating me for the rest of her days. Would I still feel the same love for an old woman?

"Almost there." She increased her walking speed, and I did too, in order to keep up with her. We passed the spot where we kissed the night before, when I ran off from her. She didn't hesitate, just pulled me right past.

Once inside, she led me down a short, dark

hallway. The bedroom was off to the right. There was a frilly blanket and two teddy bears on the bed.

I held her face in my hands and kissed her. She felt wonderful, smelled like fresh flowers.

For a few minutes, we stayed, glued to each other. Then, I undid the buttons on the back of her dress and slowly undressed her. She reciprocated, and we stood together naked.

The Need pushed every little bit of my consciousness back into a dark place. I was looking through a pair of tunnels out to my eyes, watching my body act on its own accord.

At the same time, I could feel every caress from her hands, the smoothness of her skin against mine. My body lifted her into bed and kissed her neck, her breasts, her wonderful tummy.

I heard small sighs, but there was a background noise that rumbled through me. It was like I was on a train rumbling through a mountain tunnel, and I was squinting to see out the windows.

Soon, my body entered hers.

"Tom..."

Her voice was muffled, and once again I tried to scream for her to run, but nothing happened. My cock pushed inside her.

"Tom...?"

I pushed harder, ramming into her, feeling her all around me. "Tom, what's happening? I feel sick." She tried to push me away, but I wasn't having any of that.

A wrinkle pulled down from her left eye, etching its way down her cheek.

I felt stronger, even stronger than after being with

the ghoul last night. *Oh, Janie, I'm so sorry.* She heard nothing.

"Tom, something's wrong. Stop! Please!"

Of course my body ignored her, pounding into her again and again, pulling her youth out.

Snap.

Her hair crystallized into thin gray strands. All the beautiful soft blondness was now history.

More wrinkles scraped across her face, and looking from above, I could see teeth falling out, rotten and yellowed. A cataract grew on one eye, turning the shining emerald into a fuzzy piece of mold.

How old is she getting? I gave up trying to stop my body. Now, I only wondered when it would be over.

"Tom, I'm begging you..."

Her voice was weak, unrecognizable. One of her hands came to her face and dropped on her pillow. Her arm was just a stick, bones with no meat, flaccid skin hanging like a used condom. Her breasts were loose sacks of wrinkled yellowed veins.

And still my body kept fucking her. Soon, she stopped fighting, and her eyes glazed over. I wanted to look away, but I didn't control my line of sight. My body stared at her, pounding into her dead body as it dried up. The remains of her eyes fell back into her skull, and the crisp skin popped on her face, splitting into tiny bits of dry parchment.

I felt so wonderful, so youthful. I knew I had gained much more than a single year, and still my body kept fucking the spindly corpse.

Soon, the rest of Janie's body fell into tiny shards and then popped into so much dust. My body finally stopped, and I ejaculated into the grime on the bed.

When I woke, the dust from Janie's body stuck to me in places. I was back in control.

I rubbed the grit between my finger and thumb, felt the last pangs of The Need dissipate.

"I'm so sorry." I knew I was talking to nothing, but I couldn't help it.

I thought back to that first day I had met her and wondered how things could have been different. Maybe I should have told her to go sit at a stool at the coffee bar instead of letting her sit with me. Maybe I should have just left.

Instead, I'd looked into those emerald eyes and gotten lost. I started to cry.

Accordion Season

And now, one of the more bizarre stories I've ever written. I keep imagining readers starting in on this one and thinking, "He can't really be talking about wild accordions, can he?"

You bet I am!

After I wrote this, I expected nobody in their right mind would ever want to publish it, but to my surprise it sold the first time out to Mort Castle at Doorways magazine.

Even years later, people still mention this story to me. It seems to be quite memorable.

Dad woke me at 5:00 a.m. "It's time," he whispered.

I blinked my eyes. At first I didn't quite know what was going on. It's time? Time for school? Then it came to me, and I smiled.

Dad nodded. His long brown beard seemed to glisten in the moonlight that drifted in from my bedroom window. He reached down and tugged my arm to help me out of bed. "Don't wake Billy," he said. "He's too young."

I nodded.

No school today. It's Sunday. March 25.

The first day of accordion season.

I looked back at Billy in the other bed. He was snoring softly. I grabbed some fresh clothes and snuck down to the bathroom.

Dad had said he'd get the car ready while I got changed. "What about Mom?" I asked.

"Still sleeping, too. Don't worry, we'll be back before noon."

I brushed my teeth, sort of, and ran my fingers

through my hair to comb it. I stared at my face in the mirror and wondered if I'd have to start shaving soon. After all, if I was old enough for accordion season...

Dad was moving stuff around downstairs, and I heard a couple of thumps. I froze, worried the noise might wake Mom, but everything seemed okay. I splashed a bit of water on my face to finish waking up and hurried down the hall.

I grabbed my Dallas Cowboys jacket and was careful not to slam the door as I left.

Dad was already outside at the car. He wouldn't like it if I woke Mom. He always wanted to deal with the accordions on his own.

When I climbed into our old Chevy pickup and pulled the door shut, Dad smiled at me and reversed the truck out to the road.

"How come, Dad?"

He didn't answer for a few seconds. Lit a cigarette instead, rolled his window down, and blew some smoke out. "How come what, boy?"

Like he didn't know what I meant. "How come you're taking me with you this year?"

"Well, you're turnin' thirteen this year, right? Jewish boys get themselves all done into some kinda big ceremony at thirteen 'cause it's the age you become a man. So they say, anyhow. We don't got nothing like that around here, but I figure a boy hits his teens, he's old enough for accordion season."

I should have kept quiet, but I said, "None of the other boys at school..."

Dad turned to face me, and for a moment, I thought he was going to change his mind. I got smart and shut my mouth. I didn't want him to take this away from me. I'd always dreamed of this. Wait till the guys hear about it!

Dad took another long drag on his smoke. "Most people, they don't follow the old ways. Tradition's important, though, Bud. Don't let nobody tell you no different. Should be teaching that in your social studies classes."

The sun wouldn't rise for another two hours at least, so we'd have loads of time to hunt.

I didn't know the area at all. All I knew was that there was a big campground someplace nearby. We'd just left Highway 95A, just south of Kimberley, my home town. There were no other cars or trucks to be seen—just the forest surrounding us.

Dad pulled off and followed a narrow dirt road, and for a while, branches thwacked the sides of the truck. We rocked from side to side as we crashed over rocks and downed tree limbs. Finally, we backed into an empty area between some towering Cedars. I shivered as Dad turned the headlights off. It felt like a dark curtain dropped on us.

"Help me get the gear, Bud."

I shook off my fear as I jumped out and ran to the back, lowering the tailgate. A small light flicked on.

There were two rifles, a bag full of spare bullets, a long rope, and two empty accordion cases. They were all scratched up from years of hunting. Dad'd shown me the cases last year, sitting in a corner of the basement. He'd grinned and told me all about the hunt.

"Whatcha waiting for, boy? Take the gun."

Dad had taught me to shoot a year earlier, so handling the rifle didn't bother me. But all of a sudden, I felt guilty at the idea of shooting a defenseless little accordion. Before, it seemed like an adventure; now, I wasn't so sure. I blinked away the tears in my eyes.

Now I couldn't back down. I'd asked for this, and asked again, and *again* to go along when hunting season opened.

I picked up my rifle and fished out a dozen spare bullets, pocketing them in my jacket.

Dad hefted his own gun and wound the rope around his shoulder. He looked like a cowboy in some old Clint Eastwood movie.

I smiled. I had the best Dad in town. Bruno was always bragging about *his* father and how important *he* was, 'cause he was responsible for painting all the fire hydrants in the city, but nobody was ever as good as my Dad was to me.

I clicked the tailgate back up. I knew enough to not ask about bringing the accordion cases; they'd be used to store the ones we shot and dragged home. My eyes started to adjust to the darkness. It didn't seem so bad with a rifle in my hand.

"Shh."

Dad held up a finger like he was trying to tell which way the wind was blowing. "Hear that?" he whispered into my ear.

I found myself leaning forward, craving to hear whatever he heard. There were trees rustling, a bird chirping somewhere, and—

There.

I heard it.

I almost yelled out, but Dad clamped his hand on my shoulder.

"What is it?" he asked.

"I'm pretty sure it's a 120!" I said.

Dad nodded. "120 buttons matched with all them pearly piano keys. Listen to him squeezing those bellows. The adults will be on guard, while the little twelve or sixteen basses are sleeping." He put his finger up again. "I think he's got a diatonic with him. You've gotta be careful with those buggers. Sneaky as all hell. No piano keys, just more buttons."

We crept forward, Dad in front. The farther we got, the more I could hear the 120. And Dad was right. There was definitely another sound. More of a delicate wheezing of the bellows, a milder sound. I'd heard stories of diatonics in the wild, but I'd never seen one. I heard that the zoo used to have one, but that must have been long before I was born. Now, there were only a few adult accordions there, and they never mated in captivity, so I'd only ever seen photos of the babies with only the twelve buttons.

We moved through some trees and... THERE!

There was a wide stream flowing by. Dad turned to me and said, "They always go for the water. Figure the sound drowns them out." He shook his head. "Dumb things."

The diatonic was taking the lead. She was playing some weird music.

"It's some Swiss crap," said Dad. "Or maybe German. A waltz or polka or something. She's come a long way, this one." There was admiration in his voice, and I knew he wanted her.

The accordion looked old and frail, with scratches spider-webbing its once-beautiful veneer.

"Take your aim, Bud."

I lifted my rifle and tried to get the diatonic in my sight. What a treasure that would be!

"Careful."

And then all hell broke loose. It sounded like a million accordions suddenly had their bellows yanked wildly apart, all out of synch.

My ears hurt, but that was nothing. From the corner of my eye, I saw movement above me. My rifle swiveled up and I shot, nowhere close to anything.

And then the sentry accordions dropped from the tree, landing on my back, crushing me to the ground. "Dad!" I shouted.

He didn't answer, and I knew they'd attacked him, too. "Dad, help!"

They were all over me. Three, four of them, maybe more. All 120s. I tried to kick at one, but it was wrapped around my legs and squeezing. It was still dark, and I couldn't see much, just felt the terrible pain as the circulation in my leg was cut off.

Another one sat on my chest and pinned me to the ground, while calling to its friends by the river.

And then, they started playing "When the Saints Go Marching In." Dozens of the damned things. There was no use fighting. We were surrounded.

I thought of Mom and of Billy, wondered if they'd ever know what happened to us. I couldn't see Dad, and I knew he was a goner. They'd take care of him first, same's we'd take care of the 120s before worrying about the puny 12s.

The music became louder and louder. *Oh, when the SAINTS! Go marching IN!!* The emphasized chords were all deliberately out of tune.

"Dad!" I cried, knowing it was no use. I was still pinned to the ground. There must have been a hundred of the damned squeezeboxes piling on top of me. Eventually I stopped fighting and just accepted the torture. I could barely breathe. The music grew louder and louder, less and less in tune. My head felt like it was going to explode. I couldn't help crying.

Daylight would arrive soon. No more than an hour. Only sixty minutes of this terrible noise before the accordions went back into their little warrens to hide.

I'd never survive a whole hour, and my hopes faded.

I wished I'd never turned thirteen. ❧

Way back in 1982, I wrote the first version of this story. I knew it needed work, but for some reason I put it aside and it ended up in my files of unfinished work.

That file still has dozens of stories that I really need to polish up one day.

Fast forward about 25 years. James Beach was the publisher and editor of Dark Discoveries magazine. He asked if I had a story he could buy to put in an anthology called Darker Discoveries.

For some reason, my mind drifted back to that long ago half-written story. I went to the basement and dug through my old files until I found it. It was fun collaborating with my younger self to get this story polished.

I got the basic idea for this story after a drive through Death Valley in 1982 (hence why it was started that year). It was ridiculously hot and incredibly barren landscape. I kept notes as I drove with my family, praying the car didn't break down.

When a story is inspired by a real place, it always feels more real itself, at least to me.

"SURE IS HOT OUT THERE."

Not again. Sheesh, one day I'll try to figure out how many times I've heard that line since I opened *Marie's* eleven years ago. Yeah, one day.

Hmm... maybe I could hold a contest and give a tank of free gas to the thousandth customer who says it or something like that.

If it's not the heat they start off with, it's some pimply-faced eighteen-year-old boy staring at me like I should be happy to jump his bones right there.

I shouldn't really complain, though. Most of the customers I get are tourists who missed the last gas station in Quartzsite and realized too late they need to fill up their tanks. I've got a big sign about a mile down the road warning them that *Marie's* is their last chance until Congress, which is about seventy miles northeast of here on Highway 60. It's not really true there's lots of other gas stations before then but it helps business and nobody's ever come back to say I lied.

I get the occasional tourist coming into the gift

store, too. Postcards, belt buckles with cacti embossed on them, cheap leather belts I've had brought up illegally from Mexico you know, the usual souvenirs.

But my biggest seller is the cold beer on tap.

The guy who'd just walked in the store was wearing faded blue jeans, a light blue T-shirt covered with dark sweat stains, and a heavy brown back pack. He sat the pack down near the counter. I was almost sorry he'd come into the shop it'd been a slow day and I was thinking of closing and going to visit the oasis.

He looked around the store. "Are you Marie?"

"Sure am. Want a coffee? Beer?"

"In this weather? Do you even have to ask? What you got?"

"Just plain old Coors. It's cold, though."

He smiled and sat at one of the pink swiveling stools in the restaurant section of the store.

In southwest Arizona, in July, ninety-three degrees isn't *that* hot. I pulled the beer while taking a peek back at him. He looked to be about twenty years old or so. Maybe he was a student who couldn't get a job for the summer and decided to tour America.

"Where are you from?" I passed him the mug of beer.

"Great Falls." He took a long slurp. "That's in Montana."

"I know where Great Falls is."

He smiled again and took another drink.

"You want some pie to go with that? Fresh apple today."

He shook his head. "Thanks, but I'm not really hungry. You run this place all by yourself?"

"It's not much work. Here, sign my guest book, would you? Don't get that many people from Montana down here."

As I took the book back, I read that his name was Mike Reddy. "Welcome to Quartzite, Mike. Take a look around the store. Might find something you like."

As he finished the beer, he held up the mug and nodded for another.

He did wander over to look through my junk, picking up a glass miniature of a prickly pear cactus. He was tall, maybe six foot two or three, and he carried himself nicely. I couldn't help watching him. Comes with being a lonely thirty-two-year-old woman who doesn't come in contact with good-looking men every day.

Mike had unkempt brown hair and a moustache that was just a bit lighter in color. He had a few days' growth of beard, but I couldn't tell if that was his normal style or just from being on the road.

"This is nice," he said as he put the glass cactus back on the rack. "But no way I could carry it down to L.A. in one piece." He walked back toward me. "Gonna visit my sister there. She works for Disney."

"You hitching?"

"Yeah. Not much luck getting rides on these small highways, though."

"Some truckers stop by every once in a while. Few times a day at least. They can probably get you over to the California border if you want."

He seemed to consider the idea. "Just fuckin' hot out there, don't you think?"

I laughed and shook my head. "See that old

thermometer outside the back door?" I pointed to the corroding Pepsi-Cola meter that hung at an angle. It'd been hanging there since I bought the place and who knows how long before then. "It only measures up to one-twenty but I've seen it hotter than that. I'm surprised the damned thing doesn't explode sometimes, like in an old Road Runner cartoon. *That's* when it's hot out."

Mike whistled through his moustache and smiled. "Guess I should count my lucky pennies it's not like that now."

"George Carlyle's the guy who brings me my supplies twice a month. He's older than the hills and looks it he told me it hit one-forty back here in 1958, which was long before I was born. It's a damned good thing there's no trees around here we'd be fighting forest fires all the time."

He sat back on his stool and took a drink of the beer.

"Don't you get all weirded out running this place all by yourself? You know, scared?"

"Tell me now," I stood with my hands on my hips and smiled. "Why should I be scared?"

Mike's face reddened a bit. "Well, you're a nice looking woman, you know? All alone out here." He grabbed the mug of beer and drank half of what he had left. "Maybe I'm just too used to big cities where people have to be careful."

"Oh, I'm careful enough." I slid my rawhide belt around so he could see the knife sheath that hung at my side. I always carry an eight-inch blade with me. Sheriff Dawson doesn't much like it, but he looks the other way for me.

"I've got a cell phone programmed for a one-button call under the till that can bring help if I need it. And of course there's old Sue."

"Old Sue?"

"Over there. It's about time for her tea break."

"Cell phones work here?"

I stared at him. "Special frequency. It's something the locals hooked up."

I doubt he believed my story, but what the heck. I poured a bowl of tea for Sue and carried it out the side door, setting it down in front of her. Sue's a German Shepherd, but she's really not a very good guard dog. She's seen too many people come and go through the store to much care about them any more.

"Nope," I said when I came back into the store. "Nobody causes me any trouble in here."

Mike stared at me. If it'd been most other people asking about my protection, I might have started to wish there really was a cell phone under the till, but not this guy. He looked to be quite well-off in his Gucci sandals and the T-shirt that had a brand name swirl on his chest. On top of that, his eyes showed only naiveté and concern. I doubt he'd ever been in a street fight, let alone anything more serious.

It was too bad he wasn't a bit older, closer to my age. He *was* a good-looking guy.

"Sure I can't get anything else for you? A souvenir patch for your jeans? Specially made by me. You can't get a Quartzsite patch anywhere else. Or how about some sunglasses?"

He laughed and held up his arms. "No, sorry. I

really should get going." He swallowed the last inch of his beer and stared at the thermometer. "Unless you can sell me a bit cooler weather, that is."

I looked at Mike and wondered. If I took him to the oasis, there'd be no guarantee he wouldn't tell others. There aren't a lot of things I care about, but the oasis is one of them. As far as I know, I'm the only person around here that knows it exists. Since I found it last year, I've shown it to a few people, but they were all passing through like Mike, and I'm sure they never told anyone else.

"I do know a place you might like," I said quietly. "Might be a nice break for you."

"Yeah? What's that, like a swimming pool or something?"

I laughed. "Nobody has a pool around here. That'd be silly. No, this is a little place just off the highway a bit north of here. Come on, I'll close up shop for a couple hours."

"Great. Can you bring a six-pack? My treat. We can make a picnic of it." He lowered his eyes but I could see his reddened face. "I mean, if you want..."

I locked up the shop, turned off the gas pumps, and placed a large cardboard sign in the front window saying I'd be back at two o'clock. It was just after eleven now.

We climbed into my little red Civic and pulled out. There were no other cars in sight. When I tell people I live in the middle of nowhere, they usually don't understand. Driving down state Highway 60 would show them what I mean. Sometimes you can drive for an hour without seeing another car.

The road stretched out forever ahead of us, disappearing into the faint gray mountains at the horizon. Occasionally, dusty brown tumbleweeds blew across the road, but they were the only things that moved. No birds or animals or even bugs could be seen anywhere on either side of the road.

I love the desert, but it *does* get lonely.

We passed by Mile 39, nearing the oasis. Off to the right was a junkyard full of cars and buses that had been abandoned along the road.

The only vegetation was various types of cacti. There were large Saguaros, Chollas, and others I didn't know the names of.

Dust storms caused the sand to shimmer in the distance. At twilight, the images become quite frightening when the cooler winds whistle down from the mountains. It looked like where the film *The Hills Have Eyes* might have been shot, and more than once I've been out at night and caught myself looking around to see if any mutant maniacs were following me.

"Ever been to Arizona before, Mike?"

"Nope. Never been outside Montana before."

"We're almost there. It's just past Mile 40."

"What're we looking for?"

"Almost there," I said again.

Mike was looking out the windows both to the left and the right for any signs of something that might provide a respite in the heat. My old beater doesn't have air conditioning, so sweat was pouring off both of us.

After passing a twenty-five foot tall barrel cactus I

pulled the car over to the side of the road, not bothering to turn off the engine.

"Mike, you've got to promise me you won't tell anybody else about this place."

He looked at me in surprise, probably wondering what the big secret was. I figure everyone's got to have one thing in their lives that's theirs and theirs alone. Whether it's a stamp collection, a favorite place to walk in the woods, or a coveted pet, you need something that is only you own. "Please, Mike."

He stared into my eyes for a few seconds before nodding.

"Hey, sure. No problem. Nobody will ever hear of the place from me."

I placed my hand on his shoulder and squeezed. On impulse, I leaned over and kissed him on the cheek. *Salty.* He tried to kiss me back, but I pushed him back in his seat. Maybe once we got to the oasis, but not there in the middle of a freaking oven.

"Only five other people besides me have ever been here," I said.

I pulled the car back onto the highway to drive the last bit to the oasis. After a minute, Mike put his hand on my thigh. I looked over at him and saw him smiling while staring straight ahead. I placed my hand on top of his.

"How 'bout you open us a couple beers," I said.

He popped two cans and gave me one. I took a long drink, trying not to hide my view of the road with it.

Out past the hood, fluffy white clouds floated by. One was in the shape of a snowy dragon flying over top of the mountains. A knight was chasing the dragon,

THE OASIS

and I could almost make out the lance he was carrying.

"There's Mile 40," said Mike. His hand was wandering on my thigh, distracting me from the cloud dragon. My mouth was dry even after the beer.

"Over there," I said. "See those bushes that run along the side of the road? We're going behind them."

Mike seemed surprised to see the crumbly, tan-colored shrubs that seemed to grow as we got closer, until they were much taller than the car.

It was hard to concentrate on the road. All I could think about was that hand reaching down the inside of my thigh. Man, it felt nice.

"I thought only cacti grew out here."

"Nope. There's a few spots like this."

We pulled over to the side of the road again, right off onto the hard-packed dirt beyond the shoulder. Mike grabbed onto the car frame as we bounced over rocks and dead bushes.

"There's the entrance."

In front of us was an opening in the bushes just wide enough for my car to fit through. I don't remember whether I created the opening the first time I drove through or if it was there beforehand. I was pretty drunk at the time and had fallen asleep at the wheel. When I was shocked back to reality by the car jumping about, I was at the oasis.

I was light-headed and flushed as we came through to the oasis. We pulled up to the edge of the lake and Mike handed me another beer. He was speechless at the sight.

The dead land had ended just beyond the bushes. Here, emerald-green grass ran for miles in front of us, and a cool wisp of wind was spreading waves through it. The temperature had dropped twenty degrees. I peeled off my blouse and lay down on the grass beside Mike, just soaking in the sun. Without even looking, I knew his eyes were nailed to me. I never felt shy at the oasis.

Blue jays and robins flew about us and one even landed beside us, coming close enough for me to pet it. The oasis was filled with the sound of their songs.

After another beer, I grew bolder and pulled off the rest of my clothes. I yelled to Mike as I jumped noisily into the water and swam out to the middle of the lake. Mike stayed on the lawn, watching and smiling, but he waved off the opportunity to join me.

I swam for ten minutes or so, sidestroked back to the water's edge, and fell exhausted onto the grass. The sun warmed my body and I felt like I was in heaven.

Now you can see why I was careful about who sees the oasis. The last thing I want is to have a thousand people from Quartzsite running around and ruining my secret place.

I closed my eyes and used a finger to trace the warm sun on my breasts and stomach, again imagining Mike watching me. I was so relaxed I began to drift to sleep on the grass.

Mike lay beside me, and I could feel his body next to mine. As I fell asleep, I decided to make love with him when I woke. Even though he was young, it'd be fun. I never did it at the oasis before.

"What the *hell* are you doing?" Mike whispered to me as I awoke. Damn he was ruining the fantasy. He took a couple of steps back from me. "You're a fucking lunatic."

He stared down at me, his eyes wide.

"Mike, calm down."

The bastard had destroyed everything. The grass was gone and so was the lake. Bare dead hardpan ran beneath me, and I felt a bad sunburn on my breasts and arms. I pulled my clothes back on, turning my back to him as I did. It always seemed to happen like this. Someday, I'll find someone to really share my oasis with. But it wasn't Mike. Or Jim or Scott before him. Or the others.

I frowned at the place where the lake should have been and turned around. "You ruined it," I said. "It's all gone."

"What? Forget that shit. I'm out of here. You need help, lady. Rolling around naked on the ground in this weather like you're swimming? You're fucking nuts."

"Mike, don't. Come here." I smiled widely at him and he slowed. "It was just all a joke. Sometimes, we need something to laugh at in this heat. "Okay?"

"I'm going, Marie. Just stay away from me. I'll hitch back."

I lost my temper and took him by surprise, pushing him back hard onto the ground. Bastard thought he could ruin the oasis and then just walk away and tell everyone about it. I pulled my knife out from its rawhide sheath and drove it deep into his chest. Again, *again*. A dozen times. A silent tear fell down my cheek when I ran out of energy to stab him.

I'd been sure he would be different, but he was just like all the others, coming to the oasis and then wrecking it.

I pulled Mike's body over behind a group of small shrubs and pushed it to the pile with the others. They stank.

I drove back to the store quietly, drinking the last can of beer. It was warm.

At least he wouldn't be telling anyone else about the oasis. *Bastard.* I washed up in the bathroom as soon as I got back, thinking of the cool relaxing breeze blowing in from the lake. I made a nice bowl of tea for Old Sue. As I was pouring, a man who looked to be about my age came in and browsed through the souvenirs. "Sure is hot out there," he said. 🐙

Cruel Eyes

Sometimes it seemed like I'd never be done with this story. I wrote the first version of it, and it didn't work right.

I tossed it aside for probably a year and then picked it up again and re-wrote it. It still was total suckage.

Again and again I tried to write this damned thing, and it just wouldn't gel.

Each time I tried to set the story in a different location, with different characters, but it was all crap.

Finally, after five or six attempts, it occurred to me to set the story in France at some indefinite point in the past, maybe 150 years ago.

Finally, it felt right. All those other frustrating times, I'd had the story take place in current times. It needed to be set long ago.

I was quite happy with the story as it finally turned out, but I was afraid to ever submit it to any magazine or anthology. I figured I'd get back a reject letter that said, "You really should set this in present day."

Instead of that, I held onto the story until it could be published for the first time in Little Things.

"OH, MY GOD," SAID EDWARD Lansbury. "*That's* what the judge was jabbering about. God *damn* that Frenchman."

Edward stood tall, trying to see beyond the crowd. His brown hair blew in the breeze and fell across his eyes. He shook his head to clear his vision while clenching his teeth, frustrated at having his hands bound.

Walking toward him was a huge man, lumbering past the twelve silent observers. The dozen men were all in their dress clothes, taking their civic duty seriously. The judge's orders must be fulfilled. The huge man carried a double-edged axe that swung from one hand.

Edward glanced at his friend, Mark, who also stared at the executioner. Mark stared, his mouth open, as if he felt he was in a dream and just wanted to wake up.

"You know..." Edward couldn't finish his thought. His mind kept thinking back to the axe.

Mark nodded. The two had been friends forever,

and he knew exactly what Edward had wanted to say: *You know, we'll be dead in ten minutes.*

On the other side of Edward, Thomas whimpered. Edward shook his head again, irritated at the gusting wind. He wanted to kill Thomas himself.

The three were held with heavy steel arm bracelets and leg manacles.

Edward was the eldest and the putative leader of the trio. *So much for leading,* he thought. Now he just felt helpless. He glanced to his right.

"Lord Christ," Thomas said as he fell to his knees. His mouth was open and spittle dripped from one corner. "No. No."

Edward just glared at him. Glancing thoughts ran through his mind of earlier days, when they were teenagers with the whole world ahead of them.

"Get up, Thomas," ordered Edward. "Don't let them get to you. Keep your goddamned dignity."

"I don't want to die."

"None of us do. It's..."

Edward felt the urge to run as fast as he could, run all the way back to England, but he knew he needed to accept his punishment with dignity. With his feet chained, the dream of escape was futile to consider in any case.

On his other side, Mark didn't say anything, just watched.

The three friends, all in their early twenties, stood in a deserted courtyard. It'd been abandoned for years.

The executioner moved to the chopping block and examined it.

Small, dusty-brown weeds grew sporadically

throughout the courtyard, and that light, cool breeze blew, announcing winter was on its way. Even so, Edward felt sweat trickle down his face, catching on the stubble of his cheek. A spindly crab-apple tree stood fruitless in one corner of the yard.

He tried to kick Thomas, to force him to stand, but his legs couldn't reach because of the chains. "Come on, mate. Don't be a fool. You don't see Mark and I behaving like that."

"You bloody idiot," shouted Thomas. "Can't you see? They're going to cut our damned heads off!"

"There's nothing to be done about that now, is there? Stand up and die like a man. You're embarrassing yourself and Britain."

Mark hadn't spoken a word since they were led in by the guards who wore their bright blue uniforms, and who either wouldn't or couldn't speak English.

One of the guards moved to Mark and pushed him. He had no choice and started to walk toward the sixteen-inch wide tree stump in the center of the court.

"Guess this is it, then."

Edward watched as Mark shuffled forward, with a melancholy expression on his face.

Mark hesitated and turned to the others. "Melanie turns seventeen next month. I never told you, did I? We were going to get married after her birthday. Her parents made us promise to wait until then. We wanted to surprise everyone. Big engagement party, wedding-of-the-year in Ambrose... Now, she'll never know what happened to me."

Edward took a step closer to his friend. "I'm sorry I

got you into this. We should have stayed in Paris like you wanted."

"We were all in the mood for a bit of excitement, weren't we? A bit of adventure, maybe some romance? It didn't take much convincing to get us to come with you. What happened wasn't your fault."

Thomas moaned. Edward and Mark both looked at him with anger in their eyes. Edward spat in his direction.

It'd sounded good. A chance to explore the countryside, since none of the three ever expected to be back in France again. The colonies overseas were making noises about independence, and Edward expected the call to come soon to quiet them down. When that was over, they'd planned on opening a small print shop in the lower east side of London. Together. Maybe they'd start a newspaper or print some books of poetry or politics. The three friends could never agree about what they would print, only that they wanted to print *something*.

Edward was keen on publishing pamphlets on the occult. Ghosts, automatic writing, astral traveling, and other supernatural phenomena had always fascinated him. He studied everything he could find on the topic and always felt impassioned for more. Surely, others would find books on the subject just as intriguing.

Thomas finally pulled himself up from the dirt and walked toward the others, his cheeks stained and his voice shaking. "Okay," he said with a tremor. "Okay."

Edward smiled at Thomas. He was the only blond among them and the best looking. Thomas never had any trouble getting girls with his long blond mane, never really understood there ever could *be* a problem.

Edward hated him and let his smile disappear. *How could we have been friends for all those years?*

As they stood, dwarfed by the huge deserted courtyard around them, two of the guards walked over and grabbed Mark, one on each arm, dragging him the rest of the way to the wide, squat stump. The stump itself seemed ancient, but it was still sturdy. Razor-sharp lines spider-webbed the top surface, documenting a history of past executions. Dark stains covered all sides.

One of the guards tried to push Mark down to the stump. "Wait," he pleaded. "Almost forgot."

The guard held him firm, while Mark looked at the executioner.

Edward stared at the man who would be his own killer, too. He was huge, easily six foot three and very heavy, three hundred pounds or more. He was dressed all in black, and he wore a dark cloth mask that covered all of his head except for an open rectangle for his eyes.

Cruel eyes.

Mark shuffled over to him and carefully reached into his side pocket, grasping with some difficulty at his money bag. He tossed the bag to the ground at the man's feet and looked into his eyes with a silent appeal. The executioner didn't react except to grip his axe a bit tighter. Edward thought he saw the man give a small nod, but he wasn't sure.

A guard grabbed Mark's hair and smashed his head to the stump, opening a large gash in his forehead. Mark cried in pain. The teeth that spilled out of his mouth were the least of his worries.

Edward and Thomas couldn't see Mark's face—his cheek was pressed to the stump, so they only saw the back of his head—but they heard his mumbled prayers.

The executioner stood at Mark's side, planting his feet squarely and gripping his long-handled double-edged axe firmly. The shaft was about four feet long, sturdy, and old. The sun glinted off the freshly honed edges. His arm sleeves were cut short, and Edward could see his muscles rippling.

He lifted the axe far above his head and swung hard and fast. Edward grimaced and closed his eyes as the blade struck, and he heard Mark's head fall with a heavy thunk into the wicker basket in front of the stump.

Thomas began to cry openly, falling again to his knees. He didn't care that he'd pissed himself.

Mark's body smacked to the ground. A pool of blood flowed over the edge of the stump.

The executioner jabbed his blade into the wood and rushed to the basket, retrieving Mark's head. Edward watched in horror as he lifted the head up by its hair and stared into the dead man's eyes. Blood oozed in large globs from the neck, and Edward could see the spinal cord and bones jutting out below. His stomach heaved, but nothing came up; they hadn't eaten for three days, not since they were locked up after the arrest.

Edward knew what the masked man was doing. Some men don't die immediately after being beheaded. Their mind refused to let go, their souls continued to be aware of what was happening to them. *Like chickens*, he thought. *Just like beheaded chickens running around headless.*

The executioner gazed into Mark's eyes, looking for hints. He wanted to know what it was like to die and was looking for answers directly from the dead. Edward imagined the man looking into thousands of corpse eyes, hoping in vain to find an answer.

What comes after?

"Christ almighty," said Thomas between his cries. "He's crazy. Dear God, how did we get into this?"

Edward barely kept the contempt from his voice. "How did *we* get into this? Don't you mean to ask how *you* got *us* into this?"

He looked again at the grotesque scene at the chopping block. He'd heard the idea before while studying his books on the paranormal, and the concept intrigued him even as he was repulsed by the executioner's search. That was surely what the executioner looked for—hints from living dead men.

Edward dismissed Thomas with a frown. The three had been friends since childhood. When Edward suggested a France trip to Mark, they knew they had to ask Thomas as well. For almost two decades, they'd all been together, and they couldn't just abandon Thomas now. In truth, Edward supposed they were jealous of his easy ways with women and his prize equestrian shows, but Thomas had also grown to be a snob over the years, putting down other friends of Edward and Mark. He would denounce anything that he deemed to be beneath him, which covered a great deal of territory, and would nag at them until they denounced them, too.

When they drank together, which was often, Thomas frequently grew outspoken, insulting everyone nearby and reverting to the street language of their childhood. More often than not, Edward and Mark were the objects of his abuse.

Edward and Mark couldn't find a way to part ways with their former friend.

Thomas never met a pretty girl he didn't want to bed, and his bright hair and flashing smile usually won the day. If not... well, Thomas always got his own way, eventually.

The three had arrived in Aix-les-Baines a few days earlier.

Edward led the way into the village inn, as always, marched to the owner and asked for three rooms, speaking in English. None of them spoke much French.

"Monsieur?"

"Rooms. Three." He held up three fingers and slid three gold coins across the counter. The innkeeper picked them up suspiciously and, after careful inspection, handed three keys back.

Edward nodded and walked back out, looking for the blacksmith. More gold changed hands, and their horses would be cared for.

"How'd you find this village?" asked Mark.

Edward laughed, "It's the farthest place we could ride to in one day from Paris. We're seeing the real France now."

The rooms were fine, and they met in the lobby to walk over to the closest pub for dinner.

After they'd downed six jugs of watery beer, Thomas started to lose control of himself, as the others knew he probably would. He swaggered as he walked, insulting all the other patrons of the pub, and without warning, he hauled a waitress out into the alleyway behind the building. She looked to be about fourteen.

Edward called to him, "Don't be stupid. This isn't London."

"She's only a fucking whore," he yelled back. "Don't worry about her. Just a bitch that needs her goddamned Frenchie mouth shut up for her."

"Come on. Leave the girl alone."

"Mind for yourself. This slut's mine." Edward and Mark stood by and watched as Thomas beat and dragged the girl out into the darkness, screaming. They didn't know what to do but instinctively stood in the doorway, blocking any of the shocked patrons from following. Some pack instinct told them to stick together, even though they knew this was very wrong.

No resistance came, as there were mostly older people present with no strength and less courage. Edward heard the girl scream as Thomas raped her behind the pub. Nobody spoke a word until he returned.

"Damn, you shouldn't have done that, Thomas."

"*Fuck* what I shouldn't have done. Bitch wouldn't even speak goddamned English to me."

Mark stood and put his jacket on. "Let's get out of here. Back to the inn."

An hour later the soldiers came for them.

As Edward looked down at Thomas sobbing in the dirt, it almost seemed impossible he could have taken the girl the way he did. His bold swagger and loud talk was gone now, replaced by slumping panic and illiterate mumblings.

Equally inconceivable was how he himself had frozen and let the rape happen. Maybe he deserved his punishment as much as Thomas earned his own.

The executioner shook Mark's head and more blood spurted out onto the chopping block. Bits of flesh scraped off his face.

"Merde!"

He threw the head down roughly, knocking the basket over. When the head stopped rolling, the executioner turned his attention back to the other two prisoners. One of the guards cautiously moved in and retrieved the head and basket.

Another moved toward Thomas.

"No, don't, please. Not me. Take *him*. Take Edward. I didn't know. I wouldn't... " Tears rolled freely down his cheeks, and he slumped again to the ground.

"Thomas, don't be such a coward."

"No, I..."

He looked up to the executioner as he approached. *"Take him! Don't kill me, please!"*

The masked man pulled him to his feet and dragged him to the block.

"*He* raped the girl. It wasn't me. I didn't do anything. I—I tried to talk him out of it, but he was crazy."

"Thomas, don't be an ass. He doesn't understand a word you're saying."

"*Shut up, you bastard. Shut up! It's your damned fault we're here!*"

When they were at the tree stump, still sticky with Mark's blood, the executioner stopped and stared at Thomas, holding out his hand. Thomas looked back at him blankly. The huge man grunted a command in French and pointed to the small sack of gold that Mark had given him.

"You want my money, too?" He shook his head and began to laugh between cries. "My money? A lot of good that did for Mark."

"Give him your money, Thomas."

"Hah." He stood and stared at the executioner, spat in his eyes. The guards ran over and knocked him down to the chopping block. The executioner lifted his axe, but not as far as he had with Mark. When Thomas was set, the axe drifted down slowly, almost leisurely, the executioner letting gravity do all the work.

Thomas screamed as the axe bit into his neck, not cutting all the way through.

"You poor bastard," whispered Edward. "Damn, why didn't you just give him the money?"

Thomas was rolling around in the dusty courtyard, his blood spurting from the large gash in his neck. His windpipe was severed, and his screams turned into a wheezing sound as he choked on his own blood. His face was turning blue, and his eyes were frantic and haunted. Edward stared in disgust at the mess.

The guards and executioner just stood and

watched.

After several minutes of suffering, Thomas's body stopped jerking. He was propped back on the stump and the beheading completed. The executioner picked up his head but then bounced it away; there was nothing to be learned there. He felt through Thomas's pockets and pulled out his money bag, tossing it over to lay with Mark's.

The horrible death left no trace of remorse behind the executioner's mask. His eyes stared at Edward with animation and joy. Evil eyes.

Curious, cruel eyes.

Edward shuffled to the block, staring at the two discarded bodies, wondering what would be done with them when everything was over. He was trembling at the sight of the remains of his friends and felt his neck constricting.

What would it feel like?

He didn't want to die any more than Thomas had, but there was nothing left to do about the situation. He reached into his pocket and tossed his sack of gold to the ground with the other two. If he had to die, it wouldn't be like Thomas had, and the only thing his money could buy now was a fast death.

He stared again into the executioner's eyes. They were large, black, hypnotizing. Edward felt that he could see for miles into those eyes, and he had to shake his head to stop the eye-lock. "Make it quick. Please."

He tried to think how to say "Please" in French, but even that minimal phrase was lost to him. His mind was shutting down, panicking. He felt himself trying to pull back, resisting dying with honor. Everything inside him told him he should run. He breathed deeply and forced his feet forward, putting his head gently to the block.

The stump was wet and sticky. The blood stank. He closed his eyes but then snapped them open again. He wouldn't miss a single second of life, even if all he could see was the deserted wasteland of the yard, surrounded by crumbling brick walls forty feet away. The copper scent of the blood made him gag.

"Maintenant," said the executioner. *Now.* Edward could see the axe being raised from the corner of his eye. It disappeared quickly from his view and then came slicing down toward him.

A million years seemed to pass in an instant. He wondered if his mother would hire a search team, if his lover would remember him a year hence, whether his life had any lasting meaning of any kind.

The pain was much less than he would have thought.

Less pain? He was surprised he could feel anything at all, but he did. He opened his eyes, which had closed themselves as the axe descended. He saw deep sunken eyes staring into his own and realized his head was cut off from his body, but he was still alive. The executioner was holding him up by the hair. He wheezed but couldn't breathe. *Oh, dear God*, he thought.

The executioner's eyes were full of life, and Edward thought he could hear him mumbling before the sound turned into a dull roar. Fingers gripped his cheeks. Edward tried to open his mouth to bite the thumb, but he could no longer move any part of his face. He couldn't even blink. He was suffocating. His head swelled like a balloon, his vision clouding with purple haze.

No. I will not give in. Edward stared back at the executioner, glaring deep into the hypnotic pools. He forced himself to concentrate on the man in front of him, staring further into his eyes. The stare was returned with eagerness, and again, Edward thought he could make out faint noises. He refused to break eye-contact, his brittle connection to life, but he felt himself drifting away, losing consciousness, the purple haze overtaking him.

With the last burst of will he could find, he reached out furiously with his mind.

Edward looked down at the limp, severed head in his hands. He blinked and felt his warm breath reflected inside the dark cloth face mask he wore.

"Qu'est-ce que...?"

The head he held was his own. Shocked, he dropped it and stepped back, looking down to see he was now inside the executioner's body. The head rolled to rest at his feet, eyes staring up at him. He fell to his knees, trembling, watching the last remnants of terror staring back at him before the eyes glazed over and were still. For a moment, he recognized the cruel gaze of the executioner, who'd found his answers at last.

Edward caught his breath and felt his new body carefully. "Mon Dieu." His voice sounded deep and coarse, and he almost didn't notice he was speaking

French. He reached out and touched the bloody head beside him. Already it was beginning to cool. Ants crawled toward the neck.

The guards left the courtyard after cleaning up the mess. Edward sat alone against the crab-apple tree until nightfall, staring at the stump and the walls of the yard and the birds that cackled noisily overhead. The breeze was getting stronger. As the sun set, he picked up his three bags of gold, took off his mask, and walked out to the village, quietly humming a French lullaby. 🌑

The Slow Haunting

Del Howison is the owner of Dark Delicacies, a wonderful horror store in Burbank. He is also the editor (along with Jeff Gelb) of the Dark Delicacies anthologies, of which I'm a big fan.

I was thrilled when Del asked if I'd be interested in submitting a story for the third volume in this terrific series. Of course I said yes immediately, even though I had no clue what I might write.

Slowly the basic idea of the story came to me, and I started writing, without having a clue how to put together an ending that made sense. I trusted that something would come to me in time, and it did.

I look back fondly on this story and feel it might be one of my more underrated stories.

"You didn't kill me, Timmy."

"Don't call me Timmy. You know that. It's Tim... but I *did* kill you."

"It was an accident."

"Why are you here?"

"You know."

"I can't see you. Turn on the light."

"Can't do that. I can't touch anything. My fingers go right through. It's pretty weird."

"Does it hurt?"

"No."

"Why aren't you in heaven?"

"You know."

"I'm turning the light on."

Tim climbed out from under the covers and walked to his bedroom door. He blinked as he snapped the light on. He hadn't been sure where Dennis was. His voice seemed to come from everywhere.

"Here," said Dennis. "Right where I belong."

Tim looked up at the top bunk bed, and sure enough, there he was. He looked the same as he always did, sitting cross-legged in the middle of the mattress, arms back as if supporting himself.

Would that work if he can't touch anything?

Looking at Dennis was like looking in the mirror. Same dirty blond hair, same round face and blue eyes, same small mole on the right cheek.

Dennis smiled. "You don't seem surprised to see me."

"I never felt you leave."

Dennis floated down to the rug and stood face to face with his identical twin. "We've been together since we were born. Can't change that now."

Tim moved to hug Dennis, but his arms fell through thin air and he jumped back in surprise.

"You look real."

"I am real. To you. But things work differently now."

"How long can you stay?

"As long as you want me, Timmy."

"It's Tim."

Three months earlier, Timmy's mom sat on his bed, beside him.

"Timmy? It's time to get up."

She swept the hair out of his eyes and touched his cheek.

"We all miss him, but we have to carry on. Today's the big birthday for you. Moving your age into double digits. It'd be a good time to..."

"He would have been ten, too."

"Yes, and we'll always remember him on your

birthday. And on Christmas and on summer holidays, when you two would be out throwing your baseball around, and on the first day of school, and on every other day of the year."

"It's my fault."

"Don't ever say that, Timmy. We know it was an accident. You were both curious about the gun. We should never have had it in the house."

Her eyes watered, but she kept her voice firm, not wanting to cry again in front of him. "If it's anybody's fault it's mine. I should have told your father to take the gun with him when he left."

Silence covered the room like a blanket of snow. She heard the tick-tock of the Spider-Man wall clock and the swoosh of a car as it drove through the wet streets outside.

"Timmy?"

"I think I should be called Tim now."

"Okay."

"We stopped calling him Denny last year. I should have done the same. Timmy is for little kids."

She saw a forced smile on his face and stood back so he could climb out of bed. The frame creaked. The noise had never bothered her before, but without the constant chatter between the two boys, every sound seemed out of place.

Tim didn't play any baseball that summer or any of the summers following. Eleven years old... twelve... thirteen... Somehow it wouldn't be the same. The twins had played ball together since they got their first T-

Ball set when they were five. They graduated to Coach Pitch at seven and spent most of their waking time in summers playing.

But now Dennis wasn't there to catch Tim's pitches, and Tim couldn't be Dennis's fielder when he'd hit fungos in the park.

Their fifteenth birthday was on March 15.

"Beware the Ides of March, Timmy," whispered Dennis just before daylight.

"You say that every year."

Dennis didn't answer for a few moments. Tim yawned and rubbed his eyes, waiting for a bit of sunlight to start the day.

"Let's play some baseball this year."

"You can't play."

"Sure I can. I'll have just as much fun as you will."

Dennis had aged along with Tim. They were still mirror images.

That Saturday in late May Tim picked up his glove, went to the ball field, and joined a pick-up game. He played second base and standing right beside him was Dennis, as he always was. Dennis wore his own glove and smacked his fist into it as they both set their stance for the batter.

Tim never talked out loud to Dennis when anybody was around, but he could still talk to him in his mind. Maybe that's where Dennis talked, too. Tim never really understood how it all worked that he could hear Dennis but nobody else could see or hear him.

In the third inning, the batter smacked a grounder up the middle. It was bouncing between Tim and Dennis, and both of them moved to the middle to try to get the ball. It went right through Dennis's mitt and into Tim's. Things like that still surprised him and he dropped the ball.

"Darn."

"Don't worry," Dennis said. "You still stopped it from going to the outfield."

At the end of the game Tim asked Dennis, without moving his mouth, "How'd you get the glove?"

His twin shrugged. "I get whatever I need. That's just the way it works."

They walked side-by-side down the street toward home. They ducked into a 7-Eleven and Tim bought a Coke. He knew Dennis would find a way to have one in his hand when he next looked.

The sun was hot, but Tim didn't feel like rushing home. Burbank might have hot weather, but it was nothing like the heat in their apartment. Mom always promised to find a bigger place with air conditioning, but it never worked out. She worked in a nearby bookstore, but money was always tight since Dad left.

The boys walked through Valley Park and found a cool spot sitting at the base of a shade tree. They drank their Cokes and watched people walk by.

"You ever wish things were different?" asked Tim.

Dennis had never hesitated in answering Tim, and so he was surprised that he didn't hear the answer rumble around his head.

"Dennis?"

"Oh, well, sure. I wish I was still alive. Who wouldn't?"

"It was an accident."

Again Dennis didn't reply. He just finished his Coke

and then tossed the empty can into the air. It disappeared.

"You know that, right?"

"Yeah, Timmy. I know what happened."

"It's Tim."

"You need to ask Lisa out."

"What?"

"She's just waiting for you to ask. I listened to her talk to that new girl the other day. You know, the fat thing. Lisa told her you're cute."

"*What?*"

"Just trust me. Lisa's hot. Ask her to a movie or something. We'll all like that."

Tim didn't know what to say. *Lisa?* Did Dennis really hear her say something?

But then, why not? A bunch of other kids were dating. He picked up his glove and smacked it.

"We should get home. Mom's making macaroni casserole."

"Again."

"Again."

The next day, Tim saw Lisa at the water fountain outside home room. She was wearing a light blue skirt that showed her long legs. To avoid staring at them, he wondered what it would be like to touch her dark, curly hair.

"Go on."

Tim moved a step closer but froze when Lisa finished her drink and looked up at him. When she smiled, it felt like his guts were going to fall out.

"Hi," she said.

"Hi."

"Did you want some water?"

"Jesus, Timmy, just ask her."

"Keep quiet."

He nodded to Lisa. "Hot day." He started to turn the water on and when he was looking down, he asked, "Would you like to go to a movie sometime? Or something?"

A million years passed in silence. The water ran down the drain while he watched with a parched throat.

"Sure," she said. "That sounds like fun."

Six weeks later, she kissed him. They were holding hands and walking home after the last day of school. She stopped walking, turned to him, and out of the blue leaned to him and kissed him.

"Wow, that was nice," he said when she pulled back.

For once, Dennis kept quiet.

That night, Tim woke in the middle of the night. He'd dreamed of Lisa again, and he had a huge erection. He wasn't surprised. He often woke this way after dreaming of her, and he started to stroke himself, thinking of the day when they would be together. He knew it would happen one day, thought she wanted it as much as he did, but he also knew he was too afraid of screwing things up to try anything.

He thought of feeling her boobs and touching her between her legs, wanting her to touch him as he was doing to himself.

"You should move faster with her."

Tim jumped and pulled his hand back. He pulled the blanket back on top of him that he'd moved aside earlier. "Jesus, you shouldn't be spying on me."

"You know she wants you to."

"Shut up."

"I see it in her eyes."

"What do you know? You died five years ago. You never had a girlfriend. You don't have a clue what it feels like."

Silence filled the room, and Tim felt terrible. He'd never wanted to bring up Dennis's death. His erection wilted away.

"Dennis? I'm sorry. I shouldn't have said that."

Still nothing. Tim climbed out of bed and flipped the light on. The top bunk was empty.

In the years since Dennis was killed, they'd lived together with their secret friendship. The bond between them was stronger than between any other friends Tim knew of, and he would never endanger it.

"Dennis? Come back. Please."

He pulled out the chair from his desk and sat, staring at the bunk beds. After a moment, he noticed the tick-tock of the clock and glanced at it. 4:42 a.m.

The gun was supposed to have been locked up in the cabinet near the bathroom, but the whole apartment had been turned upside down. Dad was leaving, and neither Tim nor Dennis knew why. Mom spent all her time in her bedroom crying. She only came out to go to work, and when she arrived back home, she brought fast food for the twins' dinner. For two weeks, they lived on burgers, pizza, tacos, and wings.

Then Mom started to be okay. She never did talk about why Dad left, and he never came to visit them. Tim only saw him the one time, at Dennis's funeral. Even then, they didn't even find a way to say "hi" to each other. Dad sat at the back of the church with a woman Tim didn't recognize.

The cabinet wasn't locked.

It must have been due to the rush of Dad moving out. He'd been grabbing things all over the place, throwing them inside two ratty suitcases, glaring at the boys, and yelling at Mom who yelled right back.

The twins mostly tried to sit on the couch, holding hands, hoping the fight would just end.

Dad yelled one more time at Mom, and then he stormed out and slammed the door. After crying for an hour, Mom washed her face and left too. Tim knew she was going to the bar down the street. He hoped Dad would be there, too, but that seemed like a slim possibility.

"What a mess."

"Yeah."

There were clothes scattered through the apartment, some of Dad's, some Mom's, and even some of the boys. They picked up their own clothes and took them to their room. There was broken glass in the kitchen and papers covered much of the hall floor.

"I think they're bills or something," said Dennis.

"Hey, look."

The cabinet door was ajar. Through the glass

window, they could see the gun.

"Wow. I'll get it," Dennis said as he swung the door open and grabbed the gun.

"Let me have it. I saw it first!"

"No, I've got to—"

"Damnit, Dennis, you can't have everything and—"

Tim pulled his mind back from that awful day and focused again on the top bunk.

For the first time in his life, he felt alone. The invisible elastic band that always connected him to Dennis had snapped, and he was adrift, as if sailing off on a lifeboat by himself.

He opened the top drawer of his desk and pulled out his scrapbook. Inside were photos of him and Dennis, several from the last year before the accident. He touched Dennis's pictures and tried to smile, but nothing felt right.

Tears fell down his cheeks. He blew his nose and wiped his face before flicking the light back off and heading back under the covers. All thoughts of Lisa were gone. He just replayed memories of Dennis and himself in his mind for about thirty minutes. Finally he drifted off to sleep.

"Hey, sleepyhead. Time to wake up."

"Dennis?"

"Who else?"

"You're back!"

"I couldn't stay away. I missed you."

Tim stood beside the bed and stared up at Dennis. "It's Saturday. Wanna hit a movie this aft?"

"Sure."

Tim got dressed and they went down for breakfast. As always, Dennis paced around the kitchen and living room, waiting for Tim to eat his cereal. Mom read the newspaper and drank a black coffee.

"You should try a coffee sometime," called Dennis. "We're getting old enough."

Tim shrugged and answered silently, "Doesn't smell very good."

"Lisa'll like you better. Make you look grown up."

He finished off the Rice Krispies and rinsed his bowl in the sink.

"She wants you to grow up faster. Wants you to fuck her."

"What did you say?"

"Tim?" Mom looked over at him. "I didn't say anything."

"No, it's okay. Sorry, Mom. I was just..."

"Talking to Dennis again? I thought you'd stopped that."

Dennis started laughing.

"Do you ever feel that he's still here?" asked Tim.

Mom put her paper down. Dennis stared at her and then back to Tim.

"I feel him every day. I'll always have him."

"Bullshit," Dennis said. "She's got nothing."

"Yeah," said Tim. "It just feels like he's right beside us sometimes." He looked over at Dennis, who now was wearing his spring jacket.

"Oh, aren't you the funny one."

"We'll never forget him." Mom picked up her paper again.

Tim grabbed a lacrosse ball and his baseball glove and walked over to the schoolyard. The back of the school was solid, no windows, and he tossed the ball at the wall. It bounced back just as hard as he threw it, and it smacked hard into his mitt.

For thirty minutes, Tim threw the ball over and over. Dennis dodged in front of him, trying to block Tim's view. The normal game they played.

"I meant it," Dennis said. "She wants to fuck you."

"Don't say that. She's nice. She wouldn't talk like that."

"Sez you. Just go for it. She's waiting for you to find a way."

The next day, Tim met Lisa in the afternoon and suggested they go for a walk through the woods in the park. Almost nobody ever did that, because there weren't any normal walking paths. You had to pick your way among thick trees.

As they moved into the forested area, Tim clenched his mouth and took hold of Lisa's hand. She didn't shake him off, just smiled.

"That's nice," she said.

"See," said Dennis. "Told ya."

They found a clearing in the middle of the woods, sat down, and talked about school. They laughed, and Dennis just watched. At one point he rolled his hand in a circle. *Get a move on.*

During a lull in the talk, Tim leaned over and kissed Lisa. They kissed for a long time, and Tim felt unbelievable. Lisa placed her hands behind his head and he tried to copy her.

Go for it.

She was driving him crazy and that gave him courage. He moved his hand under the front of her T-shirt and lifted up to cup her breast. He couldn't believe he had the nerve to do it.

"Hey!" Lisa slapped his arm away. "What do you think you're doing?"

"I—I thought…"

"I'm not that kind of girl. Besides, we're only fifteen, for God's sake. I thought you liked me."

"I do. I *really* like you."

She stood up and crossed her arms. "I'm going home."

"I'm sorry."

"You can come with me if you want or you can stay, but I'm going."

He rushed to keep up with her as they headed back out through the trees to the street.

"Lisa, I'm really sorry. I was just being stupid."

She slowed her walk a bit and looked at him. "C'mon, let's get home."

Dennis laughed on the way out of the woods and all the way home.

Later, Tim asked him, "Why'd you lie to me?"

"Just trying to help. I thought she wanted it."

"You said you *knew.*"

"Yeah, well. I was wrong. But at least you got to feel her boob."

Lisa and Tim were eighteen when they made love for

the first time. It happened in the back of Tim's ten-year-old, second-hand Taurus, and this time it was Lisa who engineered things.

Dennis sat in the front seat and didn't make a sound.

They were twenty-one when they got married. Dennis was Tim's unofficial best man, standing right there along with the rest of the wedding party. He wore a matching tuxedo.

Lisa's parents were happy to splurge for a huge ceremony. "As long as you understand we won't pay for another one," her father whispered to her that morning. "So, make this work."

Tim's dad wasn't invited.

Lisa's father walked her down the aisle. She was the most beautiful bride in the world, and even after all these years, Tim couldn't believe how lucky he was to be with her.

Every day is devoted to you, my love. He would never tell Dennis but for the first time ever, Dennis was not the closest person to him and never would be again.

Tim's voice cracked when he said, "I do." His hand shook as he slipped the ring onto her finger, not caring one whit that he'd be paying for the diamond for the next three years. She was worth every penny.

Through their courtship, they'd talked about everything to do with their future. Career aspirations, kids, houses, even what they wanted to do when they retired, though that was an unimaginable time in the distant future. She wanted to be *sure* he was the right man for her.

Their entire lives were mapped away in her mind, and he loved her all the more for it.

Dennis helped answer all Lisa's questions, which was fine with Tim. After all, they were one, and what mattered to Dennis mattered to Tim. Sometimes he just figured it out faster.

The newlyweds wanted three children, spaced over eight years. Not too close together, not too far apart. They planned to conceive their first child a year after their marriage.

Sixteen months passed.

"Tim? Look!"

She held the little plastic stick up to his face. "Positive!"

"Hey!"

He picked her up and twirled her around their apartment. When he put her back down, he stared at the test. "You're sure?"

"Well, these things are never one hundred per cent, but I'm as sure as I can be."

"Get her a glass of wine to celebrate," called Dennis. "Piss her up!"

Tim ignored him. "We need to get you to the doctor to double check."

They kissed. The elastic bond between Tim and Dennis was definitely weakening as the bond grew stronger with his own family.

Seven months later, Lisa delivered a perfect set of identical twin girls. They named them Patricia and Denise.

Patricia was Lisa's mother's name. Tim said he wanted to name their other daughter Denise, to honor his long-dead brother. Lisa thought that odd, but she liked the sound of the name.

"Denise is the pretty one," said Dennis. "Of course."

Tim laughed. "Just like I'm the more handsome of us."

Dennis spoke more somberly, "I feel like I'm their father as much as you."

Tim just nodded and smiled. *Not a fucking chance,* he thought.

Having his brother's ghost around was second nature, and he could always carry on separate conversations with him and with Lisa whenever he needed to. Some things, though, were better left unsaid.

Lisa never suspected he was talking to a dead man.

Tim could never imagine how his life changed after the girls were born. They became his first thought every morning and his last thought at night. He held them in his arms every evening, waiting for them to fall asleep. And when they learned to smile, he knew he was totally sunk. His whole life was devoted to the girls.

Lisa didn't mind. She never felt ignored or neglected, and she appreciated all the time Tim spent taking care of them. It gave her a chance to escape after being with them all day while Tim was at work.

Even Dennis didn't mind. He seemed to love the girls just as much as Tim.

"I wish I could hold them," he said one night.

Lisa was out picking up a couple of groceries, so Tim talked out loud. "We're awfully lucky. Everyone says so."

Dennis reached his hand to Denise and pretended to pat her hair. Tim thought he felt more involved in the family when he acted out like this.

"Just don't leave any guns around," Dennis whispered.

Tim didn't answer. He was shocked that Dennis would even bring up such a possibility.

They heard Lisa's car door slam and the ghost pulled his hand back, as if he'd been caught doing something he shouldn't.

Tim automatically switched to talking to Dennis in his mind. "I wish she'd met you when you were alive."

"Well, she kinda did, since we're identical, right down to the last cell."

"We only look the same. We don't think the same at all."

Dennis shrugged and floated to the other side of the room, knowing Lisa would rush in and sit down where he'd been sitting.

"No, we don't," he said after a moment.

By the time the girls hit their ninth birthday, Lisa's long-term plan for their lives was scattered to the winds. They never conceived another child and probably never would. Neither of them wanted to go to the doctor to see who's plumbing was at fault. They were happy with Denise and Patricia.

The bigger house she had hoped for didn't work out, either. Living in Burbank wasn't cheap, and they'd only been able to afford to rent a basement apartment. Both of them worked full-time, she in the local Starbucks, and he at an auto body shop. They weren't rich, and sometimes he wondered about the end-game of Lisa's plan: retirement. He'd already passed his thirty-first birthday, and he could see tiny tufts of gray hair on the back of Dennis's head. He refused to look that closely in the mirror, but he knew what he'd see.

"Hard to believe it's their birthday again," said Dennis. He'd been missing for the past half hour, which had worried Tim.

"Where've you been?"

"Just reminiscing."

"What do you mean?"

"Sometimes, I just get sad." He walked to the window and looked outside. "Do you ever think about that day?"

Tim moved to stand beside him. The girls were in their room, napping, and Lisa was out picking up party supplies. It was still a few hours until the guests arrived.

"Sure. I still think of it all the time."

"We were nine. Just like Denise."

"And Patricia. Why do you always leave her out?"

"You shouldn't have tried to grab the gun."

Tim took a long breath and watched a car roll down the street.

"It was an accident."

Dennis said, "It's hot. I'm going to open the window."

And he did.

Tim took a step backward. *What the fuck?*

His first thought was that he'd just had some kind of daydream—imagined what he'd seen. But, no. He replayed it in his mind. Dennis had leaned down and turned the rusty lever at the top of the window, lifting the screen and pushing the window open.

"You can't do that."

"Apparently I can."

"What the fuck's going on, Dennis? How long have you been able to do that?"

Dennis stared at him. "Since you fucking well killed me." He took a step toward Tim, who stumbled back and found himself in his easy chair. "You can touch things. Why wouldn't you tell me?"

"Let me show you something," Dennis said. He moved to Tim and grabbed his left arm.

"Jesus, what are you doing?"

Dennis's fingernails were sharp. He scratched deep into Tim's arm, leaving three bright scars.

Tim stared, speechless.

"You *killed* me."

"It was a fucking accident, and you goddamn well know it."

"I remember the pain. I didn't die right away. Remember that? You shot me in the gut."

Dennis lifted his T-shirt and rubbed his stomach and chest.

"You burst my left lung and fragments of the bullet bounced around everywhere. My heart started to leak, and I couldn't get enough breath. I guess Mom never bothered you with all the gruesome details."

Tim couldn't say anything.

"You don't remember? I suppose you don't remember me drowning in my own blood, spitting up painful red vomit and looking at you for help. And I'm sure you don't remember how you just froze, didn't move a muscle to help, didn't call 9-1-1, didn't do a goddamned thing."

"I was only a little kid."

"A little murderer, you mean."

"You always told me you couldn't touch things."

"I lied."

"What's going on? Why are you doing this?"

"Because it's Denise's ninth birthday. She's lived as long as I did, and that's long enough."

Tim stood up. "You touch her and I'll—"

Dennis laughed. "What? You'll kill me?"

"It's time for you to go."

"Actually, on that, I agree. I've just been waiting for today. Waiting a long time. I've already killed her. That's where I was earlier."

"You shit. I don't believe you."

Tim pushed past Dennis to go toward the kids' room, but Dennis grabbed him. He had more strength than seemed possible, and he used it to throw Tim down into his chair.

"And I called the police to confess. They should be here any minute."

"They wouldn't be able to hear you..."

"Sure, they heard me. Probably recorded me. And my voice is identical to yours."

"Let me get to her."

Again he stood, and again Dennis threw him down,

rougher this time.

In the distance, Tim heard a siren, and in his heart he knew that Dennis was telling the truth, that Denise was dead.

"How did you...?"

"I strangled her. She was sleeping and I used every ounce of my strength to squeeze the life out of her. She tried to fight, but there wasn't much she could do. She didn't understand why her daddy was doing that."

Tears rolled down Tim's face.

"They'll find my DNA on the skin beneath her fingernails. Defensive wounds. Just for good measure I spit in her face."

Tim closed his eyes and lowered his face into his hands.

"Of course, the DNA they find will match yours. We're identical twins, after all. Even our scratches match."

Dennis rolled up his sleeve to show identical scars to those he'd given Tim.

The sirens screamed as two patrol cars pulled up in front of the house.

"OPEN UP!"

"Not yet, brother." Dennis kept Tim a prisoner in his seat.

After a moment, the police broke down the door and found Tim alone in his living room, staring with guilt into his hands. 🦋

JOHN R LITTLE

Following
Marla

Much of my work had surrounded a small number of basic themes, including love and loss. It's easy to find those ideas frequently in my stories and novels.

This time, I wanted to write a pure love story, about a man who would do literally anything for the girl of his dreams.

The story was originally published on the web site, Horror World, edited by Nancy Kalanta in 2009. I was thrilled when it was subsequently nominated for a Black Quill award.

I eventually married the girl who inspired Marla, and that journey became my very own true love story.

"I JUST WANTED YOU TO KNOW," Marla said. "It's not too late for you to change your mind."

We were in the back room of the church, just having finished the rehearsal. Most of the wedding party was hanging out in the foyer, waiting for us, but Marla had whispered something to the priest and then pulled me down the hallway to the back room.

"I just don't understand," I said. "You... it doesn't make sense."

"I know."

She had those big brown puppy-dog eyes staring at me as she pursed her lips. She took a deep breath and said again, "I faked my own death."

"You're not kidding?"

Of course she wasn't. I could see that as clear as the candles surrounding us. She lowered her head a bit, and pushed her hair back. Tomorrow, she'd have some new hair style for the wedding, but I liked it just hanging long and straight, like she always wore it.

"It was two years ago. I was married to a monster in Boston. He just hit me one too many times, I guess.

We'd been married almost three years, and every one of those thousand days was worse than the one before. He abused me in every possible way. Yelling, belittling me, hitting me so often I felt like a punching bag..."

Marla started to shake and I pulled her to me. "You don't have to—"

"And he'd rape me after hitting me. Fuck me just to hear me scream. Sometimes, though, my mind just went blank."

She pulled back and looked up into my eyes. I didn't know what to say, so I said nothing.

"You wouldn't recognize me, Andy. I was a lifeless zombie, not caring if I lived or died."

She stopped talking, continuing to look at my eyes. I tried to imagine this vivacious, beautiful, strong woman in a marriage like she described. I couldn't see it.

Marla tried to smile, but it was forced. Even so, her smile always hit me like a hammer, and I kissed her forehead, still amazed that she would agree to marry me. She was definitely out of my league.

There was a knock on the door. We both turned to look as Michele poked her head through. "We're getting hungry, guys..."

"We'll be a while," I said.

"We're ready now," said Marla. She whispered to me, "The rest can wait. I just had to tell you the hard part."

Now her smile was genuine.

The wedding was perfect.

I thought I'd seen Marla in her best form many times before, but when she walked down the aisle with her sister, I knew that I was marrying the most beautiful woman in the world.

We'd known each other for a couple of years, but our first date was exactly one year ago, on her thirty-second birthday. It seemed only appropriate to marry on the same day a year later; I wanted the day to be devoted to her. For that matter, I wanted my whole friggin' life to be devoted to her.

It sounds terribly hokey, but I was head over heels in love, and I knew my sole purpose in the future would be to make Marla happy. That's God's honest truth. Marla was on my mind every waking minute, and my feelings were even stronger knowing now what she'd been through in Boston.

I wanted her forever. It all seemed guaranteed, until we were alone in our suite and somebody knocked on the door.

We hadn't even had time to change out of our wedding clothes. The reception was underway, dinner was over, and the speeches were all done. We were just getting changed into casual clothes to go for one last dance before... well, before my fantasies would end and I would make love to her for the first time as my wife.

"Probably Janice," said Marla. "Not sure what she'd want, though."

Marla's sister was the only person who knew our hotel room number. I nodded.

She flipped the lock on the door and pulled it open. I heard her gasp and turned to see her try to push the door closed. "Ricky? No, it can't be—"

And then she was blown back, blood splashing out on her peach wedding gown. The gunshot wasn't loud, but it was very powerful. Blood covered everything, and Marla flew off her feet, landing a few feet behind.

She never moved.

I think I went a little crazy for a while. It was impossible to believe my whole life would be stretching forward without Marla.

I couldn't cry at her funeral. It was like I was looking at a jigsaw puzzle all broken apart with the pieces mixed up. The picture wouldn't come to me. It was simply not possible that the casket being lowered into the ground carried my Marla.

For a week after, I ignored the phone calls, the knocks on the door, even the cards that came in the mail from well-meaning friends.

All I knew was that I needed her back. And, yes, maybe I was *more* than a little crazy, because the only idea I came up with was to follow her. I had to follow Marla beyond death.

Before I did, I needed to talk to her sister, Janice. She opened the door at my knock and gave me a hug. She was a big woman, so different from my petite Marla that it was hard to believe they were sisters.

"I'm so sorry, Andy."

"I know."

"Would you like a drink?"

Marla always drank Chardonnay. "Do you have any white wine?"

She smiled and poured the drinks. "To her."

I touched glasses with her and took a sip.

"How'd she fake her death before?"

Janice looked at me and seemed to be thinking back. "It was so hard on her. She knew if she just left Ricky, he'd hunt her down. He was nutso crazy, but the cops could never do anything. One night we cooked up this plan. It took eighteen months to work."

"Why so long?"

"Insurance. She took out an insurance policy on herself with me as the beneficiary. Ricky was so stupid, he believed he was the one who would get the money, and that scared Marla even more. We didn't want it to ring any alarm bells at the insurance company, so we waited a long time before…"

She stopped and took a sip of her wine.

"It's okay. She wanted to tell me. We just ran out of time."

"I know. Anyhow, the two of us hired a friend who owned a fishing boat. The story was that we all went out on the ocean for a day, and Marla fell overboard. We couldn't save her and her body was never found. Of course, Marla wasn't really there that day. She was on a train to Topeka. Eventually the insurance company paid me two hundred fifty thousand dollars. I gave part to Billy, who owned the boat, and sent the rest to Marla. She used it to buy a new identity. A couple years later, I followed her here."

The house was silent except for a quiet song coming from a radio in another room. I think it was a song by the Bare Naked Ladies.

A tear rolled down Janice's cheek. "Ricky must have followed me. Somehow he must have known she wasn't really dead."

We finished the drinks, toasting my Marla one more time before I left.

I thought of having another drink or two, just to give me the courage I'd need, but no. I needed to be clear-headed if I was to follow Marla beyond death.

My kitchen

(our kitchen)

had many different knives. Marla brought a complete carving set when she moved in. They were some kind of novelty knives with long emerald-colored handles. There was a copper design snaking through them. Marla thought they were funny looking. I didn't much like them but the knives were long and sharp. The handles were firm and the blades serrated.

I took the longest one and placed it on our coffee table, staring at it from my easy chair.

"My name's Marla. Who are you?"

"Andy."

She nodded and shook my hand. That first day, she gave me that gorgeous smile. She was short, couldn't have topped five feet, but that smile shone through the whole room, making her the tallest person in the room.

"Do I know you?"

"Not yet."

I'd come to the party with my room-mate, just wanting to kill a couple hours.

Marla moved closer to me, staring at me.

"Is something wrong?" I asked.

"No, no of course not."

We kept our eyes locked. It was a once-in-a-lifetime kind of thing. Finding somebody you didn't even know you were looking for.

Ten minutes later, I held her hand. I didn't let go until I left her at three the next morning. I knew I'd found the woman I needed to be with.

The knife was in my hand. Thinking back to when we first met confirmed my decision. I couldn't let her go.

I used the blade to find a soft spot between some ribs and held the handle with both hands.

(What if I can't find her?)

I shook my worries away. I damned well *had* to find her.

My hands were shaking. I blinked and looked up at the ceiling, biting my teeth together.

And I slammed the knife into my chest as hard as I could.

Pain roared through me and pushed me down into the chair. I couldn't breathe. Somehow I'd let go of the knife but my hands tried to find it again, to pull the fucker out to stop the pain and to... to rest... and to rest... and... *Marla!...*

I wanted to blink but I didn't seem to have the muscles

to do that. I no longer felt the knife and I looked down to my chest.

There was no knife, no blood. I was wearing the tuxedo I'd worn to our wedding.

Around me was a light purple fog swirling on the ground.

Purple!

My nickname for Marla when we'd first met was Purple. She'd worn a purple dress to her birthday party and I mentioned an old poem I'd heard about a woman who promised to wear purple when she grew old.

"Marla?"

My voice didn't make any sound, but I could tell what I was saying. I called for her again.

"She's not here."

The voice came from everywhere. Or nowhere. I turned to see an old man in a wheelchair. I think he was black, but I wasn't sure. There wasn't much light.

"Who're you? Where's Marla?"

"Marla's dead. So are you. I'm the gatekeeper."

"Gatekeeper to what?"

He didn't answer, but wheeled around me. "You don't belong here."

"I had to follow her."

He didn't seem satisfied. "You shouldn't *be* here yet."

"Then let me find Marla and go back."

"Oh, if it were only that easy."

"You know who she is?"

"Everyone knows everyone here."

Here? I still didn't know where I was. Heaven? Hell?

Purgatory? Were those even useful concepts for people who are really dead?

"I came to take her back."

The man just stared at me. Somehow I knew what he was thinking even though he didn't say it: *You're not the first to try.*

The purple mist floated around my ankles, my mind turning the swirling fog into cloud-like shapes. I watched for a few minutes, waiting to see what would happen next.

Purple.

My Marla. Sometimes I seemed to catch a glimpse of her face in the mist, but it was gone before I could truly see her.

"We don't just send people back for do-overs."

I looked back to the black man, who now was younger with long brown hair. His face seemed Oriental but he didn't have an accent.

He still sat in the same wheelchair.

"How do I get her back?"

He smiled and spun around. "You can push me."

What I *wanted* to do was to spin the damned chair around and grab the guy by the throat. I *wanted* him to tell how the fuck I could get Marla back. I *wanted* him to just let me love her.

I pushed his wheelchair forward, not knowing where we were going. The chair didn't need much pressure to move, and I was pretty sure that my pushing was an illusion.

"Why her?" he asked.

I almost answered "I love her" almost as a reflex, but I stopped myself. He knew I loved her. But why? What made this girl so special?

In my mind I ran through some random thoughts about her. She was pretty, she was smart, she was funny, sex with her was inventive, funny, and magic, she liked the same books and movies I did, she appreciated me, she worked hard, she played hard, she wanted to have two children like I did, she had simple tastes (preferring fried pork chops to filet mignon), she told me every morning that she loved me and every night, she rarely wore cosmetics, she loved to hear me compliment her, she had a gentle voice and a loud laugh, she would lay her head on my lap letting me stroke her hair while we watched movies on TV, she had that alarmingly beautiful smile, she taught me to play Sudoku, I taught her to play chess, she always held my hand while we were walking together...

And a million other things about her ran through my mind.

I stopped and turned the guy around in the wheelchair.

"All my life I've built up an image in my mind of what my perfect life-companion would be. No woman ever came close. One would have the looks but no sense of humor. Another might be funny but a flake. I never found any one girl that ever came close to what I really wanted. I'd pretty much resigned myself to being alone, because there was never a woman that could meet my ideal.

"Then, a year ago, I found Marla. She didn't match *any* of my ideals. She's short. She's not blonde. So many things aren't what I thought I wanted, but I knew right away she was *it*.

"And it seemed I was equally her *it*.

"We were just meant to be together, and I am not going to fucking well give up on that now."

I'm not sure when the guy's hair had changed to white. He looked Scandinavian, I think. Long cheeks, blue eyes.

"Being without her isn't worth living," I added.

He nodded.

"You must prove that you truly will do *anything* for her."

I almost gasped. The first hint of a chance. "Anything," I repeated. "I'll do anything."

"We'll see. You must succeed at three challenges. One is physical, one emotional, and one spiritual. On my watch, there have been more than ten thousand people who've come to me as you have. Only three hundred eighty-two succeeded at the physical challenge."

"How many of them—?"

"Thirteen succeeded at the emotional challenge."

I couldn't ask.

"And of the thirteen...well, maybe you'll be the first to pass all three challenges. I keep thinking there has to be a first time. What will you do to have her return?"

"I'll do whatever I have to."

"We'll see."

"Who *are* you?"

There was no answer. He turned his wheelchair around and started to roll away. "Your first challenge is to walk to the light."

I started to follow behind him.

"Not this way. Go to the light."

I didn't know what he meant until I looked around and in the distance I could see a bright flash. It might have been a spotlight or a flashlight or something. Or a star. There was nothing else to see except the purple haze, so I couldn't tell how far away it was. one hundred feet? five hundred? A mile?

When I looked back to the wheelchair, it was gone. I was alone in the mist.

I started walking toward the light, wondering if something in the mist would try to stop me. My watch had frozen at 4:42 p.m. when I'd committed suicide, so I tried counting my steps. What else was there to do?

When I hit two thousand steps I stopped. Had to be a mile, and I couldn't really tell if the light was any closer.

"Keep going if you want her."

I spun around, but there was nobody there. I wondered if I was being timed and if I didn't get to the light in time, would I forfeit Marla?

I started again, faster.

After another three thousand paces my leg muscles were starting to hurt, but I didn't stop. I was almost sure the light was a bit brighter.

(Maybe.)

If anything, I walked faster, breathing heavily and really starting to notice the cramping in my leg.

I started to get discouraged after another ten thousand steps. Five miles? More?

And then somewhere after that, I lost track of how

long I'd marched. The landscape was all the same rolling purple mist and the damned light never really seemed to get any closer.

"It's moving away from me," I said. When I realized that, I stopped.

Could I see the light move? No. But it had to be moving away, likely as fast as I was walking. How else could I not have reached it yet?

A wheelchair rolled around from behind me. A bald woman sat in it now. She had a lilting voice. "You don't seem to want her very badly. You've got a very long way to go."

"How long?"

"*Long.*"

"It's moving away from me, isn't it?"

She shrugged. "What does it matter? It takes as long as it takes, and if you keep going, you'll get there."

"But, I've got to know how long it'll take."

"No, you just have to know you want to do it."

She rolled back into the mist and disappeared.

I walked.

"How long has it been," I asked.

"Two days."

Could it be? I'd walked for two days?

I stared at the guy. He was Chinese. "You shitting me?"

"Two days."

My legs were cruel tortures all the time. They hated me. I didn't need to eat, sleep, drink water, or anything else I should have wanted. I was dead. But, my legs cried out in pain with every step.

I walked again.

Marla and I worked together at City Hall. I worked on computer problems and she was down the hall and around the corner. I saw her sometimes at our shared printer or in the cafeteria. I never had the courage to talk to her.

Besides, I thought I'd heard she was dating somebody.

But... from a distance, I saw her. Saw her when she changed her hairstyle to wear pigtails, saw how she loved to pop a peanut M&M into her mouth as an afternoon snack.

For two years, I slowly fell in love with her, barely ever saying a word.

At her thirty-second birthday, she originally seemed surprised to see me. I'd found a way to tag along with Dan, and when I saw her there... I could see she was glad to see me. Some barrier just melted away that day; we became inseparable.

"How long?"

"Almost a year. Now you're making progress."

A year? I'd been walking for a fucking *year*, and the light wasn't any closer?

"Shit, this isn't working," I said. "There's got to be another way."

"Don't you want her badly enough?"

I hesitated for the first time. A year? But then in my mind, I saw her again, as clear as ever, that wonderful smile breaking me into little pieces.

I walked.

"How much farther?" I asked.

And I finally got my answer. "Another ninety-nine years."

And I walked again.

When I asked how long I'd been searching for Marla, it seemed impossible to believe the numbers. Two years, Ten years...

Fifty-seven years.

And she was still fresh in my mind. I still needed to walk, to save her.

I loved her too much to let her die.

One hundred years.

The light grew brighter. It was a lighthouse after all. I reached the base where a naked woman in the wheelchair met me. She was missing an arm.

"You made it."

"Where is she?"

"Soon enough."

For the first time in a century I fell to the ground. My legs were jelly and it was hard to not just die. Except I'd already done that.

The ground was slightly inclined at the lighthouse and large rocks were scattered around. The weird purple haze didn't climb the small hill and so it looked like we were in the eye of a hurricane, only this was the eye of the fog.

"Do you want to stop yet?"

Stop? How could I stop? I'd just spent *a hundred fucking years* following the woman I love. I wanted to hit the woman, but I had no strength.

"No. I won't stop until I save her."

She nodded. "You may rest."

I don't have any idea how long I slept, or even if sleep was the right word. In any case my legs relaxed, my eyes closed, and I thought of Marla again.

At some point, the guy in the wheelchair used his walking stick to poke me in the ribs. "Get up, you lazy bastid."

He was dressed in a tuxedo like me, with his hair slicked back. He frowned, as if he was just wasting his time with me.

Fucker.

I stood, my legs still wobbly.

"Ready t' give up?" His face had deep lines etched into them, as if he'd spent his whole life frowning.

"I've come this far to bring Marla home. Nothing can stop me now."

"Ya think?"

"I know."

"Second challenge. Somebody's comin' out that lighthouse. You kill them."

"Kill them? Like with a gun?"

"Strangle. Don't piss around. Just do it. No matter what."

I looked at my hands. Could I actually kill somebody in cold blood? Maybe if it was Marla's ex-husband, Ricky. Anybody else? A stranger?

Of course I could. After walking about a million miles, this would be easy.

"When—?"

The wheelchair and its occupant were gone.

I waited.

It was a week after her birthday party that Marla and I decided we were going to marry. Just seven days. We'd spent those seven days together, almost every minute. We found we agreed on everything we talked about. We both loved frog's legs and escargot, but we also both liked a Big Mac with fries and a coke.

I liked that she wanted to dance even if there was no music. We just made our own. We hummed Billy Joel's song, "Just the Way You Are," to each other as we waltzed.

We knew we'd be together forever.

I don't know how long I stood there. I thought of lying down, but what if some guy came storming out of the lighthouse and attacked me when I wasn't ready?

So I watched and waited. I have no idea how much time passed. It could have been a day or another hundred years. I just knew I had to stay focused on the lighthouse.

Then the door opened.

I had developed a new understanding of patience and a sense of purpose like nobody else ever had. Time will do that.

A few minutes passed, and I wondered if another infinity would go by, but no, this time, only a few minutes passed and through the door toward me came Marla.

She hesitated and looked behind her as she moved out to me. I'm not sure she knew I was there. She seemed to startle when she noticed me. "Oh, my God... Andy!"

We stared at each other and then she smiled. I hadn't forgotten that smile, and it melted my heart the same way it had more than a century earlier.

"Marla..."

She rushed into my arms and we kissed, a long deep kiss, and this time I didn't care how much time it took. I ran my hands through her hair and smelled her and pulled her to me and stared into those amazing brown eyes.

"I can't believe you found me," she said. "I've been locked here so long."

"I know. I've been following you."

"But what do we do now?"

And then I remembered what the guy in the wheelchair said. *Somebody's comin' out that lighthouse. You kill them.*

"Andy?"

She kissed me again and I kissed her back. I licked her lips and sucked her tongue.

I couldn't...

As I kissed her, my hands trickled down her hair and held onto her neck. I rubbed her throat as tears filled my eyes.

"Andy? What—?"

I pressed my hands harder and squeezed her neck. Her beautiful neck.

Marla realized what I was doing. She couldn't talk, but I could see the pleading in her eyes. *Stop.*

I didn't stop. I squeezed harder, even though every ounce of my being shouted at me to stop. I could barely see Marla through the tears, and I couldn't help but think I was betraying her. I just prayed that I was right, that this wasn't the real Marla, that I needed to kill this fake in order to save *my* Marla.

Her eyes continued to stare at me, begging me to stop. I wanted to stop so very much. She tried to fight me off, but nothing could loosen my grip after all I'd been through.

Eventually, her beautiful eyes glazed over and her arms fell to her side. She felt like a bag of raw meat. I lay her on the ground, but I kept squeezing her neck. I wasn't going to take any chances.

"She's dead."

I think she was Japanese, but I'm not sure. I was still covered in tears. "Tell me it wasn't really her."

The wheelchair moved around so the girl could face me. "I won't tell you any such thing."

"What?"

"Go into the lighthouse." She rolled into the door that Marla had come out of.

I looked down. Marla's body was gone.

Her lips had felt so soft on mine. I had to believe I'd done the right thing, and I followed the girl into the lighthouse.

There was an auditorium inside. I'd long ago given up any pretense at trying to understand how things worked here, so I just accepted that more than a thousand wheelchairs were all lined up with a thousand faces staring down at me. Maybe ten thousand. Or a million.

Behind me, on a table lay my Marla. There were no marks on her neck. She wore her peach wedding dress.

"Do not go to her. She is sleeping."

I turned back to the crowd. None of them had spoken; all of them had spoken.

"I need to take her back. She doesn't belong here."

Their voice was in my mind. "You've completed the first two challenges. Now the third waits for you."

"Just tell me what the fuck it is and let us go!"

A short pause. One of the wheelchairs came forward. In the chair was my mother. She'd died of Alzheimer's disease a decade before my suicide.

"Andy, this isn't easy."

"My God... Mom?" I went to her and hugged her. The last time I saw her was in the hospital and she had no idea who I was.

"You have a decision to make, son."

"Mom, what is this place?"

"It just is. We may be able to chat later. Now you need to make your choice."

I stood back from her. Her dark eyes were as clear as they were when I was a teenager. She nodded as if listening to me tell her my grades.

"You can't both go back. Only you or only her. You need to decide which it'll be."

I turned to face Marla, moved a couple of steps toward her. She looked at peace. After all this time, we couldn't be together?

"That's not right," I said.

A murmur of laughter came from the people behind Mom.

"You should go back, son. Look at her. She's already dead and doesn't know you've come for her. She'll wake in her own wheelchair and she'll fit right in. You should just go back. Go live your own life."

"I need to help her."

I looked around. If one of us had to stay with the dead...

"It won't work that way, son," Mom said. She reached out a hand and touched my arm. "You interfered. If you stay, you won't be with us. You'll be in an endless mist alone forever."

"What?"

"Exiled. For all eternity. No chair for you."

Marla's hand was cold, but I loved holding it anyhow. She was what I had wanted my whole life. Would she forgive me in time if I left her dead? My Marla...

I stared into her face forever, touched her cold cheeks and put my hand on her breast for the last time.

When I turned back to my mother and told her my decision, my voice cracked.

We were just getting changed into casual clothes to go down for one last dance before... well, before my fantasies would end and I would make love to her for the first time as my wife.

"Probably Janice," said Marla. "Not sure what she'd want, though."

Marla's sister was the only person who knew our hotel room number. I nodded, but inside me I felt panic. Something was very wrong.

"Marla, no!" I grabbed one of our emerald-colored knives and ran toward her.

Marla had flipped the lock on the door and pulled it open. I heard her gasp and turned to see her try to push the door closed. "Ricky? No, it can't be—"

I jumped and pushed her aside as the gun exploded and my guts fell out all around me. I gasped as I slammed the knife into Ricky's chest, and then I had no energy. I fell to the floor.

"ANDY!! NO!"

Marla was lifting my head from the floor and screaming. I tried to touch her face one last time, but I couldn't lift my arm. I couldn't even say good-bye. A strange purple haze seemed to roll through the room, taking me away from my Marla.

I smiled, not knowing why.

Sammy

I was tempted to correct the spelling of the title character in this book, but I eventually decided to leave it as is.

Sammie (with an ie) is the name of my youngest step-daughter, along with her sister, Emma.

Watching them grow has been as wonderful as it was watching my two older children, Peri and Christian, as they grew up decades earlier.

Before Sammie was born, her mother (now my wife) was going to name her Sammy, which was the name I used here. This story was written just before her birth.

Even after having written hundreds of stories in my career, this remains my only zombie story.

As for the dachshund in the story, she was modeled after two little wiener dogs I owned once upon a time. One of them showed up in my novella, Miranda, and the other one showed up here.

They died many years ago, but I still think of them often and miss them.

"Sammy" was originally published in the online magazine, Dead Lines.

SAMMY STARED OUT AT HER yard again. The arthritis in her wrists and ankles hurt just thinking about the mess. The twister had spared her house—well, *most* of her house—but the yard...

Sigh.

Ten years ago, she wouldn't have cared. Well, that's not *quite* true. She would have cared, but she wouldn't have been bothered.

Adam would have been there to help.

Now all she could see was a mountain of work with no reward. No teaming up with Adam to clean up the mess, no hearing his laugh and seeing his smile as they worked through things together, no hugs whenever they happened to be working in the same general area, no secret glance that said, "We'll have more fun tonight, sweetie."

No more Adam.

Just the mess.

She walked out to the garden and looked at the shredded flowers. Marigolds, carnations, mums. Now, the whole garden was just a giant bowl of coleslaw.

The dozens of hours of pain she'd endured as she kneeled to the ground during planting season... all the pain was wasted.

"Why'd you leave, me...?"

Sammy glanced over her shoulder, wanting to be sure nobody saw the mess. She had the finest garden in Ayr, but now she felt naked, exposed as a fraud.

It didn't help that all the gardens on Watson Avenue had fallen to the same fate. She didn't care what happened to her neighbors' gardens. She only cared about *her* garden.

The garden she originally planted with Adam all those years ago. Before her aching ankles. Before his chemo treatments.

Sammy raked a bit of the mess, half-heartedly, as the broken stems and crumpled flowers seemed to drain her ambition.

Why bother?

It didn't take her long to answer. As long as she was still above the ground, she'd tend to Adam's garden.

She raked more seriously, pulling up the plant roots easily.

Above the ground...

Puppy.

She steadied her eyeglasses and looked to the back of the yard. There were thick branches scattered around, cast off from the nearby oak tree. More work. She mentally tried to judge if she could move the branches on her own and doubted it.

Storm clouds covered the sky, and if it weren't for Adam, she would have waited till a better day.

He would have said, "Screw it. It can wait till nicer

weather."

"But what about...?" Sammy imagined herself pointing toward the Hendersons', next door.

He'd just laugh and kiss her. "Who cares what they think?" And maybe later, he'd make love to her. He always liked to love her when she was upset; he wanted her happy, and he knew just how to do that.

The wind blew her hair into her face and she moved it back.

"I'm going to fix it for you, sweetie."

But first, Puppy.

She took her first steps toward the back of the yard and felt the years of arthritis fighting every move. Pain bolted through her ankles, screaming at her to give up, go back inside and have a nice hot bath.

That wasn't possible until she checked on Puppy, though.

Sammy took a deep breath as she saw that the fence at the back of the property was smashed into kindling. More work.

No way I can do that, she thought. The fences had always belonged to Adam.

The tornado had ripped through Ayr at 9:00 that morning, surprising everyone. It wasn't like they lived in Kansas or something. This was the Oregon coast, and Sammy'd never heard of a twister hitting the small town before. She glanced back and was surprised again that her home seemed untouched, except for one corner where the shingles had been ripped off. The roofers were coming tomorrow.

Eight hours after the tornado swept through the back yards of Watson Avenue, Sammy kept her feet moving. The air pressure was increasing and her ankles were aching more than she could ever remember.

Loose branches covered Puppy's grave and at first she couldn't see the cross. She looked farther back and then saw the two white pieces of wood sticking out of a pile of dirt and wood about six feet away.

"Didn't last long, did it, girl?"

She walked over and picked up the sticks, leaning on the rake she'd used as a crutch while walking. One of the sticks was cracked near one end but she thought she might be able to use it still, until she had time to get a new one. The nails that connected the two pieces were still there and she was able to press them back into the holes and make the cross solid again.

Puppy had started to die the day Adam went to the hospital for the last time. She always stared out the window, but he never came back to her. Her tail never wagged again and she just seemed to mope about. Dachshunds aren't normally the brightest dogs in the world, but Puppy just seemed to know her master was leaving for good. Her personality changed that day. She ate less and less, and even though she lasted two more years, she was never the same.

Sammy buried her six weeks ago after finding her cold body laying by the front window one early morning in May. She knew she had to bury Adam's dog beside him... beside his ashes. He'd want that.

Now Puppy's grave was covered in branches, leaves, wood splinters, and other things that Sammy didn't even recognize. She couldn't tell for sure, but the grave itself seemed disturbed.

"I'm coming, Puppy..."

She grabbed the biggest branch with both hands and pulled. It was stuck on something. She pulled harder and the limbs inched toward her. There was a pile of other branches caught that came along as well. They cracked against one another as she moved them off the grave.

There was a smell of rain in the air and Sammy looked to the sky, wondering if another tornado might come along.

One's enough for me, thank you very much.

The sky was darkening and she looked at her watch. Only 5:00, but it felt like twilight. She shuffled around the branches, back to Puppy's grave.

That Saturday in May when Puppy had died, Sammy cried holding her tiny body in her lap. Time seemed to slow down or maybe speed up, somehow she couldn't decide, but then it was mid-afternoon and she took the stiff little body out and spent two hours digging the shallow grave. After laying the dog in the ground, there was only a foot or so of dirt on top.

"It's all I can manage, Puppy. I'm too old to be digging anyhow."

Now the ground seemed shallower and Sammy worried about... well, she didn't want to think about it.

She had to walk around the damned branches, using the rake as a crutch again. The grave was under the shade of the old oak tree, and it was hard to see clearly. Sammy moved closer and leaned over.

"Woof."

Sammy froze. She couldn't have heard it; her mind

was playing with her. She turned her head, so her good ear faced the ground. Silly, but she did it anyway.

She heard panting.

Sammy's heart started to race. Had some other animal gotten trapped somehow? She inched closer and got down on her knees.

"Woof!"

Puppy!

After fifteen years, there was no mistaking the sound. Adam's dog had the most distinctive bark of any dog she'd ever seen. It was wheezy, like she didn't quite want to put her full effort into making the sound. A kissing kind of bark.

She watched as the dog's snout rose up from the dirt.

"No," she whispered. "This can't..."

Then the front paws burrowed through the soil, scrabbling to pull the body up from the grave. The dog panted and its tongue hung out, covered with small white maggots.

Sammy fell back and stared. She couldn't move.

Puppy continued to dig, pulling her body up. She was even thinner than the scrawny little dog that had died not two months earlier. Patches of fur were missing and pus-covered sores covered her remaining brown fur. The thing was just skin and bones.

Then Puppy stopped digging and turned to stare at Sammy. Her eyes had fallen back into her skull and only empty pits stared at her. Even without eyes, Sammy knew the horrible thing was staring directly at her. Wanting her.

She tried to stand, but her legs were too weak.

"Adam, help!"

She felt stupid, because just for a moment she'd forgotten he was dead too. His ashes were interred in the concrete monument behind her. Her husband would be no help to her today.

The dead dog growled and bared its teeth at Sammy and somehow it continued to pull itself from the dirt.

"No. Go away."

The dog was almost free of its grave when she felt a rush of adrenaline and used the rake to help herself up.

Puppy glared at her without eyes and started to move toward her. The mouth was wide open and her teeth were sharp and ready to attack.

Sammy swung the rake over her head and smashed it down on Puppy's body. It landed with a thud and she felt awful. She'd loved the dog almost as much as Adam had.

She swung again and hit the dog just behind the neck. It yelped and growled but it moved closer. Sammy inched backward and tried to scream, but nothing came out.

Again the rake came down, harder this time, and she felt Puppy's head crush. The next blow hit the head a second time.

It took ten hard hits to the head to stop the dog. Once again Puppy was dead.

Sammy pushed the corpse with the rake to be sure. It was crushed beyond recognition.

She sat back down on her knees and cried. "My little Puppy. I'm so sorry."

And behind her, she heard a whisper near her ear.

"So am I, sweetie."

She knew that voice. Knew her love from the softness in him. Knew how he was the only one who'd ever called her "Sweetie." He'd used that nickname for the forty-two years of their marriage.

She turned but she didn't get far. His hands closed on her neck. Her last thought was that she should have checked on his ashes first, instead of the dog.

At least now, they'd be together again.

George's Head

The main character in this story is named Emma Nicole Smuck, which is the name of my other step-daughter. She was about ten when I wrote this one, and I liked having her show up in one of my stories.

This story was requested by Michael Knost, who edited several anthologies of legends from West Virginia. I knew nothing at all about West Virginia, but the beauty of being a writer is that you can imagine anything. Michael loved the story, and it appeared in Legends of the Mountain State Volume 3.

Emma Nicole Smuck sat on a boulder near the river and lay her fishing rod on the ground. Her little sister, Sammy, had gotten bored and left to walk back to the farm house and the sun was starting to go down. Emma had been out at the bank for three hours with barely a nibble.

"Stupid fish," she said.

It was Emma's twelfth birthday and when her mom asked what she'd wanted, all she could think of was a new fishing pole. It was waiting for her that morning, a shiny bright red rod with a slick reel and a brand new spool of twenty pound test line.

The perfect rod.

Too bad the fish didn't know that.

The water rushed by and Emma stared into the water. The river wasn't deep, nor was it very wide, only about twenty-five feet across, but in her imagination it was the mighty Mississippi, full of jumping catfish and trout.

Something glinted. She saw it from the corner of her eye, but when she looked directly at the spot, she saw nothing.

She moved her head a bit, left and right, and...

There!

It was on the far bank. Shiny. Not shiny like a mirror but more like snow reflecting the sunlight on a cold winter's day.

"Emma? What's wrong?"

"Sammy? I thought you went back home."

She shrugged. Sammy had her own fishing rod. Well, it was Emma's old rod, a flimsy pole made of bamboo. Gramps had made it for Emma, so she liked it and everything, but she was glad it was time to hand it down to Sammy. In four years, when Sammy was twelve, maybe she'd want a nice rod too. Or maybe not. She hadn't seemed very interested today.

"Scaredy cat."

"Am not."

Emma shrugged and moved her dark hair back over her shoulders. She and Sammy were like identical twins born four years apart. Same coal black hair, same green eyes, same smile and laugh.

Emma looked back and saw the spark of reflected sunlight again.

"What are you looking at?" asked Sammy.

"I don't know. But I'm going to get it."

"Where?"

"Across the other side."

"I don't see anything."

Emma pointed at the small white patch buried in the bank. She wouldn't have seen it most years, but the drought this spring had lowered the river level.

She took her shoes and socks off and rolled up her

pant legs to her knees. As she walked across, she found the river was deeper than she thought and much more powerful. Her pants were getting soaked. She kept walking and the water was up to her waist. It took all her concentration to not lose her footing.

"Mom won't like that!"

Emma waved back at Sammy and continued. No point going back now. Not with her sister watching her, anyhow.

The water was cold, and Emma tried to move a bit faster, but it felt like she was walking through molasses as she fought the current.

"Finally," she said as she reached the other side.

The white thing was hard, like rock, and it was buried deep in the bank. She used her fingers to scrape all the dirt away and freed it. It finally popped out of the muck, and Emma screamed.

Sammy yelled, "What happened?"

Emma dropped the skull into the river and lost her footing but recovered soon enough. She looked around in fear but saw nothing threatening. Her T-shirt was now soaked along with her pants.

"Emma, what was it?"

She reached into the water to find the skull and held it over her head.

Sammy stared silently at the clean white skull in Emma's hand.

Emma turned it and held it to her face to get a better look. The jawbone was missing but she could see a top row of teeth still there. It looked like the skull was staring at her. A chill seemed to run down her spine and for a second she thought of tossing the thing away.

"Spooky."

The surface of the skull was grainy, not smooth, and she wondered if it could possibly be real. *Probably not,* she decided.

Still, it'd make a cool addition to her desk. She could tell stories of it being a long-dead relative, and who could say otherwise?

"Em... Help."

Emma kept staring at the skull when she heard the tiny call from her sister.

"Sammy? What's wrong? It can't hurt you. It's probably just a fake."

"No! It's real!"

Emma looked at Sammy, wondering why her voice had such a tone of urgency.

There was nothing unusual going on. Sammy just stood on the opposite bank of the river, maybe hunched over a bit but otherwise just fine.

Sammy looked up for a few seconds and then yelled over to Emma. "You have to bring the skull over here right now!"

"What are you talking about?"

"There a guy here. He needs his head back. He's like a ghost or something. He's grabbing my shoulder and he's scaring me, Em."

Emma shook her head and watched the water roaring past her. She'd had no trouble getting across but she was so focused on the skull, she hadn't realized how deep the water was. Now that she knew, well, it looked harder to get back. Especially carrying the stupid fake skull.

"There's no such thing as ghosts," she called.

Emma stared at the skull again. Was it real? She didn't know what a real skull would look like. It's probably just a stupid toy.

"Em! His name is George Van Meter. He says Indians cut his head off and he's been looking for it ever since. He says that's *his* skull and he needs you to bring it back to him!"

Sammy's shriek made Emma look back at her little sister.

"What's *wrong?*"

Sammy was breathing too fast, hyperventilating.

"Sammy!! Tell me!"

"He's going to take me away if you don't give him the skull back! Em, he's pressing his hands on my neck. Hard! Help!"

"Sammy, cut it out. You're bugging me. I'm coming back."

She took a few steps forward, each one making her feel more weak than the one before. The river rushed at her and for a split second, she imagined herself being swept off her feet and carried downstate. Somebody would find her corpse miles away.

Damn!

She felt her foot slip on a stone and then she did fall. The water was about three feet deep here and she found herself grasping at rocks with both hands to stop herself from being swept away. The river was as ferocious as the Niagara, as wide as the Amazon. She panicked and found herself spitting out water and shaking her head as she sat on her knees.

"Emma..."

Sammy's voice was softer, but Emma didn't have time to worry about that. She needed to get across the river.

The skull was gone. She'd let go when she fell and it was nowhere to be seen.

"I'm coming, Sammy. Hold on."

This time there was no reply. Emma blinked water from her eyes and looked across the water. Sammy wasn't there.

She rushed through the rest of the water, not caring about slipping anymore, and as a result, she was sure-footed and reached the other side in a few seconds.

"Sammy!"

She went to where her sister had been standing, and saw only blood-stained sand. The blood was still wet.

There was too much of it. There was no other sign of Sammy.

A vision of the skull flashed through her mind, but it vanished as she ran to her house, screaming for her mom.

Flies

In early 2009, I lived in Vancouver. My best friend (and subsequently my wonderful wife) lived in a small village in southern Ontario, three thousand miles away.

We emailed to chat quite a lot, and one day, we had an email conversation that was word-for-word the exact opening of this story. The first 100 words or so were my conversation with her.

I immediately knew I could turn that into a story. Fatima thought I was crazy.

That night I wrote the first half of the story, giggling as I typed, because I loved the idea so much. Unfortunately, I have no clue where to take the story after that. I was stumped.

The next night, totally by coincidence, I watched a TV show that discussed bats. I think I may have been channel surfing, but I'm not sure.

In any case, as soon as I saw the bats, I knew the rest of the story in a flash. I ran back to my room to type it up.

For many years I was a member of the Horror Drive-In website community, which was an online forum for horror fans to meet and discuss books, movies, whatever.

Mark Sieber owned the web site and he occasionally published short fiction. He loved "Flies," and I was truly honored to have him share the story with the rest of us horror weirdos who hung out at the site.

"DID I EVER TELL YOU THAT when I was a kid I used to catch flies and then tie a piece of thread around their neck and let them go and they'd be like my pet fly?"

"No shit. Really?"

"You have to be careful when you tie the thread though. If it's too tight, their heads pop off. I murdered quite a few flies that way. Once I got the hang of it, it was much better then."

"How did you catch the flies?"

"I'd catch them with my hands. How else?"

"You used normal thread? Like for sewing? And it could still fly around?"

"Yup, that's right, just normal thread made a leash. But like I said, it took a while for me to get the right amount of pressure so that I didn't kill them. They couldn't fly *that* well. The weight of the string really slowed them down."

The two girls stared across the river, each lost in their own thoughts. After a minute, Emily turned to Sue. "Think you could still do it? But on something bigger?"

Sue didn't answer right away. She seemed lost in thought, staring out over the water.

"You gonna miss school?"

Emily shrugged. "Nah. We'll be back in grade eleven soon enough. I'm just glad we're finished with Mrs. Jameson. I'm so over her."

"Bitch."

A sweet summer breeze blew off the water and cooled their faces. Both girls wore dark sunglasses, but Sue's light complexion would have her tanned quickly. She wanted that. Emily knew Sue had always been jealous of her own dark skin. Not *jealous* jealous... more like envy.

Emily poked Sue. "So?"

Sue shrugged.

"You're like the lord of the flies," Emily said. She laughed and kicked off her flip-flops. "You really did that, huh?"

"It was really funny."

"So let's do it."

"Kay. What do you have in mind?"

Emily didn't answer for a moment. She wasn't sure that Sue would like the idea that floated through her mind. She picked up her fishing rod and started to reel her line in. Nothing was biting anyhow. Sue copied her, reeling in her own line.

Using her peripheral vision, Emily saw Sue smile.

The girls had known each other since they were four years old. They'd lived on neighboring farms back then, and although Sue's parents moved away to Chicago when she was ten, they were still best friends. They emailed and texted each other every day and Sue always visited during summertime, staying for a couple of weeks at Emily's place smack in the middle of Nowhere, Nebraska.

It was the best two weeks of the year for Emily. They camped outside, fished, wandered around the countryside for hours, and shared the farming chores. They fed the chickens together, cleaned out the barn, watered the horses, and even did a bit of plowing, with Emily's dad watching from the edge of the fields.

As they gathered up their fishing gear, Emily said, "It's like the end of summer tomorrow."

"Yeah. I wish I could stay longer. Next year, maybe I'll come here the whole summer."

"*Now* you're talking!"

They both spent some time lost in thought. Emily wondered if she'd ever actually see her friend again. Sue was dating some guy now. A Senior named Tommy something or other. If that got serious, how would she ever manage to spend even two weeks apart from him, let alone the whole summer? The prospect of losing her best friend brought sadness that washed over her.

"Hey, where to?" asked Sue.

"The barn. The old one."

"Kay."

The old barn caught fire three years ago and was ruined. Parts of the main wooden structure was still standing; it wasn't worth demolishing. The insurance money paid for a new barn. It was all steel and glinting metal and didn't look much like a barn at all.

The cows didn't care, though.

Emily liked the old barn, though. It was empty. Quiet. It was now her own private place.

She pulled open the door and they slid inside. There were no lights and the windows were all boarded up. A five by ten foot jagged hole in the roof at one end brought some light in, but near the other end, Emily and Sue stood in twilight.

The barn still stank of burnt wood and rotten hay. There was no way to avoid the stench. Somewhere in the smell, there might once have been the scent of rotting flesh as well – ten cattle – but that must have been long gone. At least that's what Emily hoped.

"I like it in here," she said.

"Yeah?"

"It's like my own place. My own hidey hole."

"What do you do in here?"

"Sometime just sit. Listen. Sometimes I go under the hole in the roof and read. Sometimes..."

Emily turned to Sue and put her hands on her shoulders, like she would a young child she was about to scold.

"You can't tell anybody."

Sue stared back and shook her head. "I got nobody to tell."

"Not your mom and dad... not Tommy."

"It's okay. Really."

Emily nodded and took Sue's hand. It felt like they were five years old again. "We have to go to the top deck. That's where he is."

"That's where who is?"

Emily didn't answer. She led Sue over to the darkest side of the barn and pointed to a wide staircase. It was built of old timbers and planks that had somehow escaped the fire. They creaked as the girls climbed.

"This used to be a place to store corn and hay and stuff. Like a silo, I think."

The stairs led to a flat area high above the ground. It was about eight feet wide and twenty feet long. The floor was solid but black from soot. There was almost no light and the girls stared toward the end of the platform where it ended at a corner of the barn.

"Over there."

"Jesus, Em, this is kind of freaky. You sure?"

Emily squeezed Sue's hand. "It's cool. But be quiet now. We don't want to wake him."

Sue slipped her hand from Emily's and followed behind her.

Emily smiled.

She walked to the corner, still carrying her fishing rod. Sue had left hers at the barn door.

From behind her, Emily heard a whisper, "What the fuck are you doing, Em?" Emily ignored her. It was just silly noise. She needed to get Bailey.

Her eyes slowly accustomed themselves to the dark, and she could see the bat hanging upside down from the roof. The roof was sloped so that at this point in the barn, it was just at the height of Emily's head. Bailey hung alone, upside down, unaware of the girls' presence.

"Here." Emily handed her rod to Sue. "I'll get him. You can tie the line around his neck."

"Oh, shit. Emily..."

"Do it!"

Sue took the rod and let a few feet of line loose.

Emily moved the final few steps toward the bat. She'd never been this close to Bailey. One more step... but then, the bat woke and started to flap his wings. She pounced at it and grabbed the bat, pinning its leathery wings to its sides. The bat hissed and tried to bite Emily, but she had a tight grip and the bat's head was too far from her hands.

"Get it!" she shouted. She turned to face Sue, who took the limp fishing line and looped it around the bat's head.

The bat fought and struggled but Emily kept a solid grip.

"Hurry," she called. "I'm not sure how long I can hold him!"

"It's trying to bite me..."

"Do it, Sue, or I'll put the damned line around *your* neck!"

Sue finished the loop and tied it. The loop wasn't tight enough to kill the bat but it looked solid.

"Hold the rod," said Emily. When she saw that Sue had the fishing pole, she threw the bat out and it flew away, squealing as it went.

"Oh my God, I can't believe you did that," Sue shouted.

The bat flew farther away and Emily grabbed the rod. "Don't let it keep going."

She locked the reel and the bat jerked to a halt and fell. The force almost pulled the rod from Emily's hands.

The bat recovered and flew to the left and then to the right, trying to find a way free.

"We did it," said Emily. "Just like your flies."

The bat flew back and forth like a kite, and the girls watched it, almost hypnotized by the shadowy figure flying through the darkness. The only sound was the whip-whip-whip of its wings.

"Emily, that's cruel. We should let him go."

"It's just Bailey. Just a bat. It's really just a rat with wings."

"I should go."

"Hold him."

"No. I want to go."

"*Take* the fishing rod, Sue. This was *your* idea."

Sue reached for the rod and took it, watching Emily's face more than the rod or the bat. She'd just taken control of the pole when the bat changed direction and flew toward the girls.

Emily could see Bailey's eyes flash red in the darkness as it flew toward her. His mouth opened and closed with a hiss. She threw her hands up to protect herself, but the bat bit her finger and held on. She screamed in pain and surprise and shook her hands as hard as she could.

The bat flew off and landed in Sue's beautiful blonde hair. Its claws buried in her locks and it started to bite at her. Emily was pretty sure the dark splotches that started to spread were red.

Sue screamed and dropped the fishing rod and tried to reach back to knock the bat from her hair, but she couldn't get to it.

"Help me! Emily, help me! It hurts so much!"

Emily froze, not knowing what to do.

Sue jumped and shook her head. "EMILY!" She moved and suddenly she disappeared as she fell off the edge of the platform. One more scream was choked off halfway through. The fishing pole followed her down.

Emily stared at the edge of the platform, wanting to hear Sue. Hear anything. All she could hear, though, was a sucking sound. She imagined Bailey sucking on the blood, now with no resistance.

"Sue?"

Her call was so quiet. She could only whisper.

"Sue?"

She kneeled down and crawled to the edge, looked down, to see the remains of her best friend. 🜚

I'm proud to be a Canadian, even though many of my best friends are American.

It's not often I write with a purely Canadian focus. This is one of those rare times.

During the horrible war in Afghanistan, a Canadian reporter was killed by a roadside bomb. I remember reading about it and hearing about it on the news, and a while afterward, I wrote this story.

I hope everyone can identify with the feelings in the story, regardless of where they live.

MY LITTLE JILLIAN CAME HOME LAST NIGHT.

It's been such a long time. I call her "my little jillian" because she's such a cute, tiny girl. She's not even five feet tall, but she's just chock full of cute. She's got this amazing smile that only I ever get to see, and the most beautiful green eyes that just sparkle full of love whenever I see her.

Her size never interfered with her abilities—as a person and reporter she was the tallest person I know.

Jillian has been away for two years, and I missed her terribly.

We met at work. She was a reporter and I was a layout manager at *Canada News,* the weekly magazine that still manages to hang on, even though Canada's press has mostly been wiped out. I saw her the first day she started working there. It was September 10, 2001, and she was writing a story about... well, truthfully, I don't recall what it was about, because she never finished it. The following day changed the world, and she scrapped whatever she was working on to write instead about the Canadians who were killed in the terrorist attacks in the twin towers.

She wrote with such passion and emotion that she won awards for that piece. She didn't care about that. All she cared about was the "thank you" emails and phone calls she got from the dead's loved ones.

Everyone wondered where the hell such a talented writer had come from. Out of nowhere.

Over the years, she was always writing about the major international issues Canada was involved in. I never knew how she figured this stuff out.

I once asked her, "How do you know who to call or what to ask?"

She just laughed and said, "Anybody would know."

Anybody?

Nobody else got quotes from the 7/7 terrorists in Britain about their thoughts on Canada. Nobody else had a secret interview with Jean Chretien the night before he announced his resignation. Nobody else had official quotations from Chinese Premier Wen Jiabao prior to Stephen Harper's first state visit.

I was always so amazed. Even after we lived together, I never figured out how she did it. She just *knew* things. Her cell phone always had whatever phone numbers she needed, she remembered every e-mail address she ever wanted to use, and everyone always took her call.

That part I understand. If you ever heard her soft lilting voice, that always had undertones of laughter and smiles, you'd talk to her, too. She entranced everyone.

She finally came back to me last night. Back to our home.

That day we met, back in 2001, I felt my life change. She just looked so freaking cute! My little jillian was talking on the phone with somebody when I first noticed her, laughing her way through another series of wonderful quotes that she typed up as she talked. I thought she looked amazing, but I never said anything to her. Not for more than eight years. See, she was married to somebody else. I was, too.

I kept my feelings to myself all those years, seeing her every day from across a dozen desks, talking to her once in a while in the lunch room, watching her pick up her work at the central printer.

My heart ached to be with her.

Things change. My wife left me, and when that happened, all I felt was relief. I wouldn't have had the courage to ever leave her, so I was stuck with my secret love for Jillian while living a fake life with a woman I no longer knew or cared for.

I still couldn't have my dream girl, though, because she was still married.

And then, one day, she wasn't. I never knew she'd been having trouble in her own marriage until the gossip girl in the corner started letting everyone know that Jillian had booted her husband.

Wow.

Six months later we started dating. Me and my little jillian! She told me then that she'd always had a secret crush on me.

Three months after that we bought our house together. *This* house.

Last night, at 4:42 a.m., I heard her.

"I'm home, sweetie."

I blinked in shock and surprise and godforsaken love and amazement and—

"Jillian..."

"I'm home. I'm back."

The lights were off but there was no mistaking the outline of her body and that amazing soft voice.

She was naked and she climbed into bed beside me. I only ever wore a T-shirt at night and so our bodies melded together like they always did, as if we'd never been apart.

I touched her face lightly with my fingertips. "My baby... you're back."

Even with almost no light, I could feel her mouth pull up into that wonderful smile, and I needed to kiss her. I was still half asleep, shocked awake, and questions that should have been asked didn't come to my mind. All I cared about was that she was home. I kissed her gently, licking her lips and then feeling the electricity as our tongues touched.

God, what an amazing night.

Two years ago, we had our last meal together. Seafood linguini. We always made it together. Fried shrimps, prawns, and scallops mixed in with a nice rose sauce and poured over the pasta. It was our favorite, especially since we always hugged and kissed when we were cooking. That night was no different. It was such a joy for both of us.

During dinner, she broke the news.

"I want to do a story about Afghanistan."

"Sure. That sounds right up your alley." I thought for a minute. "Actually I'm surprised you haven't done a story about it before. Other that that one piece where you interviewed that retiring army guy. I can't remember his name."

She wiped a bit of sauce from her mouth. "I want to do it right, so I'm going there."

"To Afghanistan?"

"Kandahar."

"Oh." I thought of the dead soldiers being carted out of southern Afghanistan, but I tried to sweep that from my mind. "You've never really done that kind of thing. Can't you do the story by phone?"

"The last troops are leaving soon. I want to see what it's really like for them. The last stand, so to speak. What do they feel? What do the Afghans feel about us leaving? I want to be there, to get the story perfect."

She smiled at me. *That* smile. "I have to do this, sweetie."

I nodded, not able to say anything. I had no right to try to stop her. I tried to smile, but I'm not sure how successful I was. She knew me inside and out. When we cleaned up the dinner dishes, I stopped and held her to me tightly. I didn't have to say anything.

Our laptop was sitting on the kitchen counter, playing songs from a 70s radio station on iTunes. Stevie Wonder started singing *You Are the Sunshine of My Life*, and I swiveled my little jillian into a nice slow dance.

As the song came to a close, she looked up to me and touched my face. She wasn't smiling now. Her face was full of love and concern.

"What is it, baby?" I asked.

"I leave tomorrow."

Tomorrow. The word that's haunted me for so long.

That night we made gentle love, caressing each other's bodies, touching, kissing, licking, until we finally both came and our passions were satisfied. We snuggled together under the blankets, with lots of "I love you"s and more gentle touches and hugs.

It was very late before we were able to fall asleep.

She was supposed to be gone for seven days.

Instead, we were apart for more than two years. It was actually two years, three months, and six days. Yes, I counted.

Jillian phoned me when she got settled into her temporary home near Kandahar Air Field. The Canadian Forces were dwindled in numbers and it looked a bit like a ghost town. Most of the remaining soldiers were focused on the security of the air field itself.

She sounded excited to be there, and I knew that she was going to find the perfect angle for her story. It'd be a story no other journalist could tell, because that's just the kind of work she did. She was unique.

Jillian e-mailed me every day, for five days.

On day six, I heard nothing from her.

When she slipped into our bed this morning at 4:42 a.m., it was magic. My little jillian had come back to me. Her hands felt my cheeks and she kissed my chest and she told me she loved me over and over again.

"I'm sorry it took me so long to come home," she said, "but I'm here now."

I was still confused but my body reacted to her touch. She put her hand on my cock and I just wanted her so very much. I pulled her face to me again and kissed her, more passionately this time. She climbed on top of me and I felt her direct me inside of her. God. It'd never felt so good.

She leaned back and bounced on me, and I couldn't help myself. I came almost immediately. It felt like a new experience, like something I'd never felt before. She came shortly after I did, and then collapsed onto my chest.

We held each other for a long time, and I could feel tears leaking from my eyes. I was so happy. My girl was home again.

"What happened?" I finally asked. "How can you be here?"

She rolled off me and lay beside me. I pulled her to me and vowed never to let her go again.

"We'll talk in the morning, sweetie."

"Kay," I said.

She was yawning and snuggling in under my chin. That was what she always did before falling asleep. I rubbed her hair and kissed her forehead and soon I could hear her soft breathing as she fell to sleep. I didn't want to let her go, and I just held her until I, too, fell into a sound sleep.

Two years, three months and two days ago, my little jillian went missing. There was an attack at the air field and Jillian was kidnapped. She was never found. I was notified the following day and told that the army was optimistic about her return. *Right.*

I knew that if they ever found her body, there would be a knock at my door and some big honcho army guy would be there to tell me the news.

The knock never came.

When we woke up on the day she left for Kandahar,

I felt like I was glued to her. I couldn't leave her alone for a single minute. I helped her pack and she even pretended that I helped her decide what to wear for the trip.

I couldn't say good-bye when we got to the security desk at the airport.

"It's okay, sweetie. I'm coming back. I absolutely promise you."

And she did.

This morning, though, instead of finding her cute little body snuggled up to me, I found a pile of dust. It was spread out on our bed, in her body shape. Some of it was still on my chest, in the form of her arm.

I touched some of the grains of sand as I waited for the doorbell to ring. ☙

The Wishing Stones

This story is another example of me collaborating with myself.

I wrote the first draft of this many years ago. My eldest daughter, Peri, taught me about wishing stones when she was ten years old. She also had a doll she called Heavy Baby,

Those two elements came together in this story, but it didn't feel right to me at the time, so I put it on the shelf with a hundred other unfinished pieces.

A quarter of a century later, I remembered the story, and I hunted down the draft version. I liked it enough to rewrite it and have it published.

Peri is now in her forties, but I love her just as much as I did when she was ten.

"OH, DAD, MARTY'S CRYING *AGAIN.*"

I stared at Jodi, frustrated. Of course Marty was crying again. This is not rocket science; it's what he does.

Up to then, it'd been a beautiful September afternoon. Eighty degrees, a cool breeze blowing off the lake, and not a cloud in the sky. Figured it'd be a good day to take the kids on a little nature walk in Lynn Canyon, about an hour's drive from our home in Surrey.

The drive out was heaven, since Marty fell asleep as soon as I packed him in his car seat, and the whole sixty-five minute drive was draped in silence. Even Jodi seemed to appreciate the quietness and sat silently in the passenger seat beside me.

When we arrived at the park, it was a different story, and Marty started into his normal routine. Crying.

It's not his fault. Really, it's not. He's only six fucking months old. But sometimes, the crying gets to me as much as it does to Jodi. I keep thinking I'm doing something wrong, that I'm a failure as a father, but the doctors just say he'll outgrow it.

He was born two months premature, and maybe that has something to do with it. Just a tiny thing, five pounds no ounces, and so frail. He looked like he'd crack just from us looking at him, but he always had that pair of powerful lungs, right from day one.

Mary died in the hospital, and she only ever saw Marty once before she died. Her death multiplied all the stress by a million times, and I don't think I'll ever be over her. She was the only woman I ever loved, and deep in my heart I just *know* she'd be able to calm Marty down. She'd be the good parent.

Jodi wasn't very impressed with the park until we climbed down the embankment and found the river at the bottom. I'd carried Marty in a leather backpack and was surprised that he didn't cry on the way down to the trail to the bottom. He laughed and gurgled at me whenever I had to stop to catch my breath. Even Jodi laughed at me as she skipped ahead.

When we finally got down to the Capilano River, Jodi decided that it wasn't really that bad a place to spend an afternoon after all.

"Look at all the pretty stones, Daddy!"

We sat at the river's edge, the cool water splashing near us, and Jodi picked up a handful of small stones to throw in. Marty sat and patted his hands in the water, lifting them up in surprise when they got wet. It was a perfect afternoon.

The three of us walked around at the bottom of the Canyon for forty minutes or so. It was a nice change from sitting around the house or walking to the small park three blocks north of us. Gordon Park has an adventure playground for Jodi and some baby swings and slide for Marty to play on, but it's not the same as a real outdoorsy place. *This* felt like a different world, where anything was possible, even making a family to be together.

Jodi collected a small pile of stones, packing them into the pockets of her jeans until there was no more room. "Look, Daddy," she said just before we left. "A wishing stone."

"Yeah? What's a wishing stone?"

"Look, see the line?" She held up a gray stone with a white stripe circling its center. "That makes it a wishing stone. You throw it in the water and make a wish. The Lollipop Lady told me that."

"Who's the Lollipop Lady?"

Jodi scrunched up her face, looking at me as if I were stupid. "She's the lady at the school who helps us cross the street. She's got this stop sign she holds up to the cars, you know? It looks like a big lollipop, so we call her the Lollipop Lady."

"Oh."

"She says if you make a wish and throw your wishing stone into water, the wish comes true."

She showed the stone to her doll, who was almost as big as Marty, and who earned her name of "Heavy Baby."

Jodi shut her eyes tightly and leaned her head back. Her mouth was pursed as if she was afraid she might say the wish out loud in front of me. She stood still for a few seconds before awkwardly tossing the stone into the river.

"I collect wishing stones in my drawer, Daddy. I bet I got about a *million* of them now."

I nodded and smiled. Normally I might have tried to calculate how much space a million rocks would take up, but right then I was too busy getting Marty into his backpack for the trip up to the top of the Canyon. He didn't want to go back into the pack and he screamed. I thought of the refreshment stand at the top of the climb. I thought of wishing stones and the Lollipop Lady. Anything to get my mind off his screaming.

"Heavy baby never screams," said Jodi.

We were halfway up the rough steps inlaid in the side of the divide when Marty finally stopped crying. I'd had a headache growing, and Jodi was getting on my nerves with her complaints about Marty. Finally we made it to the top and I ordered two Cokes and a big bag of Lay's chips. Marty drank a bit of my soda and spat it out, making a face and sticking his tongue out.

"I found three more wishing stones at the river," said Jodi. "Look at this one, Daddy. I like it best."

I admired her prize and promised myself never to go on long hikes with the kids again; it was too much work for an out-of-shape artist.

My headache stayed with me until well into the night, when I do most of my painting.

I mostly paint astronomical landscapes—the surface of Mars, the rings of Saturn or Uranus, that kind of thing. I started doing it as a hobby when I was fifteen, when I saw a book cover by Alan M. Clark that just blew me away. It was the cover of Richard

Laymon's *The Traveling Vampire Show*. The details and perspective were amazing, and I immediately knew I was meant to take his style and transport it to a different place.

I sold twenty-two paintings to the science fiction magazines for their covers. They were always after me to do more of them, but I found I could make more money as a one-man show than the magazines would pay me. At my first show, I sold thirty pieces for four hundred bucks each, and I was barely twenty years old at the time.

Ten years later, I make a lot more money for each picture, but since Mary was killed, I'm not enjoying the work as much as I used to. She was my best critic, never afraid to tell me when I was going off in the wrong direction. I finished a nice portrait of her a year before her death. She was tall with long straight blonde hair that swept back behind her ears. Her face was just a bit more pudgy than she would have liked. I helped her a little bit with that in the picture, but now that she's gone I wish I hadn't.

That night we returned from Lynn Canyon, I was working on a twenty by twenty-eight inch version of the Pleiades as seen from the viewscreen of a passing spacecraft. It'd taken me most of a week to get all the angles calculated. Geometry was never my best subject in school (I was too busy in art class), but somehow I figured it all out eventually. The Pleiades look something like a cross formed of stars, but from a nearby spaceship, they'd look more like a distorted letter S.

Marty and Jodi were both in bed by the time I

started to paint that night. I pulled out the iPod from my desk in the workshop and put the soft headset over my ears, turning up the volume as high as I could stand it. Tchaikovsky's *Nutcracker Suite* surrounded me.

Mary gave me the iPod for Christmas. Her last present to me. At first I thought the idea was silly, listening to classical music while painting.

"Just try it, Jim," she said. "What can it hurt to *try?*"

She smiled and laughed, a small dimple showing in her left cheek, and how could I have refused her then? I tried wearing it and never looked back. It seems easier to concentrate with the music on instead of the random noises that always bounced around the house.

Just as I was putting a few light streak marks on my spacecraft window, Jodi pushed open the door to my study and walked in, rubbing her eyes. Her hair was matted down and she wore her pink housecoat over her pajamas. I took off the headset and heard Marty crying. The only problem with the music was not being able to hear him; I had to rely on Jodi to come and get me when he woke up at night.

But it kept Mary with me.

"Why does he cry so much, Daddy?"

I didn't have a very good answer for that. How could I explain to a six-year-old about colicky babies, especially when I couldn't understand them myself? "It's the only way he can let us know he needs us, honey. He doesn't know how to talk like us."

"Jimmy's baby sister doesn't cry like that."

I walked Jodi back to bed and hurried into Marty's

room. His face was red and his crib was soaking wet. I changed his diaper and his sheets, took him to the living room, and rocked him as I warmed a bottle.

I usually don't mind Marty's crying myself, except when he goes on for hour after hour after hour. He was the last gift that Mary'd given me and I cherished him.

Marty took after Mary more than he did me. Maybe that's why he cries so much—Mary sometimes had an awful temper when she was angry. Marty had her nose and her smile. He even had double-jointed thumbs like her, so why not her temper, too?

After an hour, Marty was calmed down enough to fall back asleep. It was time for me to crash, too: ten minutes to three. I turned out the lights in my study and quickly fell asleep.

By eight the next morning, Marty was crying once again. I was getting Jodi ready for school when he let loose.

"Can't he *ever* shut up?" she shouted. "I'm glad it's a school day again, so I don't have to listen to him all day."

"Don't talk about your brother like that. He can't help it."

"Well, I don't like him. I *hate* him!" She took Heavy Baby and placed her neatly on the pillow of her bed. At least Jodi was old enough to make her own bed and get herself dressed most of the time. Heavy Baby sat in her usual place, perched on the pillow like a watchdog, guarding the room against unwelcome visitors.

I stared at the doll as I always did when she sat

there. Heavy Baby belonged to Mary when *she* was a little girl. Maybe that's why Jodi cherishes her so much.

Marty was still crying when Jodi left. That wasn't unusual, since he cried every day when she left. Not because she was leaving; because he was awake.

Just as she went out the front door, she turned around and yelled, *"Be quiet, Marty!"*

"Jodi, calm down. He can't help it."

"I hate him. I hate him, I hate him, I hate him! I wish he had never been born. I wish he'd die and Mommy would come back instead."

She started to cry. I hugged her and tried to calm her down, drying her tears with a tissue. At the same time, I felt guilty not holding Marty while he cried. No win.

"Come on, honey. Mommy wouldn't like you to talk like that. You'd better run off to school now."

It wasn't until after dinner that night I realized just how much Jodi resented having Marty there all the time, crying. He'd been quiet for a couple of hours and was actually eating some of his dinner when he started up again for no apparent reason.

The doctors all said there was nothing that could be done—we'd have to put up with it until he outgrew the crying.

Maybe Jodi really was too young to understand. I know I said that before, but... anyway, she lost her temper and started to yell at him again, yelling about how she hated him and how she couldn't bring any friends over to play because he'd cry all the time and ruin everything.

It hadn't been a great day for me, either. Before the baby was born, I enjoyed staying home all day, flipping between work and household duties. Paint a bit and then do the dishes. Sketch an underlay and vacuum the living room.

Mary had worked as an assistant librarian at the library. There wasn't all that much housework to do, anyhow, after Jodi started kindergarten.

Now, it wasn't quite that easy, and I could only do my painting at night, in the few hours I could squeeze when Marty was sleeping.

Deadlines were piling up.

After Jodi threw her temper tantrum and ran off to school, I paid the bills and threw a load of laundry in.

The mailman arrived, and brought me the letter I'd been waiting for: the answer from the Minerva Gallery. Finally.

I'd begun to think they'd discarded my application, and when I opened the letter, I found they may just as well have done that. They would only have room for twenty paintings, since they were doing two shows at once. That would cut my earnings in half right there. Even if the gallery only took forty percent of the gross, it still didn't leave a lot. I'd never thought of getting life insurance on Mary, and now I was surviving... but only barely.

After she died, I had three life insurance salesmen phone me, asking if I wanted to protect my kids. I hung up on the first two, but then I felt guilty and the third guy got me to sign up.

Everyone has thoughts they're a bit ashamed of now and then. Maybe it was because I'd just paid the damned bills and gotten the half-showing at the gallery, but right then, all I could think about was how much better off I'd be if the kids were run over by a truck. I'd collect a hundred grand in insurance, I'd have more time to paint without interruptions, and I'd get a good night's sleep.

I'd only lose the two things most dear to me.

I hated myself at the thought, and shook it off to think of the good things.

So, the day moved on and Jodi came home from school, immediately nattering and complaining about Marty's crying. I lost my temper even faster than she did.

"You listen here, young lady. I've told you time and time again not to talk like that. Forget your goddamned dinner tonight and go to your room. I don't want to hear from you until the morning."

She ran from the room crying and slammed her bedroom door behind her. It seemed I was yelling a lot lately. Still mad, I dumped her dinner in the garbage and took Marty downstairs for a bottle.

He ran out of energy after forty minutes and fell asleep. I carefully put him in his crib upstairs and washed my face. Then I took two Advils.

Jodi hadn't come out of her room, so I walked down the hallway and listened at her door.

She was praying. Her mother had taught her that habit a few years earlier. I didn't have much use for prayers, but neither did I discourage the practice. It was another way for her to remember Mary.

I felt like a heel listening in on her prayer, but after listening to her, I'm glad that I did.

"Dear God," she said. "Please take my brother back. I don't like him."

I felt awful hearing her say that. I guess it doesn't say very much about me as a father when something like that happens. Her voice trembled and it hit me hard.

"Please take him back, God, and let me have my Mommy instead."

I opened the door of her bedroom and saw her sitting on the edge of her bed, her arms folded together, appealing to God. She wiped her face with her arm.

I broke down; no matter what else, I loved her very much.

As usual Heavy Baby sat at the head of the bed, waiting to be cuddled. It almost looked like it was the doll that Jodi was praying to.

"Honey," I whispered. "Come here, darling."

She looked at me, knowing I must have heard her, and she seemed to be afraid of what I might do to her, which was only natural after my earlier outburst.

"Come on... why don't we have an ice cream cone together?"

I smiled to show I wasn't mad at her. How could I be mad when it was my fault she felt as she did?

I tried to spend as much time as I could with Jodi over the next few days. By Saturday, things were back to normal, the tension eased. She hadn't yelled about Marty since that Monday and I hadn't lost my temper with her.

The forecaster called for a nice weekend. Skies were clear, and although there was a bit of nip in the air, we spent much of Saturday afternoon out in the back yard. Marty squawked when I put him in his red spring jacket, but the moment passed without a cry. The summer before, I'd installed a swing set with two chain swings, a see-saw, and a slide.

As I sat holding Marty on the see-saw, Jodi climbed to the top of the slide, which was only about four feet off the ground. She was waving to Marty, trying to catch his attention. "Hi, Marty! See sister?"

All of a sudden he started to cry again. I put both feet to the ground to stop the see-saw and bobbed him on my knee, but he wailed away.

"Daddy!"

A crash. Jodi yelled, and I just saw as she hit the ground after falling from the top of the slide. Fortunately, she'd put one hand in front of her, so she didn't hit her head. She sat in a crumpled heap, trying not to cry.

"I hurt my, my, my hand, Daddy."

I rushed to Jodi, carrying Marty over my shoulder. "Let me see, honey."

There was a one-inch long scrape on her right palm. It was raw and covered with thin lines of beaded blood.

"Is everything else okay? Can you walk?"

She stood and nodded. "I'm okay." She rubbed her hand on her jeans.

"We'll get you cleaned up. Let me just try to calm Marty down first."

We all walked back to the house, me carrying

Marty, who was still crying, and Jodi rubbing her hand on her pants all the way.

Before following me into the house, Jodi pulled out one of her striped pebbles from her pocket and tossed it into a small puddle. As the stone hit, some mosquitoes jumped up from the surface and flew away. She mumbled as she threw her wishing stone.

I warmed up another bottle for Marty. We were almost out of formula, too. I'd have to get some money from somewhere soon. In a way, it's fortunate I'm an artist. If I could get Mary's mother to watch the kids for a day, I could take the bus downtown and paint some portraits for tourists. It's an easy way to pick up four or five hundred dollars. The tourist season was almost over, though, and after that it would be harder to meet the mortgage payment.

Jodi cleaned herself up from her fall and holed herself away in the basement to play while I watched Marty. As it turned out, between trying to keep him calm and worrying about the money problems ahead of me, I forgot about Jodi's scraped hand until three hours later.

Marty was down for a nap, laying quietly. When he was like that, you wouldn't think it possible for him to be such a terror when awake. All children look like angels when they sleep.

I pulled the door to his room halfway shut and walked down to find my daughter. She was laying on a couch in the TV room, sleeping while the latest Harry Potter movie played in the DVD player. I turned the movie off.

"Jodi?" I shook her. "Jodi, come on, wake up."

"Huh?" She rolled over and opened one eye. "Tired, Daddy."

"I want to take a look at your hand, honey."

She started to whimper. "I'm *tired*, Daddy."

"Just for a sec. I want to be sure it's clean."

She closed her eyes again and stuck her arm up toward me. No scrape.

"No, the other one. The one that was bleeding."

"Oh, Daddy, I want to sleep."

I pulled her left arm up and looked for the scrape. Puzzled, I looked again at her right hand. There were no marks on either one.

"Jodi? Which hand did you hurt?"

She blinked her eyes. "What?"

"When you fell off the slide. Your hand was bleeding. Which one?"

She shook her head. "I didn't fall off the slide."

"Come on, honey. When Marty was crying out in the yard this afternoon. You were climbing on the slide and fell off. Your hand was bleeding."

"I didn't fall anywhere."

I looked at her hands again before putting them down reluctantly. "Sure, pumpkin. You go back to sleep."

I picked her up as she slept and carried her to her room. I thought back to her tossing her stone into the puddle earlier. "I wish I didn't fall," she'd mumbled.

I took the kids down to English Bay the following Sunday. The city had organized a picnic for July 4th. We had a lunch basket and I picked up a six-pack of

Coke on the way. The weather cooperated with us at first, but as the day continued, large black clouds rolled in from the Pacific, and cool winds sprang up with them. The sun retreated, and by three-thirty, the waves on the beach were capped with white foam. Too cold to stay anymore.

People ran for cover as the rain began to fall, and the organizers pulled out large plastic canvasses for their electronic music equipment.

The rain hammered down harder than I could remember ever before. I had to drive back home at ten miles per hour – it was impossible to see anything out the front windshield even with my wipers going their fastest.

And the baby cried.

Jodi sat beside me, while Marty was in his car seat, alone in the back. He was scared of the noise and the pounding of the rain, I guess. He cried and coughed himself into spasms of choking. I pulled off the road several times to try to calm him down, but it didn't last.

"Oh, why can't he just shut up?"

"I'm doing the best I can, honey. Just try not to think about him."

She paused before talking again. "The Lollipop Lady doesn't believe in colicky babies. She says he's just spoiled."

"Well, the Lollipop Lady doesn't know very much, then."

"She's got a little baby that doesn't cry."

"Jodi, I don't want to *hear* about her baby. Marty is *our* baby, whether you like it or not."

"Well, he can't have Heavy Baby today."

She crossed her arms and pouted. Marty seemed to like Heavy Baby, maybe even more than Jodi. Maybe cause they were about the same size.

The rain let up a bit when we were halfway home, and by the time we pulled into the carport, the sun was starting to peek out from behind the clouds again. The only reminder of the storm was a group of huge puddles laying around the yard, and a spray of water falling from a hole in the eaves trough near the front yard.

"Can I play outside?"

Marty was still whining.

"Okay, just don't get into any mud or anything."

I put Marty in his playpen while I took off my jacket and tried to tug his off. That just upset him more. I could feel a headache coming on, and I prayed for the next six hours to go by quickly, so that Marty would be asleep and I could relax with my painting in the study.

Finally, Marty calmed down. He sat in his playpen with his pacifier, and he rolled around, smiling, and trying unsuccessfully to sit up. My headache stayed, however, and I swallowed three Tylenols, hoping they would help.

Sunshine bathed the front window. Looking out, there wasn't a cloud to be seen. Good old Seattle.

Jodi was sitting on the front step with Heavy Baby and a small pile of her wishing stones. She was tossing them into a nearby puddle.

One, two, three, four, five. Then she went to the puddle and retrieved them. Start again.

I opened up one of the side windows to hear what

she was up to.

"I wish my brother was dead." Toss. "I wish he was *dead*." Toss.

Marty was cooing in his pen and giggling. I thought of asking Jodi to come see him now, but it wouldn't have done any good. As soon as he started to cry again, she'd forget the good times.

I thought of the Lollipop Lady. I'd never met her, and now I was glad. She was probably a perfectly fine old lady, who liked to talk to kids as she helped them across the street.

I preferred to think of her as an old hag with a crooked nose, smelly teeth, and a hatred for little kids, trying to get them into trouble. Maybe one day, she'd "accidentally" trip one of them when a car was rushing by, or cast a spell on a kid by using her damned wishing stones. She'd have a crooked back and a wooden cane and—

"Daddy?"

Jodi was smiling at me. It was nice to see.

"I'm hungry. Were you asleep?"

"No, honey. I'll make some Kraft Dinner for supper. How's that sound?"

"Okay."

"Why don't you go play with Marty?"

"I think I'll just go to my room and play with Heavy Baby."

The day seemed to drag on and on. Marty wanted to be held all the time, and Jodi was being a little brat, nagging about the noise that Marty was making.

Finally, they both ended up in bed. Marty wasn't all that interested in going to bed at first, but he settled down about ten o'clock. I was tempted to take a night off from painting, but the exhibition was only a week away. I wanted to finish my Pleiades picture and give it a few days to dry.

The painting was one of my best, and I was sure that I would get a good price for it. I'd start at fifteen hundred and see what kind of interest I got.

The last touch to the painting was to add some gray shadows behind the window in the spaceship, to hint at the aliens inside. You could barely notice the contrast unless you looked closely in good lighting. Fine details like that are my trademark and make the work worthwhile.

I painted until my eyes started to blur over and my legs became sore from standing so long. I was amazed to look at my watch and see it was three o'clock. Not that I hadn't painted that long before, but it was a rare night that Jodi didn't come down to get me to calm Marty down.

As I peeled off the Walkman, I heard him. He was crying in huge whooping coughs, racking his lungs in spasms.

"Marty! I'm coming!"

I ran up the stairs as fast as I could. Something must have been wrong—he only cried that loudly after a long time. He must have been crying for a half hour or more. And Jodi hadn't come to get me.

Marty was soaking wet and trying desperately to sit up. He'd been sick in his crib. Dried vomit stuck to his blue sleepers.

"Okay, Marty. It's alright, baby."

I carried him into the bathroom and cleaned him up, irritated that Jodi hadn't called me. I put on a bottle and carried him into the living room, turning on the radio. He liked music, and it sometimes calmed him down. This time, the music didn't help, but the bottle did, after it warmed up. I lay him down on my lap as he took huge glugs of formula. After four ounces, he was back asleep. It still amazes me how little kids can change their moods in moments.

I put him back into his crib and pulled his light yellow blanket over him. Then I walked angrily into Jodi's room and shook her roughly.

She didn't move.

The next few days are pretty much a daze for me. The police arrived soon after I called. I sat quietly in a corner of Jodi's room, not really believing that she was dead. How could she be dead?

There was a group of men with cameras wandering around, and one detective in charge. He tried to get me to call a lawyer, but I wouldn't.

"Suit yourself," he said.

He asked me a bunch of questions I couldn't answer. I cried and moved to her body before they carried her out. Her cheek was cold when I kissed it.

"I don't know," I said to the detective. "She was fine when she went to bed. Fine."

"We may have to have an autopsy done, sir."

I nodded. As more officers arrived, Marty woke up. I went in and cuddled him. I'd lost Mary and somehow

I'd lost Jodi, but I still had Marty.

The days seemed empty without Jodi running around and complaining and asking questions and laughing, but after a few weeks, the pain started to diminish. When the police found out that Jodi had been recently insured, they came back to ask more questions.

The only thing I couldn't tell them was how she died. They wouldn't have believed me. Maybe the Lollipop Lady would have, but not rational, logical policemen.

When I'd come into her room that night, Heavy Baby wasn't down at the end of her bed guarding the room, like she normally was. She was close to Jodi's contorted face. I'd seen that doll for years, even before Jodi was born, since Mary used to bring it out once in a while and sit with it, remembering her childhood.

The doll normally carried a totally ambivalent expression. It's mouth was straight, not carrying the slightly upturned smile that was there that night. Its arms weren't flexible, but they were in a different position from the way they'd always been before. I know that sounds impossible, but I *saw* it. Ten days later, the slight smile was gone, and the arms were back to hanging stiffly at the doll's side.

Heavy Baby wasn't alive anymore.

"I wish that Heavy Baby was alive," Jodi had said. I burned the doll and threw the rest of Jodi's wishing stones into the woods at the back of the house.

Now I always remember the way Jodi had been: long, blonde hair and a smile with two teeth missing. It's only on the occasional evening, when the wind is blowing up a storm and the windows are rattling that I remember how I found her that night, with a blue tint to her face, bulging eyes, and ten very tiny red welts cupped under her chin.

I think Heavy Baby liked Marty as much as Marty liked Heavy Baby. 🌿

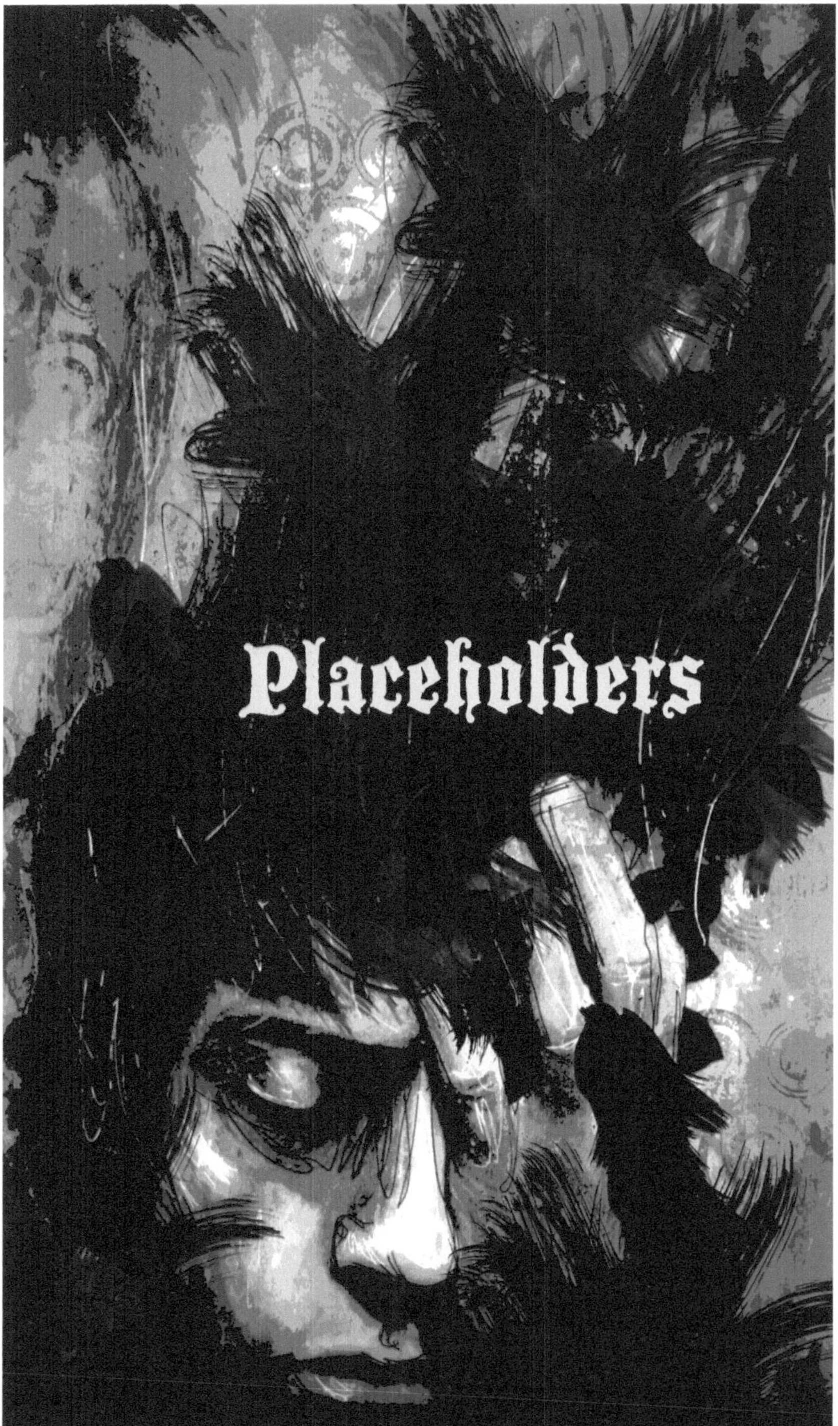
Placeholders

This story started out as two dreams I had back-to-back. I woke up and knew immediately I had to write this one. I loved the idea, and even today I think this may be the best story I've ever written. Miranda might have been more popular, and it's a tough call between the two, but this is the one that means the most to me.

The timelines in the story are quite complex, but most readers will never notice if they were bang on or not. As the writer, I didn't have that luxury, and it took a lot of planning (some in retrospect) to be sure everything was fitting together.

There's one other note about this one. When I wrote it, I was in immense pain from a herniated disk in my neck. I could barely move, and typing was absolute torture. I had tears streaming down my face from the pain.

I couldn't stop, though. The story was too important, and it had to be written.

Necessary Evil Press published Placeholders as a chapbook. It sold out very quickly, and that edition is rare, and hopefully the people who own a copy enjoy it.

Part I

I DREAMED OF THE FIRST TIME I kissed Josie Kopechne. She radiated that brilliant smile of hers, beaming as she leaned in toward me.

My future wife, our first kiss. Heaven. The best day of my life.

Then my eyes snapped open. The vision of Josie vanished in a flash, a memory lost forever. I could feel her leaving me, while at the same time knowing that I never actually met anybody named Josie Kopechne, let alone married her.

For a moment, it felt like I had lived a double life: one where I was so deeply in love with Josie, devoted to her happiness; and another very separate life without her. I was stretching back to *that* life the life without that kiss but I could remember no details. My mind was a blank slate.

Josie pulled farther away, and I knew she wasn't

really my wife. Sadness washed over me, having lost a woman I had never met.

"Get back in line!"

I jumped a bit as somebody punched my shoulder. "Fuck off," I snapped as I turned to face the guy.

"Get back in line, soldier! We've got no time for this shit now." He pushed me toward the other men ahead of me, all of them hunched over and ignoring the skirmish.

What the fuck?

An airplane. Jump suits. The deep groan of the plane as we flew... where?

Men lined both sides of the plane, hunched over, steadying themselves against the rocking.

All dressed in parachutes. Including me.

"Shit, you got the wrong guy," I said. I turned to the officer behind me. I didn't know how to read the stripes. Was he a sergeant? A captain? I didn't care as long as he didn't expect me to walk out that open door ten feet in front of me.

I felt the cold air streaming in and could see the ambient lighting cast from the wings, aimed to partially illuminate the ramp leading to the gaping hole.

"Number one, go!" the officer snapped.

The first soldier ahead of me casually jumped out of the plane and into the night sky. Here one second, gone the next. It was pitch black, and I had no idea how he knew where he would end up.

"Go, go, go!"

The fellow right in front of me dropped out of the plane.

I would be next. I'm terrified of heights. My head ached, and I grabbed onto the side of the airplane frame.

"No, I can't. I don't belong here."

My heart pounded, and I pushed back to the wall of the plane. *How the hell did I get here?*

I was hooked to a tether connected to the ceiling of the plane. When the guy in front of me jumped, I saw the tether pull his ripcord automatically.

"Go, now!"

I froze. "No, I can't. I'm not "

The officer grabbed me. "You spineless puke. You are *not* ruining this mission. Get going." He pushed me.

Out into nothing.

I felt my stomach lurch as I tripped on the edge of the plane floor. Falling. A blast of cold air pushed up into my face, and I'm sure my heart stopped for a moment.

"Help!" I couldn't stop yelling. My arms and legs pinwheeled as I grabbed at empty air. "Help!"

The sound of the plane grew fainter and was soon gone altogether, replaced only by the ceaseless roar of the wind. I was falling to my death. "Please, God, help!"

I looked up. It was dark, and I couldn't see my chute in the pitch black. Something was wrong. I hadn't been jerked back up when the chute opened. I was still falling as fast as I had on my first step out.

My parachute hadn't opened.

I couldn't breathe. I tried to gulp air, but my panic wouldn't allow any to enter my lungs. My frantic efforts to grab onto something, *anything*, had caused my pinwheeling to slow down, my outstretched arms and legs providing a bit of stability.

Out of the corner of my eye, I saw one of the other guys fly up from beneath me, as he drifted safely down to earth. I was crashing down at a million miles an hour.

Gotta be dreaming. "Please wake up," I prayed. But I knew this wasn't a dream. Another minute or two and I'd be dead.

I tried to concentrate. My parachute hadn't opened. *There must be a backup.* I grabbed at a yellow plastic cord hanging from my chest and pulled.

Nothing.

Oh, my God, I'm going to die. "Please, help," I whispered.

I still couldn't breathe. All I could hear was my own voice screaming as I slowly twisted through the night sky.

Within seconds, I saw the ground below me. It was on a weird angle, but there was no question it was getting closer to me.

Panicking now, I spun more wildly, and I lost the view of the ground for a moment. When it returned, I could see individual trees and bushes illuminated by the full moon laughing above me. I was aimed toward an open area, covered with bare grassy fields and lots of large rocks.

"Josie!" I screamed. I closed my eyes before I crashed to the ground, breaking every bone in my body and dying instantly.

Time passed. I can't say exactly how long. It's like when you're in a relaxing, dreamless sleep. You know time passed, but you have no way to tell how much.

The world was idle.

Until I awoke.

And felt the last vestiges of a dream fade away. A dream about Felicia, the woman I almost married. She was Spanish, and I met her on a grand fishing holiday in the Canary Islands. It was the trip of a lifetime, especially when Felicia came into my life. But it wasn't to be a happy ending. We had two wonderful weeks together, but then she went back to her life in Madrid. I flew back home to Boston. Six months passed with many fleeting dreams of following her to Spain. I always missed her, especially in the middle of long, lonely nights.

But that wasn't *my* life.

It was somebody else's. The love I felt for Felicia was fading as I felt myself bobbing in the water. Droplets splashed up onto my face, waking me completely.

I was treading water. Must have been doing it for some time, ever since...

What?

My arms were already tired. No life jacket. I spit out the salty water that was splashing into my mouth and looked ahead. Nothing but water as far as I could see.

"What the fuck?"

I kicked my legs and turned in a circle. About thirty feet behind me, I could see the last remains of a bubble-stream surfacing.

That's where we went down. Somehow I knew that but couldn't put my finger on *what* exactly went down and who *we* were.

I finished circling. Nothing to see in any direction. I was alone. My head was starting to get heavy, and I had to paddle harder to keep my mouth above the water.

There was no debris, no leftovers from the accident, nothing to help me float.

The water was frigid. As I paddled, I clenched my hands and could feel the tips of my fingers were already numb.

"Oh, my God."

The only sounds I heard were the waves splashing up against me. I didn't even see any birds. Did that mean I was far from shore? Sure looked like it, with not a hint of land in any direction. Oddly, panic didn't set in right away.

I stretched my hands again and then noticed: they were black. I pulled my arm out of the water and saw that the whole thing was black. And my chest. And presumably the rest of me.

How could a skinny white guy from Kansas end up in some black guy's body?

"Kansas," I said. Was I really from Kansas? No, that was the guy in the airplane—the guy who was married to Josie Kopechne.

The memory of my chute failing and me crashing to my death struck me with terror, and I found myself sinking. I scrambled back to the surface and spit out more seawater. I remembered the impact, the searing pain as my bones turned to powder, and all my nerves exploded in an instant, blinding nova.

I was dead.

But now I wasn't.

"Boston. I'm from Boston," I said. I needed to say something out loud, just to hear my own voice. Then I shook my head. "No, that's not me. That's whoever owns this body."

I tried to think of who I really was. Before the water, before the airplane.

Nothing came. The earliest thing I could remember was the fading dream of Josie Kopechne. Before that... my memory didn't give up any clues.

I shifted onto my back, trying to put more emphasis on my legs, which still had a lot of strength and giving my arms a badly needed break.

I wasn't wearing a shirt, nor shoes. Just a pair of white shorts that had seen better days. My watch was stopped at 7:42. I didn't know if that was a.m. or p.m.

My arms were well-muscled, but I had no idea how long I had been in the water. I needed to conserve my strength.

For what?

I didn't have a good answer for that.

The bubble-stream eventually stopped, and I no longer had any idea where the boat or plane or whatever it was had gone down. I wondered if other people were trapped inside the husk at the bottom of the ocean.

I knew it was an ocean because of the saltiness. That's *all* I knew. The water was cold, but that didn't help me much. I had no idea what time of year it was or where on Earth I might be.

Someplace where birds don't go.

The air was cool on my cheeks, and as time passed the water seemed to grow calmer, the splashes on my face more like fleeting kisses.

Once again, the vision of Felicia came to mind. Dark hair, darker eyes, a fiery Latin temperament that left me wanting more every time I saw her.

I shook her from my mind. The sun was drifting lower to join me in the ocean, and I kept taking brief glimpses of it, watching the tiny color shifts. When I first awoke, it had been bright yellow, burning in the clear, blue sky. Now, the light was bronze, shading toward a burnished orange. I had nothing else to do except to note the almost imperceptible change from one tint to another.

As the light changed, my skin grew darker and darker. I tried to imagine living in this black man's body, somewhere in Boston. I had none of my own history to compare his life to only his misty haphazard memories.

Felicia. That was about all I knew about him. I remembered the feel of her lips on mine as we danced, her soft perfume, the brightness in her eyes.

Was I the only person out here, or were there truly other corpses already providing nourishment for the fish at the bottom of the sea?

Just as that thought hit me, I felt a nibble on my toes.

I thrashed about and swam away, kicking myself as far away from that spot as I could. I had hoped for some type of rescue plane to find me, but despair was starting to set in.

"Fuck," I said. "Nobody even knows I'm here."

My shoulder muscles were aching with a pain unlike anything I could remember. Hot stabs burned into me with every slight twist or paddle.

From somewhere, a line from a Bill Cosby recording sprang into my mind: God asking Noah, "How long can you tread water?"

The bottom of the sun was kissing the sea. The orange had given way to a deep red with just a hint of purple, and the beautiful reflection raced across thousands of miles to meet me. A flash of green sparkled just for an instant, and I wondered if I imagined it.

It was almost peaceful.

Almost.

My left arm locked, no longer able to move. It was a dead piece of meat hanging from my shoulder. I kicked my legs faster to compensate, but even so, I started to swallow gulps of water.

The sun fled, abandoning me. Only a radiant purple glow remained, and that grew darker with each fearful glance.

My right arm was full of painful needles, and I could no longer flex my hand.

So tired.

I couldn't last much longer. I choked down some more seawater, spitting out as much as I could.

Soon, the sky was black. Stars shone above me, calling to me. I heard them whispering, "Richard, Richard..."

And so I finally remembered my name. My *real* name.

I closed my eyes to hide from the hateful stars taunting me. Resting, hoping to have just a short nap, knowing at the same time that sleep would be the death of me. Maybe that would be an improvement.

Finally my right arm also gave up, refusing to fight for me any longer. I had no more tools to battle with.

I stopped trying, feeling the blessed peace from my agonized muscles for just one moment before I sank.

I held my last breath as long as I could, maybe thirty seconds or forty. My lungs started to quiver and fight. I was sinking deeper, and I had no way to know which direction was up. Everything was black, and I had become totally disoriented. I panicked and started to swim again in a random direction, my dead arms waking up for one final push.

I needed one last chance. My tortured arms tried to find the surface. My eyes bulged, seeing nothing. The remaining air in my lungs forced itself out in small bubbles. I fought not to breathe.

Finally I lost, and my mouth opened. I breathed deeply, needing so much to fill my lungs. The sea burned all the way down. I thrashed and swallowed again, and the pain was so terrible.

I fought only for another few seconds before I died once again, my last thoughts turning to Felicia.

Time. Time. Blank memories full of nothing.

When I woke, my lingering dream was of Annie. She was a farm girl that I met at the Seventh Baptist Church in

(Missouri?)

somewhere. My life with her was already draining from my mind. I grabbed onto the last bits of love I had felt for her. My wonderful farm wife. So thoughtful and caring. God, I missed her touch. Her beautiful young smile staring down from above me as we made love on our honeymoon.

My eyes didn't want to open at first, but I knew I had to force them. A sinking feeling crawled around inside me; I knew I was going to die again.

Annie.

I could still remember her scent, but it was fading with all my other memories of her.

I managed to pry my eyes open just a thin slice. My vision was watery, clouded, and no amount of blinking would clear it up.

My mind was just as foggy as my eyesight. I heard noises that I thought were cicadas, but I knew that wasn't right. I couldn't move.

Beep, beep, beep.

Not cicadas. Electronics. I shook the tears from my eyes and could see tubes stretching upward from my arms. *A hospital*, I finally realized.

The noises got louder, hammering my ears. "Stop that," I said, hearing my own raspy, slurred words and wondering if anyone else would be able to make out what I was saying.

"Jimmy?" A woman's voice echoed from far away. "You're awake!"

At first, I heard, "Imm. Oaway," but after a minute, I was able to understand her words.

"What happened to me?"

After a short pause, I heard, "Don't talk, Jimmy. It's

too hard on you."

She couldn't understand me. My mouth barely moved, and I could feel my teeth were mostly missing. Everything hurt. I shook my head as hard as I could and forced my eyes to focus.

An old woman stared at me. She looked like a witch in a children's fairy tale. Dirty, thin gray hair and a wrinkled mask for a face made it difficult to look at her.

"Who are you?"

I must have spoken more clearly because she answered, "It's okay, Jimmy. It's Annie."

"You're not Annie! Where is she?"

She dropped her smile for a moment, but she recovered and reached to touch my face. I tried to pull away from her.

A man joined her. It took me a moment to decipher his words. "He's getting worse. He might not recognize you anymore."

She looked to the man. A doctor? "Damned cancer."

He nodded and put a hand on her shoulder. "We'll help as much as we can in these..."

I didn't hear the rest of his sentence, as I fell back asleep.

Dreaming of my beautiful Annie again, I woke up without the beeping to keep me company. I was able to open my eyes more easily and saw the light was much dimmer. I didn't know how much time had passed and tried to see a clock, but I couldn't find one.

"You're awake."

I turned my head far enough to see an old man lying in a bed next to me. His voice was weak, tenuous, immediately making me wonder if he was on his last breath.

"Yeah," I said. "I'm here."

My voice sounded better than I remembered it from earlier, but that may have been wishful thinking. I wanted a glass of water.

The other man didn't say anything for a while, and I wondered if he had died. After about ten minutes, he finally spoke again. "This is the worst yet."

"The worst what?"

"Death."

Although I heard him clearly, my mind didn't seem capable of understanding him. *I'm not the only one?*

I did my best to turn to my side, but I didn't have any strength.

He continued, "Others were faster. This is too fucking slow. Too painful."

"You died before?"

He didn't answer.

"What're you here for?" I asked.

"Same's you. Liver cancer. Spread all over hell's half acre now, but that's where it started."

Liver cancer. Just like me.

"And the other times?"

He farted and sighed. "Not so hard," he said. "You get used to the dying, just not the goddamn endless pain."

"How many times have you died?"

"Sheesh, I dunno. Maybe a hundred. How about you?"

"Twice," I said. "This is three."

"Got a lot ahead of you."

We were both quiet for a while. "A hundred?" I asked. "Why is this happening to us?"

He didn't answer, and after a while I could hear soft snores.

I was drugged in the hospital most of the time and couldn't think straight. My only lucid moments were those like now, in the middle of the night, the longest period between shots of Demerol.

The pain bit into me. With the light low, I felt alone and frightened. My midsection was ruptured and dead. I imagined the cancer eating me up inside as it spread through my organs. It was almost impossible to get enough air, as if I were breathing through a straw. Every part of my body ached, and I couldn't help but call for the nurse to give me another shot a couple of times each night. They usually refused, saying it was too soon. Sometimes I fainted from the trivial effort of pushing the call button.

The guy beside me never told me his name.

There were only a couple of other times we were both lucid at the same time. He tried to tell me his theory of what we were.

"Placeholders."

"What's that?"

"We're here so somebody else doesn't have to go through the suffering."

"But why us?"

"Never figured that part out. Maybe we're assholes. Deserve all this torture, and the guys we're replacing don't."

I wasn't sure I liked that idea. I didn't *feel* like the kind of person who deserved this.

Then again, I had no memory of my true life. All I knew was my name: Richard.

"You dream before you go to a new body?" he asked.

I nodded as I reached for the call button. The pain was too strong. Even the bit of information I was getting wasn't worth the price.

"Wives. Women I loved."

"I dream of children. Loving children who smile at me, love me... Maybe I was a child molester."

What would that make me? I wondered. *Did I beat my wife? Kill her?*

He stopped speaking. A few hours later, they carted his dead body out.

I was alone again.

The following morning it got even harder to breathe. My imaginary straw collapsed. I banged on the panic button, but I knew nobody would get to me in time. The hospital wasn't very efficient.

It wasn't like drowning, when I tried so hard not to open my mouth. This time I gulped as much as I could, but nothing came in.

Out of frustration, I beat my chest with my fist, begging my lungs to work. No good. Eventually I grew tired, and all I could see was swirling spots.

The pain. The pain.

I lay still, trying to be calm, and after another five minutes of torture, I died. I think Annie was with me and held my hand.

My fourth death was quick. I woke in the middle of a

crosswalk, jumping from an air horn as a semi ran over me, crushing my legs. I lingered for only a few moments filled with agonizing pain.

Number five was easy, too. I was shot in the face. A bank robbery gone bad. A bullet took out my left eye and lodged in my brain. The doctors could do nothing but put me out of my misery.

I'll never forget death number six. I woke up with my wife staring down at me. My wrists and ankles were tied to the four posts of our bed.

"Jen?"

"You fucking shit."

I didn't know what she was talking about. I almost never know anything about the people I'm replacing.

She took a long carving knife and cut off my cock, then shoved it in my mouth while I was screaming. She covered my mouth with duct tape, so I couldn't make any noise. I choked as blood dribbled down my throat.

Then she took her time dissecting me.

Part II

PLACEHOLDERS.

The term still seemed weird, and I wasn't sure I liked the implications. The good people didn't have to suffer since I took their place. Why?

This was the longest I'd been able to think about things. I'd been in this body for about an hour, sitting beside a small stump in the sand.

To the west, I saw a trail of footprints winding toward me through the desert. My footprints. They stretched as far as I could see, back over a small ridge in the sand. The closest thirty feet weren't so much prints as drags. I must have been crawling toward the stump when the sun set.

I'd awakened with my right cheek buried in the sand. Grit filled my blistered mouth. The sun was rising and was already as hot as a blast furnace.

I patted my clothes, but I had no water. I was wearing blue cut-off shorts and a matching tank top shirt. As my normal disorientation wore off, I realized I was female.

The last wisps of a dream faded, and I tried to catch snippets before it was lost for good.

Holding Mike, feeling his touch on me.

That's all I had.

My tongue was swollen. Even though I felt okay right then, it seemed pretty clear I'd be dying of thirst this time.

I stood and pulled my long hair back behind my shoulders. My arms were burned from the sun, blistered and cracked. Without much thinking, I touched my breasts and then my crotch. This was so much stranger than waking up in the body of a black man or any of the other men I'd taken the place of.

A small wind raised a dust pile that snaked past me, and more grit covered my face. I started to cough. Stupidly, I hadn't closed my eyes quickly enough and the sand burned inside them.

I sat back down by the stump and blinked tears, freeing some of the dirt.

Wiping the few tears onto a finger and then licking them did nothing to help my thirst, but it was worth a try.

The sun was well above the horizon now, and the air burned all around me.

"Mike?" I called.

There was no answer, of course, but I could remember fleeting images of him kissing my nipples and thrusting himself inside me. The last image faded into the drifting desert, just a mirage folding itself into extinction.

Part of me wondered where a stump could have come from in the middle of all this sand, but ultimately I just accepted it. I'd seen too many impossible things to worry about something that was simply implausible.

I stood on top of the stump and stared out onto the wilderness. Sand as far as I could see.

Except.

South.

A bright reflection. The sun was bouncing off something metal. It looked like an umbrella or a telescope. Or some place with water.

"Hey, hey," I said. I jumped to the sand and started to jog, but each step pulled me down like tar. My feet sank about three inches, so I slowed myself to a walk; that way, each step was easier.

"Don't get too optimistic," I warned myself. "You know how this shit's gonna end."

It didn't matter. Even now, my tenth time, I didn't want to die. There was a part of me that fought every time fought for the body I owned as if it were my natural one. Fought for the chance of a release from the endless cycle of pain and death.

"Hello!" I shouted. My voice was hoarse and my throat sore.

As I walked, the glint of the sunlight on the metal thing disappeared and then reappeared. At one point, I had to climb a dune, and lost sight of the light for about ten minutes. I couldn't help feeling a bit of panic, sure I had only imagined the reflection, but when I crested the top, it was back.

As I walked down the other side of the huge dune, I could finally make out what it was: a rotting sky-blue Chevy Silverado pickup truck. It was buried to the top of its tires in sand, like a lumbering creature sinking in the primordial ooze.

My heart sank. The truck could have been there for fifty years for all I knew.

I stopped walking and stared. There was somebody in the driver's seat. Shadows covered him, but I could see a tangled beard. His head lolled back between the headrest and the window, his body slumped like a rag doll. Without thinking, I crossed my arms across my breasts, once again startling myself.

"Hello?" I called again. My voice was much smaller this time. It was like when I was young

("Why are you doing this to me?" Natalie cried.)

and my heart seemed to skip. Was that a memory? It was almost gone, though. All I could hang onto was the name *Natalie*.

I closed my eyes, begging the memory to come back, but to no avail. Sweat rolled down my face as I stood still. I wiped my forehead and figured I had nothing to lose by seeing if the guy in the car was dead or alive.

"Hey!"

He didn't react to my shout. I moved closer and poked his arm by reaching through the broken window. He turned his head and opened his eyes, staring at me without saying anything.

I wondered if he thought I was just a dream. A mirage. A fantasy. Old man wakes up in the middle of the desert to find a young brunette smiling down at him.

"I saw you from back there," I said, waving to the distance. "You got any water?"

He grinned and shook his head. "Nope. 'Course not. Supposed to die here again. What good would water be?"

I stared at him, trying to be sure I'd heard him right. Die *again.*

"Did you mean that? Dying again?"

He opened the door and unfolded himself out to stand beside me, stretching his arms up to the sky. "Damn hot day again. Fuck're you?"

I answered without even thinking. "Mandy. I'm from Miami. Who are you?"

He slammed the door shut and wiped the sides of his face with his filthy hands. "Name's not important. I'm just a placeholder. Probably you, too. You wouldn't be out here with me otherwise."

There it was. Another one.

I didn't know what to say. I found myself nodding.

"What time for you?" he asked.

"Ten. I've never been a girl before. It's weird."

He shrugged. "Happens all the time. Law of averages and all that. This is fifty-seven for me. Fifty fucking seven."

He looked drained and haggard, like he'd been out here a lot longer than me. Or maybe it was just that he was in an older body.

"Where'd you get that name from?" I asked.

"Placeholders? My word. Figured it fits."

"An old guy used that term not that long ago."

"That's *my* word. Where'd you hear it?"

"Hospital. We were both dying of liver cancer."

He stared at me, looking at me from top to bottom, like I was from a species he'd never seen before.

"I guess that'll be me."

We were both quiet. Could it be? Was he really the

guy from my third death?

"He said he died more than a hundred times," I said.

"Shit. Forget about things happening in order any more."

I stared at him. Dark eyes, a grayish-brown scraggly beard. He looked about thirty going on fifty. In the hospital he'd been in his eighties, and of course he looked nothing like this.

I was guessing I was somewhere around twenty years old myself. It was hard to gauge with the toll the sun had taken on my body.

"Well, Mandy from Miami, it's nice to meet you again. I don't remember the hospital yet, but   " He squinted and licked his lips. "Hold on. Yeah. Now I remember. Not in a damned hospital, though. Richard, right? Forget this Mandy bullshit. Isn't that right? Richard?"

Richard. I remembered the stars seeming to whisper that name to me while I was drowning.

I nodded. "Yeah. That's right. I think. We met another time? Not just at the hospital?" I shook my head. "I would have remembered."

"Hasn't happened yet for you, but it will."

I had no idea what he was talking about. "What's your real name?"

"Ray."

"Well, Ray, any thoughts what we should do?"

"Don't much matter, does it? We're gonna be gone in a few hours, I figure."

"I just came from the north, and from there I could see footprints. I was going east. Maybe we should keep going that way."

"Why not? Car was only a place to sleep. Too hot to stay inside during the day."

I moved first, toward the rising sun. It was like we were marching toward our executioner, but what choice was there?

We walked for an hour or so in silence, with the sun rising higher and higher. My feet were getting heavy, and I couldn't believe how dry my mouth was. I kept scanning the horizon, looking for anything that might have water. All I ever saw was sand.

"Was there anything in the car?"

Ray was walking slower than me, holding me back; his body wasn't in as good shape as mine. Even so, I was starting to really droop.

"Ownership papers were in the glovebox. Didn't recognize the owner name, of course. Didn't expect to. Looked like the thing's been deserted for a long time. It was a 2003 model."

His voice cracked as he spoke, and when he got to the last phrase he stopped walking and hunched over, his hands on his knees.

"Don't know if I can go much farther."

I walked over to him and put my hand on his shoulder. "Sure you can."

He lifted his head up, and we walked again.

I wasn't sweating any more. It was too hot for sweat to bead. My face was dry parchment and my arms were on fire.

"Do you remember the first one?" I asked. I was mostly trying to get his mind off the walking.

"Sure. Everyone remembers their first time. Isn't

that what they say?" He chuckled.

I didn't look back to him, just waited. Part of me didn't care if he just dropped dead. I doubted he could help me understand what was happening to us.

"I was murdered," he said.

"Really?"

"Strangled. Wasn't much fun."

"None of them are."

We lasted another hour or two. I'm not really sure how long. My vision was blurring, and it was hard to concentrate. I couldn't swallow.

"Too hot..." I mumbled as I tried to just move one foot in front of the other. My toenails were painted red, but the flesh around them was almost as bright a color. Strips of skin burned off where the hot sand kept flowing into my sandals.

I looked back, and it took a minute to realize Ray was long gone. I don't know where he dropped, but I could only see my own prints lazily winding their way up to me. I hunched over and took the same position he had earlier, with my hands on my knees. It hurt like hell, but if I didn't support myself that way, I knew I'd fall onto the burning desert floor waiting for me.

I think I managed another hundred feet. The sun was directly overhead. I tried to undo my tank top, vaguely thinking I could somehow use it for shade, but I couldn't manage the buttons. My fingers were charred sticks.

("Richard, no!" yelled Natalie.)

The echo of some original life washed over me. An

image of Natalie flashed in my mind. She had big auburn hair that always bounced when she walked. I saw her looking over her shoulder at me. Beautiful, a laughing smile that seemed to show more white teeth than should be possible. Eyes that captured everyone and...

That was all.

Natalie. Were you my wife? Did I hurt you?

I fell, and I couldn't even scream when the sand swallowed me and smothered the small amount of remaining life from my body.

I was reborn again. Agony hit me immediately. There was no time to realize what was happening. Too fast. I died.

It was now time for number twelve.

I dreamed of Jamie. She was my first love, when I was fifteen. Sometimes, when we were alone, I called her my *Moondreamer*. She wouldn't let me use that name in public, but I always loved it. It described her perfectly. Her long blonde hair spilled down her back and it always took all my will power not to hug her all the time and play with her hair behind her neck.

She always wore a smile, and her tongue licked her lower lip whenever we met, a subliminal but very erotic invitation.

We were each other's first lover, and were destined to be together forever.

My heart ached as her image faded and fell by the

wayside.

(Moondreamer, don't leave me!)

I woke.

The woods were quiet and eerie. I was walking quietly along a path made of bark mulch. All around me were towering pine trees. The only sound I could hear was my jacket rustling against the bushes. The path was too narrow, and I was lost.

"Jamie!" I found myself shouting. I guessed that she and I must have wandered into a forest for privacy, and somehow we got separated. The image I carried of Jamie had faded to a wispy ghost. I vaguely remembered loving her, but her face was gone.

The air was cool. I couldn't tell if that was because of the time of year, the time of day, or just the immense shade from the stands of trees.

How would I die this time?

Most times I replace someone, the circumstances are staring me right in the face. A gun. Fire. Cliff. Water. Hospital. This was different. I seemed to be lost in the woods, but nothing threatened me.

The forest was quiet, and that raised my alertness. Nothing came easy for me, and if I was here, that meant something awful was just around the corner. I could hear my heart beating.

Tree branches slapped me in the face as I walked. There was no way to know which direction I was heading. I couldn't see the sun, and whatever light did make it through the forested canopy was filtered and directionless. As I walked, even that small amount of light started to fade. It was dusk.

That's when I stepped into the rusty bear trap.

The hinged teeth slammed shut on my ankle, and my world exploded in pain.

I think I fainted, but I can't say for sure. All I know is that I found myself on the ground, my leg seemingly on fire from pain and barely able to move. Every slight movement sent new tremors of agony screaming through my body.

Small shrubs covered the ground, and eventually I was able to gather the strength to move the brush aside to see my leg locked inside the large spring-loaded trap. The steel jaws dug deep into my flesh. The metal was crawling with orange flakes and looked like it had been sitting here for years. Maybe decades.

"Help!"

I'm not sure why I bothered to call out. Instinct maybe, some still-functioning need to try to live. Useless, of course.

I lasted three days and was so happy when I finally died.

(Natalie looked down from above me, and I smelled roast leg of lamb broiling in the oven. It was her favorite meal and, as a result, mine.

She laughed and hugged me, and I couldn't have been happier.

"I love you, Richard," she said. Just then she glanced behind me.)

There was fire all around me. I screamed from the pain. My clothes were on fire, and my skin was baking off. I could see some kind of sticky fluid on my arms. The pain caused me to double over. The fields around me were covered with other people on fire, all screaming.

A woman waved her arms at me. She was Oriental, and I felt love for her, my sweet Dung Bi'nh. *Beautiful Peace.*

She fell to her knees ten feet from me. She reached out an arm for a second, then dropped it. I could see farewell etched on her singed face. Somehow I pushed my mind through the pain to see aircraft flying above us. Did they drop something on us?

When I breathed, fire shot down my throat. I choked and cried. I watched Dung Bi'nh and wanted so desperately to help her.

Other screams joined ours as the fire consumed us. My eyeballs popped, and I collapsed, trying to crawl toward my wife. I didn't make it, and I died with her agonizing screams pushing me down into darkness.

I wondered briefly if she had been taken by a placeholder. I hoped so.

Part III

BEFORE WAKING UP TO MY thirty-first death, I dreamed of Natalie again. I could see her full hair and even fuller figure as she walked around the kitchen wearing a white apron over a frilly pink dress.

She didn't talk to me this time, didn't shout "No, Richard!" and didn't look distressed. It was a quiet time, reflective, as the smell of a spiced cake wafted from the oven. I saw her count out some birthday candles ten and I wondered if she was counting them for a child we shared. A smile played across her face as she rubbed each candle between her fingers.

Natalie looked toward me. I knew she couldn't really see me, since I was only seeing *her* in my imagination, but my mind lifted the corners of her mouth into that smile I had seen so many times before.

She faded as I regained my consciousness. I felt no pain. Yet.

I loved my visions of Natalie and just wished I could see them more often. Now her memory faded again, and only a dispersing phantasm was left of her, and even that tried to hide from me.

I couldn't see, even though my eyes were open. Night time? Not likely. No stars, no light of any kind. The air was stale and dusty. I was lying on the ground and a rock bit into my side. I coughed from the dusty air.

"Hello?"

The voice came from only a few feet away. He sounded scared.

"Hey," I answered. "Where are we?"

There was a brief pause before he said, "We're in a mine in Ohio. Collapsed. Trapped."

He lit a match. "Found a book of matches and a lantern. Figured no point lighting it if I was alone. Saw you stretched out there and couldn't wake you."

I recognized his speech pattern immediately. "Ray?"

The match burned down to his fingers as he held it up to stare at me. "Shit!"

He lit another. "Let me get this fucker lit." He touched the match to the mantel of the small lamp and it glowed brightly. "Didn't want to waste oxygen if I was all alone."

He put the lamp between us. I sat up and rubbed some of the dirt off my arm. No question, we were royally fucked. We were at the end of the mine, just solid rock before us. The tunnel only ran about twenty feet behind us before it was completely blocked by the collapsed roof. It was pretty much a formality; I wouldn't be there if I wasn't going to die.

Two flashlights were discarded on the ground, both with dead batteries.

"Now, Sonny, tell me how you know my name. My

real name."

"C'mon, Ray, you remember. We met in the hospital once and then we died together in a desert somewhere." He just shook his head, so I added, "We're both placeholders. I was a girl that time."

"Whatcha call it?"

"Placeholders. We take the place of people who don't deserve the pain."

I paused and stared at him. "You don't know the term? Now, that's weird. It was you who taught me that word."

"You talkin' nonsense, boy."

"My name is Richard."

"You still talkin' nonsense, *Richard*."

"What number is this for you?" I asked. "This is my thirty-first."

"Forty-two. Never met anyone else like me."

"You'll meet me again. I've already met you twice. The last time you said you'd died fifty-seven times."

"*Told* you it was forty-two."

I moved a bit closer so I could see his face reflected in the lantern's light. He was in his early twenties this time, just a kid. My first instinct was to feel sorry that such a young guy had to die, and then I shook off that silliness. His face was covered with grime and I imagined mine was, too. Dark hair, clean lines. Whoever owned this body before Ray was a good-looking kid.

He was black. So was I.

He seemed to be still thinking about me having met him before but finally shrugged it off. "Tried to move some rocks, but they're too heavy. Couldn't budge the fuckers."

I took his words as an invitation to try myself, and I halfheartedly tried to lift one of the rocks. No chance. Even if somehow I had moved one, rocks covered the shaft from floor to ceiling and there was no way to tell how deep.

"Did you yell?"

"Sure I did. Nothing at all back."

"Yeah. Well, not really a surprise, is it?"

He shrugged. "We could turn off the lamp. Save oxygen."

"Nah. What's the point?"

I stretched and could just touch the roof of the tunnel. Wooden beams crisscrossed the ceiling. When I stood still, the place was dead silent. Not the slightest trace of a sound.

I sat down beside Ray, reclining with him against one wall. "Have you ever suffocated before?"

"Not 'xactly." He waited and added, "Strangled, though."

"Your first death, you were murdered, right?"

He glanced at me and didn't answer. I could tell he didn't like that I knew things about him.

There was something about his eyes. The furtive glances he took at me, like he recognized me but wouldn't admit it. I moved to the other side of the tunnel and stared at him. The light was already starting to dim, but I could still make out the eyes, surrounded by filth and

("Who are you?" she cried.)

the memory was gone before I even knew it was there. Natalie again.

I felt sad, like I was losing my best friend every time I caught a snippet of a memory about her.

I'm not sure how long we sat there not speaking. Ray stopped glancing at me after a while and just hung his head, closed his eyes, and occasionally sniffed. I closed my eyes, too, and maybe I slept. I'm not sure.

"We're in 1958."

My eyes snapped open. "What?"

"Found a company ID card in my pocket. You prob'ly got one, too."

Sure enough. The card was just a flimsy green cardboard thing. It was wrinkled and faded, but I could see a renewal date of May 16, 1958. My name was James Carvard. I worked for the Southern Ohio Mining Company.

We were getting less oxygen with each breath.

Here was the only other placeholder I'd ever met, and we were just pissing the time away. "What do you remember about your real life?"

"Nothin'."

"Well, you know your name. What else?"

He shook his head. "I just have flashes of kids. I dunno."

I had nothing to lose, so I asked, "Ever remember anybody named Natalie?"

Ray didn't answer for a long time. "Wish I had a cigarette. Is that too much to ask?"

"Who killed you?"

"What?"

"That first time. You know who strangled you?"

"Nah. Never know shit about the fuckers I'm taking

over."

The lamp was flickering. "Might be running out of fuel," he said. "Looks like we're dying in the dark this time."

The light cast harsh lines on his face. He yawned, and the shadows made his mouth look like a black hole.

"I fell from an airplane my first time. Parachute didn't open." As I spoke, I stood and felt around in my pockets to see if there was any other information. I'd already done that after I found the ID card, but I couldn't help trying again.

"Never had that one," he said. "Second was murder, too."

"How?"

"Strangled again."

I looked at him. "Really? The same thing twice in a row?"

He looked back at the pile of rocks. "First ten were all being strangled. All different places, different people doing it, but all the same in the end."

I sat back down. "Never figured out why?"

He just stared at the ground and drew a figure eight with one finger.

He never answered my question about recognizing the name Natalie before we both suffocated.

Waiting to die again. Number 121.

This time, though, something was wrong. I was back in another hospital, but I couldn't move.

Even my eyes were stuck in one place. I couldn't

look in any direction other than where they happened to be pointing. Sometimes I saw Claudia when she leaned over me. I think she kissed my cheek, but I wasn't sure. I couldn't feel her touch me. She didn't talk to me much.

Not surprising. I was a vegetable.

I didn't know how long I'd be there. It felt like it'd been an eternity already, but maybe it'd only been a year. I kept wishing for her to pull the plug on me, but she never said anything about that. She often held onto a big silver cross that dangled around her neck.

The first few times she visited me, she cried. Not after the first year, though. Her visits were shorter, and she looked at her watch a lot.

The days were long. I thought of my lovely deaths. After the first fifty, I stopped fearing them. Then I started looking forward to them, enjoying the last pinch of life being pulled from me. Knowing I'd be back alive soon always put a whole different perspective on dying.

The moment of death became a game exactly when would it happen? How? I never died the same way twice.

No doubt, I was the right person to be a placeholder.

But here my eyes stared unfocused toward a light green ceiling. Claudia was young, no more than twenty-five. If I was anywhere near the same age, I might have fifty years of this ahead of me.

I started counting days. There was little else to do, and almost twenty-two thousand immobile and terribly lonely days went by before I finally died.

I woke with visions of Natalie in my head. Her image was much clearer now, memories of the soft roundness of her cheek next to mine and her perfectly manicured fingers holding onto me.

She gazed into my eyes and I could see the tiny angel-hair lines pulling out from the corner of her eyes. She didn't know I could see the dark roots of her hair beneath the auburn surface, didn't know that I was the only person who could distinguish the smell of that hair after she colored it. I loved her hair all the time, but it was different after she colored it. Stronger. Fuller.

I was quietly waking up in my soft bed, stretching my arms back and blinking my eyes open.

And there she was.

Natalie sat on the edge of my bed and looked down at me.

My Natalie.

"Hey, Mister," she whispered. "It's your special day."

Confusion washed over me, and she must have thought I was just not quite awake yet. She laughed and poked a finger into my ribs not hard enough to hurt, just enough to make me flinch and sit up. She often did that when I took too long to crawl out of bed.

"Natalie?"

She laughed and wagged a finger at me. "You might be ten years old now, Richard, but that's nowhere near old enough to call your mother by her first name."

Mother? Richard? She called me Richard.

I was in my own body.

I tried to stand up, but I couldn't help staring back at her.

"You look like a lost puppy," she said. "Did you have a bad dream?"

"I guess I did." My legs felt watery, and I wasn't sure I knew how to use them. Twenty-two thousand days laying in a hospital bed will do that to you. My muscles were fine, but my mind wasn't used to sending the right commands to move them.

"Get dressed then. I've got a fun day planned for us."

She left me alone, quietly clicking my bedroom door shut behind her. She gave me one of her little uplifted-corner smiles as the door closed.

My room was foreign to me. There was a Detroit Tigers pennant on the wall in front of me, along with a couple of newspaper articles tacked beside it. I looked to see the date of the paper: July 28, 2019.

The rest of the walls were bare.

The bed sheets were a mess, like I had been thrashing around all night long. A dresser with four drawers held my clothes, and I fished around for a T-shirt while checking out the rest of the room. A small table held school books and a computer monitor and keyboard, two pairs of shoes sat in one corner, and a round mirror hung on the wall near an open window.

I had no idea what I really looked like. The tee shirt I had selected dropped from my fingers as I shuffled to the mirror. Part of me didn't want to know, but I couldn't understand that.

I stared at my face looking back at me.

I had blond hair, a bit stringy and long, touching

my shoulders. My eyes looked brown, I thought, but it was a bit dark still in my room, and I wasn't absolutely sure.

Although I knew I was white by looking at my hands, I was still surprised to see my face in the mirror. It was covered entirely with long scars. I leaned closer and saw that there was no part of my face unscarred. It was a canvas of deeply etched red and brown furrows, top to bottom. I couldn't help but think I was looking at the rough leathery skin of a gorilla. It was grotesque, and it was me.

No eyebrows.

My lips were partly grown back, but I licked them and couldn't really feel any sensation.

The nose was a crumpled brown mess, just a lump of scar tissue. I realized I had been breathing through my mouth since I woke.

I don't know how long I stared in the mirror before I found the nerve to touch my face with the tips of my fingers. The skin felt like rubber, tough and thick. Both my hands found their way to my cheeks, and again I remembered Natalie

(Mom)

pressing her own cheek to mine. Laughing with me.

She never flinched when she looked at me, just loved me for who I was.

I wondered if I had been hurt this badly in a fire or something like that, or had I just been born this way? Either way, it didn't matter to her. She loved me.

And I loved her back with every ounce of myself.

A tear dropped from my eye, and I quickly wiped it

away. What was a rubber face compared to the atrocities I'd been through?

Or had I?

Was there a chance I'd really dreamed all that?

All one hundred and twenty-one times? I picked out random bits of memory. Being ripped apart by wolves, falling off a cliff, being murdered in so many different ways.

Kissing Felicia. Making love with her. Pushing my cock deep inside my Moondreamer.

I almost laughed. No way a kid just turning ten knows how all that felt, and I definitely remembered every bit of it.

But now it was over, and I was back where I belonged. With Natalie. With my mother.

"Richard! What's taking you so long?"

I quickly got changed and felt how strong and limber my arms and legs were as I hopped down the stairs to the kitchen. My nose might not look like much, but I could easily smell the spiced cake baking. The blue birthday candles were counted out, lying perfectly parallel on the counter.

"Smells good, Mom," I said.

She smiled at me and said, "That's for dessert. After a lamb roast."

An odd sense of déjà vu flushed through me. Came and went and left nothing other than an odd memory. Really, more like a memory of a memory. I shook it off and took Mom's hand.

That day, we went to watch a spy movie at the theater that Mom thought I'd like. As we walked from where the car was parked to the entrance, I saw people take surreptitious glances at me, and I could imagine them thinking, *Look at that monster!*

Mom didn't seem to notice.

We had popcorn and a hot dog, since it was still a long time till dinner. The movie was boring, but I pretended to like it.

She gave me a card about two inches by three just before dinner. "Have fun with it."

I looked at the white card and smiled back. "I will," I promised. I couldn't very well tell her I had no idea what to do with it. Probably something to do with the computer; I'd figure it out later.

She laughed and gave me a hug. "Hope you're hungry. Dinner's ready."

She looked down at me, and I smelled the roast leg of lamb broiling in the oven. It was her favorite meal, and, as a result, mine. She laughed and hugged me. "I love you, Richard."

That sweeping almost-memory swept over me again, and I felt a chill.

"Mom? We've got to go."

"Go? Go where? It's dinner time."

As she turned to face the oven, I saw a shadow cross the kitchen table. I turned to see a stranger standing there. He looked frantic thirtyish, with dirty, long, greasy hair and a scraggled beard. He was wide-eyed and held a gun out in front of him. His hand shook.

"Mom!"

Natalie turned back and gasped. "Who are you?"

"Give me your money! All of it!"

As he spoke those words, I knew that I wasn't really

back in my own time for good. I was still a placeholder, but this time, I was a placeholder for myself.

A sense of calm came over me, and all I wanted to do was protect the wonderful woman who didn't see that I was a monster.

I knew Natalie kept a gun in her bedside table. With there being just the two of us in the house, she always worried about security. The gun couldn't help us now, though.

I ran out between Natalie and the man.

"Richard, no!" she shouted.

His eyes glanced down at me and his arm wavered, the gun moving away from her. I saw his hesitation and jumped at the gun, using both my arms to knock him backward as my body rammed into his chest.

"Fucking shit!"

"Run, Natalie!"

He was on the ground now, his arm pinned down by my body. I looked up to see Natalie still standing there, frozen by fear, but then she took a step toward us.

The man saw her move and flicked his hand up before I could knock it back down. The gun shocked me with its noise. Natalie fell. I panicked, and he was able to push my ten-year-old body off him easily.

He kicked me in the stomach, and I flew to the bottom of the kitchen table, not able to see Natalie. The wind was knocked out of me, and I was dazed from the kick. He kicked me again and again. My arm was broken. I couldn't help whimpering as I lay immobile under the table.

I didn't want to see what happened next. I could

hear Natalie's cries for the next several minutes. "Why are you *doing* this to me?"

He hit her somewhere, and she was crying softly, but the worst was yet to come. He raped my mother there in front of me, with me not being able to move, not being able to help, not even being able to cry out.

When he was done, he shot her again.

And then he came back to me. My face was filled with tears, but my prior deaths made me not the slightest bit fearful.

"You fucking pig," I whispered. I spat in his face.

He smiled as he pulled the trigger, killing me.

The sun was shining down on me as I tread water, watching the slipstream of bubbles slowly die down. The water was calm, the saltiness biting my taste buds as I slowly rolled over on my back and looked around. Nothing.

I couldn't get my mind to worry much about the water; only Natalie filled my thoughts. My wonderful mother who wouldn't run away to save herself because she'd wanted to save me.

"Hello!" I knew it was pointless to yell, but old habits die hard. I glanced down and saw my arms were black.

That's weird.

The memory came from such a long time ago. I was reliving my second death. Visions of Felicia pushed aside Natalie to take center stage in my mind. I missed Felicia and wished I'd had more time with her before she went home.

After a long while the sun set, and I no longer knew where the plane or boat or whatever had sunk.

I remembered kissing Felicia, feeling her body against mine, that last time we parted and she smiled that dazzling white smile that always shocked me with its intensity. She was entrancing, which was why I was flying to Spain to surprise her. Flying the cheapest charter flight I could find that would get me to Madrid as fast as possible before June 21. I would be knocking on her apartment door on the longest day of the year, bringing her a bouquet of yellow roses and a bottle of Rose wine.

The night before I'd phoned her, telling her I had a big surprise for her.

My arms were getting too tired. I thought of just letting go and sinking, but dying was never that easy. My body would never give up without a fight, no matter how much my conscious mind might want it.

Besides, I was fascinated by being a repeat placeholder. Why would I go through the same death again? And why did I remember more this time around?

In the end, it didn't make a difference. My arms locked and I sank. I still fought, but my lovely death won. Number 123 ended the same as all the others, with no answers and only more questions.

Part IV

I OPENED MY EYES AND FELT the cool grass all around me. Lying beside me was Adam, sleeping in the soft forest. I loved him.

I could smell the fresh scent of spring flowers huddled around the trees and hear soft chirps from above. It was completely relaxing and peaceful. I didn't think about Natalie, didn't think about being a placeholder. I was just being Jamie.

Adam and I were both naked, and in my half-wakefulness I used a finger to draw lazy patterns on my belly and breasts, eventually cupping my right breast in my hand, as Adam had done before he fell asleep.

"My little Moondreamer," he'd whispered as his hand slipped off my body and his eyes closed. I wondered how long ago that had been.

"Jamie." I almost jumped as Adam sat up beside me. He yawned.

My nerves were on high alert, sitting here in the forest with Adam. Where was the danger? I'd been inside Adam's body when he died in the bear trap. Why Jamie now?

"Adam, let's go back."

He laughed. "We can't do that."

"We can't?"

He stood and picked up his T-shirt that lay discarded along with the rest of our clothes. I wanted him to lay back down with me, kiss me and make love to me again. Even though I knew those were actually Jamie's last wishes before I replaced her, it was hard to shake them. Her body remembered. I didn't know what he meant about not being able to go back.

"Not now, not ever." His voice was harder now.

Adam's face was in shadow, turning him into a stranger. His normally kind face was gone, and it seemed he had made a decision while I thought he'd been sleeping beside me. He opened his backpack, and then he turned to face me with a long knife in his hand. I glanced between that and his cock hanging below his shirt, not understanding.

"I know about you and Dan."

"What?"

"Give it up. It's too late." As he moved to me, he added, "I'm sorry, my Moondreamer."

Suddenly the knife was above his head, and he slammed it down with both hands into my chest. I could feel the blade going all the way through and out my back.

"I'm sorry," he said again. "But I can't share you."

I couldn't talk. I couldn't move. My arms fell to my side as the incredible pain and shock took over every bit of my being.

I didn't know if Jamie had been with anyone named Dan. I knew almost nothing about her, except her love for Adam. I tried to reach for the knife, but my hand was too weak I couldn't budge it.

Blood filled my mouth. I choked and started to black out, the pain overcoming me. My body wanted him to know. *It isn't true*, but there was no way to say it. I could barely move my hand. Adam walked away, leaving me to my pain.

At the end, I smiled, remembering how he was about to step in the bear trap and suffer much longer than I had.

After waking up by the tree stump in the desert, I immediately knew where I was. I'd had a number of quick deaths after being killed by Adam, and now I was back in Mandy's thin body, stranded in the middle of a desert.

The sand was gritty in my mouth, making me choke for a minute. I looked around in vain. Nothing was any different than the last time I was here.

Except this time, I remembered more.

I remembered riding in a dune buggy with Mike, my boyfriend. We'd had a fight the night before. I'd looked forward to this trip forever, it seemed, ever since I was a little girl. *Egypt*. The sheer foreignness of the place had called to me since I'd first seen the Pyramids in a Mickey Mouse cartoon.

More than just Egypt. The Kharga Oasis, west of Luxor. It was in the middle of the Western Desert, a true oasis, surrounded by impenetrable sand, blowing history all around. The Oasis was a small village surrounding a lake more of a large pond really, but enough to support a few hundred families. I'd talked Mike into going with me, and while he reluctantly agreed, he just wasn't interested.

Last night was the kicker. He said he was going home with or without me. Back to New York, back to civilized Manhattan, away from the beggars who always demanded *baksheesh*.

"We've got to go out to the desert," I said. "Just once, and then..." I shrugged, letting him think I'd go home after that, but I knew there was much more I wanted to see. "It's been my dream," I added, even though he already knew that.

I didn't know how much he hated me until he pushed me out of the dune-buggy. I watched as he drove off, back to the town of Qasr. I refused to shout, knowing he'd be back for me, that he was just trying to scare me.

But he didn't come back.

And eventually I started walking, but I didn't really know where I was. Mike had been driving, silent as I just soaked in the dunes. He'd always had a terrific sense of direction, while I had none.

My foot prints stretched out to the west, and I remembered the glint of light I should be able to see to the south. Ray would be there.

It took an hour to walk, longer than I remembered, but I found Ray asleep in the sky-blue Silverado, just as he'd been the first time.

I stuck my hand through the broken window and poked him. "Ray! Wake up!"

"Huh? Fuck're you?"

He turned a bit to the side and stared at me.

"Good-looking girl, whoever you are."

"I'm Mandy from Miami," I said without thinking. "I mean, my real name is Richard. I'm a placeholder, just like you."

The wind whispered

("Run, Natalie!")

but the memory was lost again. It didn't matter. Whenever I had time with a slow death, if I concentrated hard enough, I could pull back bits of Natalie. It was like remembering a dream after it had started to evaporate; if I tried hard enough, I could hold onto a fragment or two.

"You know about placeholders, huh?" He climbed out the window and added, "Thought that was my word."

"Yeah," I said. "You taught me."

"Fuck you talkin' about?"

"We've met before. A few times."

He just stared at me, mostly at my tits, making me feel like I should cross my arms, but I didn't. "Don't remember that."

I explained how I'd met him in the hospital, then here in the desert, and then in the collapsed mine. He just listened and finally added, "Yeah, I remember the mine now. Didn't recognize you."

His tone was oddly dismissive. What I'd just told him wasn't important to him at all, but it was to me. He was the only other placeholder I'd ever met. Why didn't he want to understand what was happening to us?

"Where to, Mandy from Miami?"

The first time we had walked east. I almost

suggested that again why not? but then

"The Silverado had to get here somehow."

"No shit."

"I mean, there must be a road somewhere nearby. They run east-west through the desert. Let's go south, see if we can find it."

He shrugged, not caring.

We walked south for awhile, neither of us saying anything. Ray finally broke the silence. "You like being a girl?"

Did I? "Old hat now," I lied. It was still weird to me, but I saw how he looked at me earlier, and I wasn't sure I liked where he might take the conversation.

"I always liked it," he said. "Liked to feel my tits and pussy."

I ignored him, staying a few feet ahead.

After about fifteen minutes, I saw the road. It was almost invisible, just a harder surface packed into a nearly straight line. It was covered with sand, but the slight texture change was easy to see if you knew what to look for. Expert nomads could drive straight through from Egypt to the Atlantic Ocean, making it look like magic. Or so Mandy had been told.

"Guess you were right," said Ray.

We walked eastward on the road toward the blazing sun. It was just as hot as the first time, and it was futile to think the outcome would be different. In fact, I had long ago stopped imagining not dying. Dying is what placeholders do.

When Ray started to lag farther behind me, I slowed my pace.

"You remember much about your real life, Ray?"

He took three more steps before answering. "Sometimes. Not very pleasant memories."

A flashing memory of my melted little monster face in the mirror made me nod, but I knew that my time with Natalie must have been mostly good. I'd loved her too much.

"What exactly do you remember?" I asked.

"Just bits and pieces. Snatches of hints. I think I was one of the bad guys."

That surprised me. "Why?"

"I killed people. Robbery, I think. Not really sure." He stopped walking and looked at me. "Rape, too. At least I think so. Maybe I fucked kids, too. I don't really know. Why else would I always dream of kids?"

I looked at him as he sank to his knees. The sun had beaten him to the ground and his spindly arms were the only things keeping his head from crashing and burying itself in the sand.

With no regret, I walked away, my mind thinking back to that day

(my tenth birthday)

when Natalie died.

It was like looking through a kaleidoscope, the images so scattered and not at all unified into a whole. Lamb. A spy movie. Candles. Mom being raped. I might have walked for an hour, not even feeling the heat any more, just concentrating on sifting through the faint echoes of that day.

I stopped and turned back. Ray was nowhere to be seen. I wondered where he was, and that made me realize I wasn't thinking straight any more.

Probably just as well that he wasn't there. I'd just

remembered the face of the man who killed my mother, and I knew the look in his eyes was the same as the man I had just abandoned to the desert. And I remembered the speech pattern.

Ray had killed Natalie. And me.

My next ten deaths were all memorable but unimportant. I was tortured, killed by a crazy wife, killed by a crazy husband, smashed to bits twice in car accidents... terribly painful, long or short, all the same deaths I was used to.

Then I met Ray again.

We were in a small airplane, sitting in the only two seats. We were both strapped in, but he was the pilot, with a small wheel teetering in front of him. I was a passenger, a fat white guy wearing a chocolate business suit.

Ray wore a dark blue jumpsuit and a white tie. I guessed the flight was a low-cost short-distance charter.

The grinding noise of the plane shook us, and I wondered if we were already on our way to crash. Turbulence sent us into a short dive that wrenched my stomach, but the autopilot leveled us back out. It seemed we'd have a few more minutes before crashing.

"What the hell?" Ray yelled.

Both of us had taken control of our new bodies at the same time, but he pushed himself back into his chair, looking around with big eyes, his head swiveling, not believing anything he saw.

"Ray, calm down," I said. He was a skinny kid,

looked to be barely out of his teens, and the remnants of his host seemed to have as much influence over Ray's emotions as Ray himself did. I wondered how someone so young could have a pilot's license. He pulled off his flight helmet and stared at it. Disbelief washed over his face.

"Calm down? CALM DOWN? How the hell did I get here? Fuck're you?"

"Ray, c'mon. You know who I am."

"Don't know shit, man. Just tell me this is a dream."

"Sorry."

It took me a minute to remember that this was the guy who killed me. And Natalie. I found myself breathing faster and my anger rising. If not for him, I'd have lived a normal life, at least as "normal" a childhood a disfigured little monster of a boy could. An image of Natalie formed in my mind. She smiled at me, and her beautiful hair bounced on her shoulders.

I rarely have time to play *What if?* What if Ray hadn't broken into our home? What if he'd just taken the money and let Natalie and I live?

I'd never have become a placeholder, never spend eternity dying

(chasing)

over and over and

Chasing? Is that what I was doing? Chasing Ray?

"What do I do?"

His panic swept my memory away. I wanted to hit him. My hands were clenched, and my teeth bit into my tongue. Actually, I didn't just want to hit him; I wanted to kill him. There it was. My chance to take revenge was there, and I was damned well not going to pass it up. I owed that to my mother. I unhooked my seat belt.

"Gotta be a dream."

"No, I'm afraid not."

It must have been his first time as a placeholder. He really didn't know what was going on.

I stood beside him and found the foggy memory of him killing Natalie. His eyes seemed to beg for help while I placed my hands around his neck and slowly squeezed.

"This is for my mother," I said. I looked right into his eyes, but there was no understanding there. He must have thought I was a lunatic. I didn't care a bit. He fought me, but I was much bigger and stronger. He didn't have a chance. Turbulence shook the plane again, and it took several minutes for me to complete my revenge. I ignored his feeble attempts to stop me from stealing his life.

The plane crashed not long after that, but I died happy.

I met Ray nine other times over the next hundred or so of my deaths, and every one of those nine times, I killed him with my bare hands.

Slowly, the realization came to me that my being a placeholder wasn't some type of punishment. It was a reward. I was being allowed to get satisfaction for the pain he had caused me.

By that last time, I felt the last of my rage dwindle away from me with Ray's dying breath, and I knew I wouldn't need to kill him again.

"Goodbye, Ray," I whispered to the corpse beside me in the small life boat. He was a thin, sickly woman this time, and killing her was easy. I pushed her body overboard and started to row away from it. The water lapped over her body, and she slowly sank below the surface.

Every time I'd killed him, I remembered more clearly him being there, pointing the gun at Natalie and breaking my arm, raping her and laughing about it as I watched him.

My animal urge for revenge was finally satisfied.

After a few days floating and starving in the life boat, I fell asleep for the last time in that body.

"Richard, you silly thing! Wake up!"

I snapped awake, hearing Natalie's wonderful voice calling me. She was standing in the doorway with that laughing smile on her face.

She sat on the bed beside me. "Hey, Mister. It's your special day."

I rubbed my eyes and stared at her. She laughed. "You look like a lost puppy. Did you have a bad dream?"

All I wanted to do was reach up to her and hold her. She smiled and held out her arms as if to say, *Are you ever going to get up?*

My eyes didn't leave her as I climbed out of bed. When she was satisfied I wouldn't fall back asleep, she tousled my hair and went down to the kitchen. I smelled the lingering soft apple remnants of her shampoo in my room.

I touched my cheeks with both hands. The rough skin was still there, still melted and hard. Touching them seemed like a habit I must do every morning, since my body did that without me thinking about it. I walked to the mirror and once again studied the bony ridges and charred remains of my face. I felt no pity, no sorrow, just simple acceptance.

I went down to eat breakfast with Natalie, but this time I took a different route. My ten-year-old mind was barely able to understand, but there was a flicker of an ancient man stuck in that body and he knew just what to do.

Revenge was over. Now, it was a different matter.

The man came into the room and thrust the gun at Natalie, the same as he did before. He wore Ray's eyes, skittish and untrusting. The rest of his body was emaciated.

This time, though, I pulled out my own gun, the gun I had taken from Natalie's bedside dresser, the gun I knew she'd always kept there and never used. It felt heavy in my spindly hand, and I could smell the harsh metal. I didn't know enough about guns to tell the model, but I knew it had a safety. I flipped it off.

"Kid, you watch that, you gonna hurt yourself." He stepped toward me.

Ray didn't know he wasn't only dealing with a ten-year-old. Fragments of memories from hundreds of other people floated beneath my conscious mind. Like osmosis, this body remembered how to use a gun.

Natalie screamed.

I pulled the trigger, bracing my arm for the recoil. I

hit him squarely in the chest. He fell to his knees, his own gun falling from his fingers. I shot again. And again.

The sound made when his face smacked the floor turned me back into a little boy, and I started to cry. I threw the gun to the floor.

"Oh, my God, Richard!" My mother ran to me and held me in her arms, crying along with me. She kissed my furrowed cheeks and I held her close to me. I wanted to hold her forever, but she pulled away and walked to the phone, watching Ray's dead body as she moved.

As she called 9-1-1, part of me wondered whether I would die again soon, but I moved that thought away and went to hug my mother. A thousand deaths were behind me, but my life now was just truly beginning.

The True Story
of Christmas

This is a post-apocalyptic story, the only one I recall ever writing. I had this vision of a family after the end of the world, alone, and it's Christmas. What would that be like for them?

The story took on a tone that was a lot of fun. I submitted it to Cemetery Dance Publications and they immediately purchased it to use in their web site, where they occasionally published short stories. I was thrilled to have the story appear there.

This brings us to the end of the second volume of my short stories. I hope you've enjoyed these ones, and I'm looking forward to having the third and fourth volumes for you soon.

Thanks for reading!

My name is Alexander Malicious of Oz. I am twelve years old, but I was only ten months old when the whole world went kablooey, so I don't remember any of it. Daddy once told me I had a different name back then, but he won't tell me what it was. After everybody died, Mom and Dad renamed me. They never told me why.

So, it's Alexander Malicious of Oz. I think that's an okay name, isn't it? Of course nobody calls me that. I'm just Alexander most of the time.

See, there's me and my little sister, Annie Globetrotter of Harlem, and my mom and my dad, and my granny. Her name is Bermuda Short. She doesn't like that, but it's been her name for more than decade now, and she's old, so she's stuck with it.

The world went kablooey in 2021. I can't tell you what happened, because nobody will tell *me*. All I've been able to figure out is that everyone died.

They don't talk about it. I asked Dad once a couple of years ago, and he slapped me.

Mom told me once that before the end of the world,

there were lots of other people. I asked how many, and she said, "Lots! More than you could ever imagine!"

Well, I can *imagine* a lot. I think she probably means there were about a hundred people. I know that's hard to believe, because how would anybody ever remember who everyone else was? How would they find enough squirrels and berries to eat? Maybe it was really only fifty. I have a big imagination, so it was really probably smaller than I can visualize.

It was Mom's idea to write a diary. She figures since she's been trying to teach me to write for years now, I should put it into practice so I don't forget how to. Or something like that. She said to start by talking about who I am. That's pretty dull, though. I'd rather talk about it being Christmas!

I never know when it's going to be Christmas. My daddy always just announces one day that it's time. I don't know how he knows, and he won't tell me. Mom just shrugs, like she doesn't know, either.

My dad is the big boss.

Old Granny is kind of useless. No point even asking her. The best I'd get from her is a shrug. She mostly just sits on her rotting old log during the day and hardly ever talks. Mom does the talking in this family, but it's always stuff that nobody cares about.

"Looks like another nice day!"

That's her favorite way to start the morning. Well, it's pretty much *always* a nice day. After all, we're in Floreeda. It's sunny and warm and Daddy says it's always nice in Floreeda, and I have to agree. But every morning, Mom tells us it's going to be nice.

She also likes to talk about how she wonders what

we're going to do for dinner. Daddy usually is able to hunt something, and on the days he doesn't, we'll just eat berries, so what's there to talk about?

This morning, though, it was Daddy's time to talk. He came back early from hunting and announced, "Today is going to be Christmas."

I almost couldn't believe it! It's been like forever since the last time he said we'd have a Christmas. I ran into our tent and found my little sister.

"Annie Globetrotter of Harlem! It's Christmas today!"

Her eyes went wide and she jumped to her feet, scattering the half dozen bare branches she'd been playing with. "Really?"

"Yes! He just told us."

Annie paused and then asked, "What's Christmas again?"

I shook my head. "Don't worry, you'll understand soon enough."

The rest of the day was just amazing. I had so much energy, I ran through the forest to wear myself out so I wouldn't explode. And I did my chores without complaining throughout the day. That's why I decided to start writing my diary today. What better day than Christmas?

It's later on Christmas Day now. The sun is setting and Daddy is getting the fire going. He has a big stack of books lined up to burn, so he's taking this whole Christmas thing very seriously. The fire is going to last a long time, maybe all night.

Did I say how much I love Christmas?

We didn't eat today. That's part of the tradition. We save our appetite for Ye Jolly Old Christmas Feast. We are allowed to drink, though, so I'd run down to the creek a few times during the day to scoop out some water.

The last time I went, I decided to go swimming. Annie Globetrotter of Harlem was with me, and she wanted to swim, too. We both stripped off our clothes, but before we jumped in the water, she pointed at me and asked, "What's that?"

I didn't know what it's called. Mom and Dad would never tell me.

"I don't know. It's just something I have that you don't. I call it my lazy finger."

"I want a lazy finger, too! Why don't I have one?"

"Because I'm older than you."

"Will I get one when I'm older?"
"I don't really know."

"I'll ask Mom."

"No, don't. She won't like that, and if Daddy hears you, he's just going to slap you. You know that."

Annie followed me into the water. It was cool. I suppose that's because it must be winter, since it was Christmas Day. On Christmas, it snows and the reindeer jump over the moon to cool the world down.

The current was very slow, and we floated around for a bit before climbing back out and lying in the sun to dry off. The sun is hot in Floreeda, even on Christmas Day.

Annie has long yellow hair. Mom talked about cutting it one day, but Annie hated that idea. Mom cuts my hair sometimes by chopping it with a sharp rock. My hair is brown.

While we were lying there, Annie studied the thing between my legs. At one point, it decided to grow, like it does sometimes. Annie's mouth seemed to drop when she saw it change.

I just laughed and closed my eyes. I almost fell asleep, but after a while I got up and my lazy finger was back to normal. We got dressed and went back home.

"Alexander Malicious of Oz!" called my dad when he saw me. I could tell he was in a very good mood, because he called me by my full name.

"Yes, sir!" I know how Daddy likes me to answer lickety split when he calls me.

"Grab me some more firebooks to add to our stack. It's time to get the party going."

I nodded and walked to the garage. That's a hut that Daddy built when we moved here. It's built with branches and moss and is full of firebooks.

I pulled out three. One was called *Gone With the Wind*, the second was *The Stand*, and the last was yet another copy of *The Kardashians*. That one seems to have been very popular with people. I'm sure I've taken several other copies out to burn previously. I have no idea what a kardashian might be.

They were all hefty. I always grabbed thick firebooks so I wouldn't have to keep running back and forth all night.

Daddy started ripping out pages and putting them together, then he used one of his lighters to start the fire. He'd be busy most of the evening adding firebooks to keep the blaze going and working his way up to logs that would burn longer.

Somewhere beyond the forest is the great and fabulous city of My-Ami. I know Daddy went there many times when we first moved to Floreeda. He told me he found zillions of books sitting on people's doorsteps from the amazing land of Amazon. The firebooks were delivered but never picked up by people before they died. Daddy collected them all and brought them to our hut to burn.

Inside the boxes were tiny white cubes that Daddy said were to protect the firebooks. I'm not sure why they needed to be protected, since they'd just be burned anyhow, but when I asked that, Daddy slapped me, so I know better than to care about that now.

Tonight being Christmas, Daddy had taken all the white cubes and scattered them all around the campfire. He called it snow. I love when it snows! It looks so different, and it only happens on Christmas Day.

I also really enjoy watching the fire crackle and pop. We don't have enough holidays, so whenever we do get one, I always be sure to enjoy it.

The last holiday we had was Thanks-Burning. That's not a very interesting holiday, because we mostly just sit around and talk about reasons to throw each other into the fire.

The fire pit is outside our tent, and by the time the fire was going full steam, the sun had set. Mom and Old Granny Bermuda Short came out and were sitting on the log nearby. I grabbed the stump and Annie Globetrotter of Harlem sat on the ground. Only Daddy was standing, as of course was tradition.

The sky was clear, and I could see stars up above. From somewhere in the distance, frogs croaked and I could hear an owl hoot. It made me think even Bloody Mother Nature knew it was Christmas.

Finally, Daddy started to tell us what we longed to hear.

Christmas is a very old tradition *(said Daddy)*. It's a time for love and a time for joy.

The first Christmas happened more than two thousand years ago. It's hard to believe, but it's true. Back before the whole world went kablooey, people called archeologists found evidence of that.

Every Christmas we celebrate the birth of Walt Disney. Sometimes he was called Uncle Walt, because when he was born, he already had a long beard that stretched down to his knees.

Three wise asses followed the stars to find the baby Walt in the little town of Bethlehem. That's somewhere near Japan.

Uncle Walt was the son of Dog. Dog was the ancient being who invented the world. When He wasn't happy with things anymore, He destroyed the world as easily as he created it.

For a while, though, Uncle Walt became the most powerful magician in the world. He could change water into wine, part the Red Sea, walk on water, and even bring people back from the dead. He was one hell of a magician, the best the world had ever known.

When the three wise asses found their way to the

baby Walt, they brought gifts with them. That started the tradition of always thanking Dog whenever anything good happened. Today, that tradition has passed down symbolically so that everyone has to thank their Daddy for all good things.

Everything bad, of course, is Dog's fault. Everything good is done by Daddy.

Uncle Walt was nailed to a cross when he was a teenager, because everyone loved his magic tricks and wanted to see him escape. Many years later, another famous magician named Houdini also performed magical escape tricks, but nobody could ever do them better than Uncle Walt!

Walt Disney was crucified near Orlando, Floreeda, not far from where we are now. One day, when you kids are old enough, we'll do a pilgrimage to Orlando and pay tribute to Uncle Walt himself. It's something every citizen must do at least once in their lifetime. Otherwise Uncle Walt's ghost will haunt you forever.

Tonight, we're incredibly fortunate to have Ye Jolly Old Christmas Feast. The ghost of Uncle Walt led me earlier today to trap a beautiful fat raccoon, and so we can have our traditional stuffed raccoon feast tonight.

Nobody will go hungry tonight, except for possibly Bermuda Short.

We need to thank Dog for providing us with such generosity tonight. So, please close your eyes and call out three loud cheers for Dog's generosity!

It took quite a while for Daddy to skin the raccoon and rip its guts out and then stuff it with berries. Once that was all done, he stuck a metal rod down its mouth and pushed open a new asshole for it. Then he could start spinning it on the spit.

Christmas is the only day that the great Dog gives us stuffed raccoon. It's the best meal of the year. We were just about starving when the meat started to sizzle and Mom started to shuffle around, setting places at our picnic table. She brought out the good china dishes, which shone brightly from the fire. We hadn't used any real dishes for a year, not since *last* Christmas. Usually we just plop the food right on the picnic table. Nobody cares.

We do have plastic cups for water. Before it got dark, I'd taken our jug down to the creek to fill it up, so we were all set.

I could smell part of the raccoon burning just when Daddy called out, "It's ready!"

Old Granny shuffled over to the table, but me, Annie, and Mom almost jumped. We were so hungry, all we could think about was chowing down on the meat.

When we were all seated, Mom said, "Hold on. It's time for us to say grace."

Damn.

"Dear Dog in Heaven," she said. "We thank you for delivering this delicious meal to us on this very special day, and we thank you also for protecting us from the big kablooey. You are a good Dog, and we are your willing servants. We tell you all this in Uncle Walt's name. Ramen."

"Ramen," we all repeated.

"I want a drumstick!" I called.

I wasn't really sure what a drumstick was, but I'd heard Old Granny call that out one other time.

Daddy smacked me. "You get what you get," he said.

That's when the night took an amazing turn.

Another man had walked into our camp ground.

Now, if anybody ever reads my diary here, you probably are really old, like dirt, and maybe before the big kablooey, people walked into your camp ground every day. Not so with us.

I've never seen a single other person in my life.

Neither has Annie Globetrotter of Harlem, of course.

Mom and Dad acted as surprised as the rest of us, but I'm pretty sure they'd seen other people before.

The guy had a long black beard that stretched down to about his belly button, and his face had long scratches dug into it.

He stared at us like we were some kind of weird animals.

"Been watching you all," he said. His voice was full of hitches.

Daddy walked over to behind the big old oak tree, where he stashed the axe. He grabbed it with both his hands, like he was ready to chop the stranger's head clean off.

"Get the fuck out of here, Mister."

"Hey, hold on there!"

The stranger held his hands up in the air, like he wanted to push the sky up a notch. "We're just passing through is all, and it looked like—"

"We?"

"My boy." He turned and whistled.

And then *another* person came out of the forest.

Holy carp! Two new people?

"The boy is Jiminy," said the man.

"Jiminy Cricket, I imagine," said Dad. The man just stared at him, so I figured he was right. Dad's good at figuring stuff out.

Jiminy Cricket wasn't much bigger than me. He was skinny and had long brown hair. Just like me.

"Maybe you should just keep on walking," said Dad.

"Looks like you're ready for dinner. It'd be awfully kind of you to offer some."

"It's not just dinner," I blurted out. "It's *Christmas* dinner!"

"Is it now?"

"Yup! See all the snow?" I pointed at the small white cubes.

"Well, it sounds like we came along on the right day. It'd be a very Christian thing for you to feed us tonight."

Dad stared at them, and I wasn't sure what was going to happen until Mom walked over and said, "Well, of course you can join us for dinner. It's not much, but we're happy to share what we can."

Dad was gripping the axe harder, and I wasn't sure that he wasn't going to use it to chop *Mom's* head off right there and then. He ended up grunting and motioning the two new people to the picnic table, where we all sat down. Well, all except for Bermuda Short. She just wandered off into the tent, but nobody seemed to care.

Two new people! Yowza!

The raccoon wasn't all that big, and so we only ended up with a couple small pieces each, but that's okay. Any coon is better than none!

"You know it's only October," said the man.

"No matter, Christmas is in the heart," said Mom. I don't really know what that meant. *October* sounded like some kind of weird disease. Maybe the man was crazy or something.

"What makes it Christmas today?"

"Oh, I know!" I shouted. "It's the day Walt Disney was born!"

I went on to explain about how Uncle Walt was the magician who could walk on water and how he was nailed to the cross but Dog saved him and fed him to the lions. If there was one thing I knew, it was the true story of Christmas. Once he killed the lions, he fed them to the masses, and they laughed and nailed him to a cross.

The man just stared at me. I didn't think he's very smart.

"Where you boys headed?" asked Dad.

The smaller one hadn't said anything since arriving at our camp. He just kept staring at his now-empty plate. The man said, "We were heading south, but..."

He scratched his beard and looked over at Annie Globetrotter of Harlem.

"You know, it's our responsibility to re-populate the planet. Make more babies."

He nodded at the boy and then to Annie.

Now I was totally confused. Dog is the only way to make babies. He plants seeds in the forest and pours baby oil on them to make them grow. Once they sprout, the parents come along to get them.

"She's only seven," said Dad.

The man shrugged. "Gotta be thinking about the future."

It seemed like everyone just wanted to stare at everybody else from then on. Nobody talked. No wonder Dad didn't really seem to mind the big kablooey. If this was what it was like having other people around, I was thinking maybe it's good we just had our family.

I had to pee, so I walked over to the hole in the ground over by the forest and sang "Good King Walruses" while I did it. I sang nice and loud, just like Dad does.

When I came back to the table, I asked the man, "What's your name?"

"Steve."

What a weird name.

"I'm Alexander Malicious of Oz."

"Really?"

"Yes, really."

He stared at Mom and Dad. "You really need to teach your children the proper meaning of Christmas."

Dad laughed. "Proper? Like how Jesus came down from heaven to save everybody from sin? Fat lot of good *that* did the world."

"What do you mean?" asked Annie. It was the first time she'd spoken since the strangers arrived.

"God created the heaven and the Earth," said Steve. We sinned, and He sent his only son to us, to save us for all eternity. His son was named Jesus, not Walt Disney, and he was killed by evil men, but it didn't matter, because he saved humanity anyhow and taught us how to live good lives."

"Complete and utter bullshit," said Dad.

Well then. This was getting interesting.

Steve shrugged. "Denial doesn't change the truth." Then he looked at me. "You ever read The Bible?" He pointed at one of the firebooks that Dad had brought out.

"Read it?"

"Never mind," he said. "I know the answer."

I wanted to ask who would ever read a firebook, but I knew better. I took one last nibble of my raccoon and licked my plate.

"Maybe it's time for you to head out," said Dad. "We've been trying to be civil to you, but you're in danger of overstaying your welcome."

Steve ignored Dad and looked to Mom.

"Ma'am, thank you for your hospitality. My boy and I will just curl up a while by the fire if that's okay. It's late. We'll sleep and head out in the morning."

Mom lowered her eyes, clearly not wanting to be in the middle of anything. Dad would slap her if she did.

"First light," said Dad.

We ended up not really enjoying our Christmas dinner, but a little bit of raccoon is better than plain old berries, so it could have been worse. We didn't have any dessert, though. I'm not sure if Dad found any dandelions for us to chew on or if he just decided to forget it all with Steve being there.

All in all, Christmas kind of sucked. In my mind I started to wonder if we could have another Christmas in a few days to make up for it, but I didn't want to ask Dad in case it earned me a slap.

My hand is getting tired. It's already morning and I haven't told you about what happened at first light yet, but I need to stop for now.

And I'm back.

I thought it would be good to take a break to bury Dad. Steve wasn't all that interested in helping. He'd just dragged Dad's body over to the bushes and dumped it, which seemed kind of mean to me.

Eventually I scurried around for some branches and tossed them on top of him.

Oh, right! I forgot to tell you.

We woke to screams, and it wasn't the good kind of screams. I ran out of the tent and saw Steve crashing the axe down over and over again. Daddy's blood spurted everywhere and turned all the snow around him bright red. It was really kind of pretty, but the screams kind of took away from that.

Annie Globetrotter of Harlem watched with me.

Chop, chop, chop.

I know I shouldn't have wondered what Dad's leg would taste like over an open fire, but I couldn't help myself. I was hungry again.

Eventually the screams stopped, and Dad was all beside himself. Steve just grinned and looked at Mom. Like she would ever do anything to interfere.

Then he looked at me and Annie. "You can call me Dad now," he said.

Well, okay then. After the way he handled that axe, I couldn't see much benefit in contradicting him.

"First thing we gotta do is get you clear on God, and Jesus, and the Holy Spirit."

I didn't know what to say about that, so I just stared at him. Annie, too.

"OKAY?"

I nodded. What else could I do but agree?

"Good. We'll begin our lessons later. You need to know about the birth of Jesus. He was born in a manger in Bethlehem, and he rose to become the greatest person in history."

He stared at me as if waiting for me to contradict me.

"THAT is what Christmas is all about."

I nodded.

"We'll talk about the details later. For now..."

That's when he tossed the pieces of Dad into the forest; later, I went over to find them and put them back together so I could toss some of old Mother Nature onto him.

Mom was crying, but Steve just went over and tried to hug her. She wasn't having any of that.

So, Dad Version Two is running the family now. He told me to head down to the creek to clean the axe, and then I had to use it to chop some firewood. I wasn't sure why I had to do that since we still had lots of books, but I wasn't the one making the rules.

In the evening, we sat on the picnic table and Steve, I mean Dad Version Two, started talking all kinds of carp to us about this Jesus guy. It was like this weird fantasy about how he could make bread fall from the sky and turn water into wine. Pretty familiar stuff, I know. Sounds like they just stole Uncle Walt's story and made this new guy the same.

I just smiled and nodded, but it was all ridiculous. Who would ever believe that?

Well, one person who was buying it all was Annie Globetrotter of Harlem. She sat there all wide-eyed, listening to the fairy tales.

My old daddy would have called him a brain-washer, I think.

I only asked one question. "How is Jesus related to Uncle Walt?"

I got slapped.

Some things never change.

For a fire, Dad Version Two insisted on using twigs and tree branches instead of firebooks. It seemed weird, but he's the boss, so what could we do?

Mom just sat and stared at the fire the whole time, and I knew she was thinking about Thanks-burning and wanting to throw Dad Version Two into the fire.

Come to think of it, I was thinking the same thing.

Who knows what Bermuda Short was thinking? Her brain seemed like a wasteland of porridge most of the time.

Steve's son, Jiminy Cricket, sat there poking the fire with a stick. I decided to rename him Mystery Boy Theater. I think my daddy would have liked that.

Mystery Boy Theater still hadn't spoken a word to us. He'd gone pee a couple times and didn't sing "Good King Walruses," or any other peeing carols for that matter. He has no manners.

The night ended in a very unsettled way. Dad Version Two pulled Mom into the big bed, and they had their own little kablooey, but Mom screamed a little, and I'm not sure she was really having much fun.

Speaking of that, I asked Dad Version Two about the big kablooey earlier in the afternoon.

"That was horrible," he said. "It was like God was punishing us for all the evil we do, and now it's time to redeem humanity. That's why some of us are immune to the virus, and it's God's wish that we repopulate the planet for Him."

I have no clue what that all meant, but I smiled and nodded so I wouldn't have to listen any more.

Time for sleep.

In the morning, I stretched and then immediately hopped to my feet. The sun was only barely awake, and I knew what I had to do.

The axe was just where I'd left it after chopping down the wood for the fire.

I could still smell the burned tree branches. It wasn't very nice. I love the smell of firebook ashes in the morning.

Nobody else was awake. I tip-toed to where Dad Version Two was sleeping beside Mom and made sure the first swing of the axe was true.

He didn't even get a scream out as his head was sliced off from the rest of his body, but man, what a mess the blood made! It spurted out of his neck like a fountain, and it just gushed all over Mom.

So, *she* was sure screaming.

I pointed at her and frowned. She got the message and stopped yelling her freaking head off.

I pulled the body off of her and rolled it onto the floor. It was heavy, but I eventually managed to pull it out and into the forest. I suppose I could have followed in his footsteps and cut the body into little pieces, but I just wanted to get it over with.

Once I tossed more Mother Nature on it, I went back to the creek to clean the axe.

"You killed him, Alexander," said Mom.

Well, duh.

"That's not my name any more."

She looked at me, puzzled.

"I'm in charge now. I'm Dad Version Three."

Annie Globetrotter of Harlem stared at me like I was Uncle Walt himself, her mouth wide open. Mystery Boy Theater just stared over at Version Two and didn't say a word.

I realized I should have told *him* to clean the axe, not do it myself. If he refused, I would have had to slap him.

"Why did you do that?" asked Mom.

Sometimes I think people can be so stupid. Wasn't it obvious?

"He kept telling lies about Christmas," I said. "Calling Uncle Walt a fairy tale, when it's obviously the truth."

I looked over at Annie and put my arm around her. "I needed to protect my sister from his lies."

Mom smiled.

The sun was fully up now, and our campsite was quiet.

"You," I called to Mystery Boy Theater. "Clean up the fire."

He hesitated but then moved over to the fire and stacked the unburned pieces of wood together.

Tonight we'll have a good old fashioned fire made of firebooks, like fires have been started forever.

Maybe we'll have another Christmas soon. I figure now I can decide whenever I want to have it, and Thanks-burning too.

From this point forward, we're back to the true meaning of our national holidays.

I took a peek at Mystery Boy Theater and decided I'd better hide the axe. I'm no dummy. 🐛

ABOUT THE AUTHOR

John R. Little is a Canadian writer of dark fantasy and horror. He's been publishing his unique brand of fiction since 1982. John won the Bram Stoker Award for his novella, "Miranda," and has been nominated three other times.

John loves to hear from his readers, so feel free to drop him an email to john@johnrlittle.com and let him know what you thought of this book. He is married and lives in the village of Ayr in southern Ontario.

The Collected Short Fiction of John R Little:

Vol 1: Little by Little

Vol 2: Little Things

Vol 3: A Little Bit More

Vol 4: Lost Little Tales

Fully Illustrated Trade Paperback, Full-Color Hardcover and Audiobook

Available at IndieBound, Barnes & Noble, Amazon and LycanValley.com